Holiday Express Book 3
A Sweet Historical Holiday Romance
by
USA Today Bestselling Author
SHANNA HATFIELD

Holiday Home

Holiday Express Series, Book 3

ISBN: 9798785976887

shanna@shannahatfield.com

Cover Design: Covers and Cupcakes, LLC.

Published by Wholesome Hearts Publishing, LLC.
wholesomeheartspublishing@gmail.com

To those who sacrificed so much ....

Books by Shanna Hatfield

FICTION

CONTEMPORARY

Holiday Brides
Valentine Bride
Summer Bride
Easter Bride
Lilac Bride

Rodeo Romance
The Christmas Cowboy
Wrestlin' Christmas
Capturing Christmas
Barreling Through Christmas
Chasing Christmas
Racing Christmas
Keeping Christmas
Roping Christmas
Remembering Christmas

Grass Valley Cowboys
The Cowboy's Christmas Plan
The Cowboy's Spring Romance
The Cowboy's Summer Love
The Cowboy's Autumn Fall
The Cowboy's New Heart
The Cowboy's Last Goodbye

Summer Creek
Catching the Cowboy
Rescuing the Rancher
Protecting the Princess
Distracting the Deputy

Women of Tenacity
Heart of Clay
Heart of Hope
Heart of Love

HISTORICAL

Pendleton Petticoats
Dacey
Aundy
Caterina
Ilsa
Marnie
Lacey
Bertie
Millie
Dally
Quinn
Evie

Pendleton Promises
Sadie

Baker City Brides
Tad's Treasure
Crumpets and Cowpies
Thimbles and Thistles
Corsets and Cuffs
Bobbins and Boots
Lightning and Lawmen
Dumplings and Dynamite

Hearts of the War
Garden of Her Heart
Home of Her Heart
Dream of Her Heart

Hardman Holidays
The Christmas Bargain
The Christmas Token
The Christmas Calamity
The Christmas Vow
The Christmas Quandary
The Christmas Confection
The Christmas Melody
The Christmas Ring
The Christmas Wish

Chapter One

August 1944

A fly tormented his ear, but Bryce Coleman was too exhausted to swat it away. Unless a tank drove through the tent where he rested or a bomb threat drove him to seek cover, he intended to catch a few minutes of much-needed sleep. Nothing as meaningless as a pesky insect was going to keep him from it.

The ability to sleep anywhere, anytime, was a skill he'd gained during his involvement in a war that seemed endless. He never knew when he'd be able to rest, so he took advantage of any opportunity to grab a few winks.

He breathed deeply, inhaling the scent of the food being prepared for lunch in the mess hall. The aroma mingled with cigarette smoke, the lingering odor of sweaty men, and gunpowder.

Bryce released the breath and listened to the sounds of a busy base camp. Vehicles running, men talking, equipment creaking, and footsteps marching. Somewhere in the background, a scratched record played Kay Kyser's version of "Praise the Lord and Pass the Ammunition," adding to the cacophony around him. A marching band could have performed a rousing tune two feet from his head and he wouldn't have cared. All he wanted was his sleep.

With a final deep breath, he dozed off. He had no idea how long he slept, but he awakened with a start when someone swatted the soles of his boots. Bryce jerked and almost tipped over the chair he sat in at Colonel Lee Thompson's desk.

Granted, he'd balanced the chair on the back two legs and settled his boots on top of the desk, which he probably shouldn't have done, but it felt so good to elevate his feet and rest for a few minutes.

"You are an insolent pup, Coleman," the colonel groused, glowering at him as he set the stack of files he'd used to smack Bryce on the corner of the desk.

"Like father, like son," Bryce said, sliding his boots off the desk, rising to his feet, and grinning at the officer as he offered a snappy salute.

The colonel rolled his eyes, then returned Bryce's grin. "You are definitely like your father, although I would have shot Zach if I'd found him asleep with his feet on my desk."

"Back then, you didn't have your own tent or desk," Bryce said, stretching his arms over his head, then twisting from side to side to loosen his tight muscles. His father had served with Colonel Thompson in World War I. At that time, Lee had been a lieutenant.

"True, but if it hadn't been for Zach, I wouldn't be standing here today," Lee said, shaking his head in wonderment. "I still have no idea how your dad managed to carry me to safety when he was so gravely injured."

Bryce shrugged. "Dad always says it was strength beyond his own that made it possible."

The colonel nodded in agreement, then took a seat in the chair Bryce had vacated.

When Bryce had arrived at this base camp in France four days ago, he'd been thrilled to discover a man not only familiar to him but one he considered a close family friend. His father and Lee had exchanged many letters since they returned from the Great War. The Coleman and Thompson families had even made trips to visit each other half a dozen times over the years.

Due to the nature of his work, Bryce was frequently moved from one place to another. He'd spent less than thirty minutes with Colonel Thompson upon his arrival before Bryce had been sent out with a group of engineers and railroad soldiers. He'd only returned to the camp two hours ago. Colonel Thompson had been busy when Bryce had sought him out, but he'd motioned to the tent he used as an office.

More than happy to have a quiet place to rest, Bryce was grateful three sides of the tent had been rolled up, allowing air to circulate inside. The slight breeze felt wonderful in the rising heat of the summer day.

Bryce hadn't slept in the past thirty-six hours and felt ready to drop, but he'd continue doing whatever the U.S. Army needed him to do, even if he wasn't officially a member of the American military. The past two years, he'd served his country as a civilian contractor, providing much-needed assistance with trains in war zones. If it involved a track, a train car, or an engine, Bryce was the one who knew exactly how to fix it, build it, or get the most use out of it.

Since Colonel Thompson was aware of his lack of sleep, Bryce assumed the man had awakened him for an important reason. One that would likely curtail his time spent in this particular camp. He'd traveled so much the past month, he'd lost track of his exact location a week ago.

"I know you need some rest, son, but you can sleep on the way there." The colonel pulled a map out of a drawer, spreading it across the top of his desk. He pointed to a spot that looked like nothing but forest to Bryce. "They've hit a snag on a project a few hours south of here and could use your expertise. I'm sending along one of my best engineers. Between the two of you, I'm confident you can iron out the wrinkles and get things back on track, both literally and figuratively."

"I'll do my best, sir," Bryce said, studying the map. If he wasn't mistaken, the track was being installed near an area currently occupied by Germans.

"I know you will, Bryce. I wouldn't expect anything less than that from a Coleman." The colonel stood and thumped Bryce on the back. "Head over to the mess hall and fill your belly, then gather your gear. I'll make arrangements for a car.

Be ready to leave in an hour."

"Yes, sir," Bryce said, saluting the colonel as a captain entered the tent.

Bryce jogged over to the mess tent and hurriedly ate a meal of overcooked meat and potatoes, a slice of flavorless bread, and a serving of canned peaches, which tasted delicious. He drained his cup of canned milk, dreaming of the glasses of cold milk he enjoyed on his family's ranch, then glanced at his watch. If he rushed, he could clean up before he had to leave.

The showers were empty when he carried his things inside. In less than ten minutes, he'd showered, shaved, and donned a fresh uniform. He rolled his dirty clothes inside the damp towel and tied them to the bottom of his knapsack, similar in color and design to the haversacks issued by the Army. Bryce had learned right away to carry whatever he needed with him because he never knew when or if he'd return to a camp once he was sent out on a project. Often, he went from one project to another, receiving his orders on the go. Everything he had in his possession was contained in his knapsack.

Bryce returned to the colonel's tent to find him and another officer studying the map on his desk.

"Bryce, this is Lieutenant David Kelly. He's one of the best engineers I've met, and he'll accompany you on the trip. If all goes well, you should be back tomorrow in time for supper." The colonel tapped his index finger on the map he'd spread out earlier. "Lieutenant Kelly has pertinent project details and can brief you on the way there."

"I thought you were going to let me sleep," Bryce teased as he shook the lieutenant's hand in greeting.

"You can sleep after the war is won," Lee said, offering Bryce a fatherly glare.

"Whatever you say, sir. Do you …" Bryce was interrupted as a four-door Chevrolet sedan pulled up outside. The dark color, known as Volunteer Green, would blend in well with a forested area.

A young corporal jumped out of the car, saluted the colonel and lieutenant, then glanced at Bryce. Although he wore the same clothes as the lieutenant, his lacked any insignias, stripes, or other identifying emblems.

"Ask Lieutenant Kelly if you have questions," Lee said, leading the way to the car. After the men saluted him, he handed Bryce a pistol and two boxes of ammunition.

Bryce raised an eyebrow in question, but Lee almost imperceptibly winked at him. "I already have a pistol."

"I know, but it never hurts to be prepared," the colonel said, then waited as the lieutenant and Bryce slid into the back of the car. "Be careful and stay safe. Your dad would never forgive me if I sent you off and let you get yourself killed."

Bryce grinned as he rolled down the car's window. "It's my mother you should fear, sir."

The colonel laughed as Bryce shut the door, then tapped the top of the car, letting the corporal know he could leave.

The car started forward as Bryce set his bag between his feet, tucked the pistol and ammo inside, then settled back against the seat, fighting the urge to sleep.

"Go ahead and snooze while you can," David said, setting the duffel bag he carried at his feet. "I'll wake you in an hour."

"Thanks," Bryce said, tugging his hat down to cover his face. In less than a minute, he was asleep.

"Coleman! Wake up," a voice said near his ear as a hand shook his arm. "Coleman!"

Bryce pushed his hat back on his head, yawned, and opened his eyes. "That hour sure flew by in a hurry."

David smirked and opened a file he held in his left hand. "Come on, sleeping beauty, we need to go over this information before we get there."

Bryce and David spent half an hour going over the project details and making notes for improvements as well as discussing how to handle the problem that had been relayed to the colonel.

"That should do it," David said, tucking the papers back into his duffel and zipping it shut. He glanced over at Bryce. "The colonel didn't give us time for much of an introduction. Where are you from?"

"A little town in Eastern Oregon named Holiday. My family has lived there since before it was a town. My great-granddad was one of the first to settle the area."

"Really? What is the nearest bigger town? Any name I might recognize?"

Bryce shook his head. "There isn't a town in the whole eastern half of the state with a name anyone who didn't live there would recognize, although Pendleton has been on the map thanks to the annual rodeo."

"Pendleton? As in the Pendleton Round-Up and Wild West shows and Indian encampments? That Pendleton?"

Shocked, Bryce nodded his head. "Yep. I take it you've heard of it."

"Sure have. My cousin's husband used to compete in rodeos before they wed. He mentioned riding broncs there a few times. How far is it from Holiday?"

"About two hours. Holiday is off the beaten path, on the way to nowhere, really, but there's a big lumber mill there. It used to be a top producer of gold with a variety of successful mines, including the Yellowbird, one my family owns. The mines have all been abandoned now, but they operated for almost forty years before they played out."

"Is your family still involved in mining, or is it now lumber?"

Bryce grinned. "Neither. My father's family are ranchers and have been since they moved there. My great-granddad imported Angus cattle from Scotland. Elk Creek Ranch supplies beef to restaurants and stores all along the eastern side of the state and a few in Boise, Idaho, and Portland."

"Beef, huh?" David gave him a long glance. "How'd you get so knowledgeable about trains? The colonel said you could take a train engine apart and put it back together with your eyes closed and one hand tied behind your back."

"Both sides of my family have been involved in the railroad. My father spent many years as the head mechanic at our local engine house. Grandpa Coleman was an engineer and worked every job you could think of except conductor to get there. He and my dad taught me everything they know about repairing and running trains." Bryce glanced out the window as they drove into what appeared to be an ancient forest. "My mother's father also had ties to the railroad."

"What kind of ties?" David asked when Bryce fell silent.

He'd always been cautious when sharing about his grandfather Lennox because his name was well known. His family had worried someone might hold him for ransom if they realized Bryce was related to George Lennox.

Bryce glanced over at David. The man appeared honest and upright. If he wasn't a good man, one who knew what he was doing, the colonel wouldn't have sent him along.

"My mother's father is George Lennox."

David's mouth dropped open. "*The* George Lennox? The railroad magnate? The man who owned a good portion of the railways in America along with a dozen other profitable enterprises?"

Slowly, Bryce nodded. "That's him."

David whistled softly. "He's worth millions, maybe billions."

"Maybe," Bryce agreed, wishing he could change the subject. It always made him uncomfortable to discuss his family's wealth. It was something he never flaunted and rarely discussed. He much preferred to be Bryce Coleman, grandson of a cattle rancher.

The Lennox fortune, or perhaps it was the way George Lennox had used it, was something his father had despised. If it had been up to Zach Coleman, he would have raised his family in a modest home, depending solely on the income he earned as a mechanic. However, his father-in-law had demanded the best for his only child—Bryce's mother—and his grandchildren, insisting they live in his mansion where he'd spoiled them with the best of everything.

Grandfather Lennox could be a hard-nosed tyrant when he wanted and had often thought throwing money at something could fix any problem, even if he had been a good grandfather, for the most part.

The Coleman family was so different from him. They were among the most hardworking, honorable people Bryce had ever encountered. Every day, he was grateful he'd been raised with his father's beliefs and morals instead of those held by his maternal grandfather.

George Lennox was the reason Bryce was not in the Army and was instead forced to do his part in the war as a contracted civilian. He'd been so angry at the man's meddling, Bryce had refused to speak to him the last time he'd seen him. He regretted not telling his grandfather he loved him before he left for Africa two years ago, because five months later George Lennox had died of a heart attack.

"So, I guess you grew up around trains?" David finally asked.

"I did. Dad let me work on them from the time I was big enough to hold a wrench, and Grandfather

Lennox took me on trips with him. I got to ride in the engine or the caboose, or wherever I wanted and asked the men working for him endless questions. Grandpa Coleman taught me how to drive a train, how to get the most out of it using the least fuel, that sort of thing. The rest I learned from studying books and in the field."

"Colonel Thompson said he'd never met anyone who knew more about trains than you. I suppose that's partly due to your family, and the rest is because you are a driven maniac."

Bryce turned his head to see if David was joking or serious.

David chuckled. "I heard how you skip sleep, meals, and whatever is necessary to get the job done right and completed as quickly as possible. You've made a reputation for yourself, Coleman."

"I hope it's not all bad," Bryce said with a grin. "Speaking of reputations, I heard the man in charge of this project can be a real donkey's derrière."

A laugh rolled out of David. "I heard the same thing, although not in words quite that polite. The second in command is a good man, though. I worked with him in Sicily. When we get there, let's report to him. If possible, we can sidestep the captain and get the job done without his interference."

"I like that plan." Bryce looked outside and breathed in the scent of forest along with the dust the car kicked up as it turned off a paved road and onto a narrow dirt lane. There weren't any road signs to mark the way, so he hoped the driver knew where he was headed. This close to the border of

German-occupied France, it would be easy to inadvertently cross over into enemy territory.

Taking a firm grip on his thoughts instead of worrying when there wasn't yet a problem, Bryce tamped down his concerns and looked back at his traveling companion. "What about you, David? Where are you from? Do you have a wife or family waiting for you?"

David leaned further back into the seat and sighed. "I grew up in Illinois. My uncle was a conductor, and that's how I got interested in trains. I was always fascinated by what made them go and wanted to learn how to make them run faster, better. The military intrigued me, and here I am. Eight years ago, my brother's wife introduced me to her cousin, and I knew I'd met the girl of my dreams. Three months later, we married. We have two kids. Ryan is six and Camille is almost four. I sure miss them. How about you? Wife? Kids? Although you seem pretty young to have any."

"I turned twenty-four in January, so not as young as some. I'm not married, although there is a girl back home who's special to me. We dated all through school and it seems like everyone expects us to wed someday, but we'll see how we both feel after the war is over and I return to Holiday."

Bryce had forced himself not to think about Katherine Kingston for a while. When he did let memories of her surface, it made him so homesick he could hardly stand it. Kate had been his sweetheart since he first noticed girls. She was friends with his oldest sister and was always at their house even before she became his girl, but something had held Bryce back from proposing to her.

Once he decided to head into the war, he was glad he'd refrained. He didn't want to leave behind a widow. In case something happened to him that left him maimed, he didn't want a woman tied to him if some other fellow came along who captured her eye.

David gave him an approving look. "That's a smart thing to do. So many young people have rushed to wed just weeks or days before the men shipped off to war. They hardly know anything about each other, and now they'll spend months, sometimes years apart. I can't imagine enduring that kind of separation and then going home to a person who is virtually a stranger."

"Me either," Bryce said, knowing David spoke the truth. He'd seen it happen time and again as young soldiers feared going off to war without leaving anyone behind and married the first girl who said "yes."

David glanced at the watch on his wrist, then leaned forward, looking out the windshield. "We ought to be there soon, I would think."

"The directions I have say it's another twelve miles up this road," the corporal said, glancing at them over the front seat.

"Okay," David said, sitting back in the seat.

"What about you, Corporal Matthews? Where are you from?"

The corporal looked at them in the rearview mirror, as though he was surprised to be included in the conversation.

"From Ohio, sir. Grew up in a town named Waverly. I'm the oldest of five. I have two sisters in high school and two brothers, who are eight and eleven. My dad owns a hardware store. I used to drive all over making deliveries for him, even before I had a license."

Bryce grinned at the corporal. "My Gramps let me drive his car when I was seven. I had to sit on his lap, but I sure thought I was grown up that day."

The corporal and David laughed.

"I was ten before my father let me touch the steering wheel," David said, then looked to the corporal. "How about you?"

"I was nine when I first got to drive, but Dad let me start driving by myself when I was twelve. I was tall for my age and could see over the steering wheel by then. One time, I accidentally hit the gas instead of the brake and ran into a stack of lumber behind the store. It didn't even scratch the grill, so I kept that to myself for a whole week before the guilt got to me and I confessed what I'd done. Instead of punishing me, my dad told me honesty was the best and only policy; then he gave me the keys and sent me out on an errand."

"He sounds like a great father," David said as the car rounded a curve.

One minute they were driving along the dirt road in the peaceful forest. The next, a hail of bullets hit the car.

"Drive, drive!" David shouted to the corporal, but the boy made a gurgling sound then slumped over the wheel, his foot buried heavily on the gas pedal.

Bryce started to scramble over the front seat, but the vehicle veered wildly to the left, hit a stump, and came to a stop with the front of the car nosed upward in a tree and the driver's side pinned against another towering deciduous giant.

Although he wasn't sure when it had happened, Bryce had been tossed out the open window of the car before he could reach Corporal Matthews. By a miracle, the car hadn't crushed him to death, although he felt as though every bone had been jarred loose. Shots rang around him as he waited for the air to return to his lungs. When it did, he hopped up into a crouched position and zig-zagged his way to the car. He felt a sting, then another, but kept going, focused on reaching the two men in the automobile resting at an unnatural angle.

"David?" He yelled as he took in the precarious position of the car. Something in the undercarriage seemed to be caught on a limb, and that looked to be all that was holding it upright. He feared one false move might send it crashing backward to the ground. He climbed over a tree stump and started to climb up the massive trunk. He raised his left hand to grab onto a branch and pull himself higher just as the exhaust pipe fell off the car and seared his arm as it toppled to the ground.

Bryce winced but kept working his way up to the passenger side door.

"David?" he called again.

"I'm here," a voice replied, sounding groggy. It grew stronger when he spoke again. "I'm here, Coleman!"

"I'm coming to you. How's the corporal?"

He heard rustling and the car groaned. Suddenly, a gush of boiling water washed over him as the radiator cracked open, scalding his left side from shoulder to hip. Ignoring the pain that rendered him lightheaded, he managed to climb up and wrench the back passenger door partway open. David remained pinned in place by the front seat that had been shoved backward onto his right leg.

"Is anything broken?" Bryce asked as he cautiously worked his way into the car.

"I can't tell," David said, tugging on his leg but unable to work it free. He ducked as more shots echoed around them, shattering what few pieces of window glass hadn't already cracked and fallen out. "I'm thinking the corporal might have taken a wrong turn somewhere."

"Probably. How is he? Has he said anything?" Bryce asked, carefully leaning over the front seat. At a glance, he could see the corporal was gone due to two bullets to his head, but he felt for a pulse to make sure. He edged back and shook his head at David.

David closed his eyes, as though saying a prayer for the young man's soul, while Bryce frantically worked to free the lieutenant's trapped leg. With strength borne of desperation, he turned so his back was against the front seat and pushed while David yanked upward. The second David's leg was free, Bryce grabbed his arm and tugged him toward the door. Before he slid out of the car, he handed David's haversack to him, then snagged his knapsack that had been wedged beneath the seat and slipped the straps over his shoulders. The feel of it against his burned flesh nearly made him pass out, but he forced himself to remain focused on escaping.

David was bleeding from a head wound and holding his left arm like it was broken. Bryce somehow managed to help him out of the car, then half-carried him down to the ground.

"Can you walk?" he asked as random bullets continued to knock bark off the trees around them. Either the shooters had terrible aim or they were far enough away they couldn't see their targets well through the trees.

"I'm not sure," David said, tentatively putting his weight on his right foot. It held him so he took another step, then dropped to the ground as a volley of gunfire popped around them. Bryce flopped onto his belly and crawled several yards on his elbows until he was hidden behind the trunk of an enormous tree. He looked back to make sure David had followed him.

"We can't stay here," he said, rising to a sitting position and glancing around the tree that offered protection from the shooters. "I think we should blow the car."

"Blow the car? Make it explode?" David asked, eyes wide as blood continued to trickle down his forehead and along the side of his face.

"Yes. I don't know what official papers or maps are inside it, and I'm not crawling back up there to find out. I would like to give the corporal a proper burial, but it's more important the Germans not get their hands on him or the car."

David nodded in agreement. "We've got our

bags and papers. Unless the explosion draws the whole German army down on us, it's probably the best plan to get rid of the car and anything we don't want them to find."

"Can you move on your own?" Bryce asked, slowly working his way back around the trunk of the tree.

"I think so." David pushed himself up. He took a few wobbly steps, then looked back at Bryce. "What are you going to do?"

"If you can run, now would be a good time to start." Bryce didn't wait for David's answer. Instead, he pulled a pistol from his bag, aimed for the gas tank, and hit it with his first shot. He took cover behind the tree as pieces of metal went flying in every direction; then he sprinted after David, who was now racing in earnest through the trees.

Bryce caught up with him and they kept on running until they could no longer smell the smoke from the explosion. They came to a stream, crossed it, then stopped to rest on the other side.

Up until that moment, Bryce had been fueled by pure adrenaline. But after he bent down to wash the blood from his hands and drink the cool water, he found himself unable to regain his feet.

David's wounds appeared to be mostly superficial since water washed away a good portion of the blood that had been covering him. However, his arm still dangled at an odd angle.

"Let me see that," Bryce said, pointing to his arm. David moved so he sat facing him. Bryce felt along David's shoulder, then his collarbone. "What did you say your wife's name is?"

"Natalie," David said.

"Picture Natalie on your wedding day. Recall her fragrance. Think of how you felt right in that moment," Bryce said trying to give David something pleasant to focus on. Before the man had a chance to speak, he braced David's arm and gave it a hard jerk, pulling the dislocated shoulder back into place.

David didn't utter a sound, but when Bryce finished, he rolled his shoulder and nodded in appreciation.

"Better?" Bryce asked.

"Much," David answered, then motioned to Bryce. "You look worse. Why didn't you mention you'd been shot?" he asked as he ripped the sleeve of his shirt and tied it around Bryce's left thigh. Two bullet wounds bled in his thigh, a lump on his shin made him think his leg was broken, and burns embedded with scraps of his uniform throbbed on his left arm, side, and upper leg.

"I hadn't actually noticed the bullet wounds with everything else that hurts," Bryce said, biting his lip as David tried to pull a piece of what had been his shirt from a burn on his arm. "Just leave it. It's going to take more medical care than either of us has the time or ability to deliver. If you can splint my leg, we'll keep going."

"Keep going?" David stood and glared at him like he'd lost his mind. "You can't walk on that leg. And with all those burns, you shouldn't even be moving. Are you delirious?"

"Not yet, but I reckon that'll come sooner rather than later. We need to find shelter; then you can leave me and go for help. I figure the corporal took a wrong turn on this road. If we keep heading west, we'll eventually find a road or someone who will help us instead of shoot at us."

"For the record, I think this is a terrible idea." David gathered a few long sticks then wrapped them around Bryce's leg using strips torn from the dirty shirt Bryce had changed out of earlier. When he finished, David picked up the haversack he'd set down near the bank of the stream and settled the strap over his head so the bag rested against his back.

Bryce reached out his right hand and David reluctantly took it, pulling him upright. He started to slide an arm around Bryce to support him, then stopped when he realized no matter where he touched him, it would inflict pain.

"Can you find a stick I can lean on? It might be easier," Bryce suggested, closing his eyes and drawing in deep breaths to keep from being violently ill. His stomach roiled and bile surged upward, but he swallowed it down.

David disappeared into the thick trees and soon returned carrying a sturdy branch. "Will this do?" He held the stick out to Bryce.

Bryce pulled a sock from his pack, slipped it over his left hand, blocked the pain it caused his burned hand to hold onto the stick, then took a step forward. Fire shot both up and down his leg, but he forced himself to take another step, then another.

"Let's go. Maybe by the time I pass out, we'll be somewhere safe."

David scowled as he hovered next to him.

"Aren't you just a bucket of merry sunshine?"

Bryce tried to grin, even though he was sure it looked more like a grimace. "I do what I can. Tell me more about Natalie and your kids."

If he was going to survive walking on a leg he was sure was broken, he needed something, anything, to take his mind off the overwhelming agony flooding through his body.

Bryce didn't know how long they walked, but by the time they came out of the trees in a little clearing, he knew David's daughter's favorite bedtime story and even the names of all her dolls.

"What do you think?" David asked as they stood in the safety of the trees and looked at an ancient farmhouse made of stone, surrounded by a wooden fence that had seen better days. A big barn, also made of stone, stood about ten yards behind the house. The fenced pasture was empty, and a few outbuildings appeared to be on the verge of collapse.

The place looked forsaken, but it also appeared no Germans were there. They stood and watched for a quarter of an hour, but nothing stirred, not even the breeze.

"Want to give it a try?" Bryce finally asked, taking a slow step forward.

"What's the worst that can happen?" David asked. "Someone might shoot us and put us out of our misery."

Bryce chuckled at the man's attempt at humor. The effort at laughing caused sharp pain in his side. He wondered if he had a few cracked ribs to go along with the rest of his injuries.

They made their way across the clearing and had just stepped past a weathered gate into the yard when the door to the house swung open. A woman rushed out with a rifle in her hands.

She uttered a warning in German as she held the gun, poised to shoot.

David looked quizzically at Bryce.

"She said to stop or she'll shoot," Bryce whispered without taking his eyes from the woman. Her hair was fashioned in two braids, like a little girl would wear, making him question her age. She could have been thirteen or thirty, but he had no idea which was more accurate. She had on a loose worn shirt and an equally worn pair of trousers with a hole in the right knee. Her feet were bare. If they'd been back in the States, Bryce might have called her a hillbilly based on her appearance. Behind her scowl and wary eyes, he couldn't tell much else about her.

"You speak German?" David asked, sounding awed by Bryce's knowledge of the language.

"German, thanks to my grandmother, and French due to my mother's insistence I have a well-rounded education." Bryce kept his voice low as he conversed with David, then turned to the woman and smiled. He raised the hand not holding the walking stick in the air in a gesture of surrender and spoke to her in German. "We mean no harm, miss. We only seek a place to rest this evening."

"You speak German?" she asked in English.

"And French, and a little Italian," Bryce said, his smile widening. "We really don't mean any harm. Our car ran off the road and crashed. We need to get back to our base, but we aren't exactly sure where we are."

The woman sighed and lowered the gun slightly, although she still kept it pointed at them. "There's an American camp about twelve miles that way," she motioned to the west, "but you can't walk straight there. The river must be crossed at the bridge, and it's half a day's walk to the south."

"Are we currently in Germany or France?" David asked, taking a small step forward.

"At the moment, Germany, but I hope by the end of the war, this land will revert once again to France."

Bryce could hear the woman and David speaking, but they sounded far away. His vision grew cloudy and he felt like he was being sucked underwater as the world around him began to darken and waver.

David grabbed his good arm and kept him from falling over. "Please, miss, my friend here is in bad shape. May we please have shelter for the night? I promise we'll not cause any trouble."

"How do I know you aren't pretending to be injured?"

David frowned and pointed to the blood caked on Bryce's leg. "Does this look fake to you?"

The woman sighed a second time and set the gun inside the door of her house. She motioned to them, flapping her hand forward. "Come on, but just so you know, I don't have much to offer."

"As long as you have clean water and a spot on the floor where we can rest, that's all we ask," Bryce said, aware his words sounded slurred.

"You better hurry before he faints," she said, reaching out to help Bryce over the threshold and into her home. He drew in a breath, inhaling a faint fragrance that smelled soft and feminine. Something about it reminded him of his grandmother, Cora Lee.

Three steps inside the door, his leg gave out on him and pain swept over him with such force, he crumpled to the floor. The last thing he remembered was looking into a pair of bright blue eyes framed with a halo of golden curls.

Perhaps the woman in the farmhouse was really an angel in disguise.

Chapter Two

Britta Webster glanced from the man on the floor to the soldier hovering over him. She had an idea the Americans were holding something back from her. If they wanted her help, they'd better tell the truth.

Since one of them was currently unconscious, it left the other one to do the talking.

"What's your name?" she asked as she stepped across the prone man on the floor and over to the stove. She built a fire in it, then filled a large pan with water to heat. It had been so warm out that day, she'd avoided heating up the house with the stove, but now it couldn't be helped. Hot water, and plenty of it, would be necessary for cleansing wounds. From the looks of the two Americans, she was going to need a lot of water. She filled another pan and set it to heat.

The man watching her every move nodded politely to her when she glanced at him over her shoulder as she scrubbed her hands at the sink. "My name is Lieutenant David Kelly. This is Bryce Coleman."

Britta studied the man on the floor. He was tall and sturdy with broad shoulders, but he looked terrible. She noticed what was left of his uniform had no emblems or insignias on it, nothing to identify his rank. "What's his title?"

"He doesn't have one. He's a civilian contractor."

Britta's brow wrinkled as she gathered a stack of rags from a shelf beneath the counter and a fresh bar of soap. "I don't understand what that means."

"It means he is not a member of the United States military but voluntarily offered to help the Army for the duration of the war."

"He volunteered for this?" She waved her hand at his inert, injured body. "The man is …" She recalled the word she wanted, "crazy."

The lieutenant grinned. "Perhaps, but he's a good man. I'd sure like to help him stay alive, miss. I appreciate you letting us come inside."

"You didn't just have an accident with your car, did you?" She pinned him with a knowing glare. "Germans shot at you. Is that it?"

"Yes, miss," he said, nodding in agreement. "We were on our way to help with a new rail line our troops are installing, but our driver took a wrong turn, we think. Germans shot the driver, killing him, and the car crashed into the trees." He tipped his hand upward to demonstrate the position of the car. "Mr. Coleman was tossed out of the car and I was pinned inside. He climbed up to the car and helped me out, after being shot mind you. After I was safely away from it, he went back and blew up the car to keep the Germans from it. We've been walking for hours."

Britta felt bad for these men who'd journeyed so far and what they'd been through. She might be half German, but she despised them. Despised all of them except for the one who'd been her father. "I'm sorry, Lieutenant. I haven't heard anything about a new railway going in, but I don't often go into our village. It's safer staying here."

"Is the village occupied by Germans?"

"It depends on the day. The last time I went for supplies, there were Germans everywhere."

The lieutenant frowned. "When was that?"

"Two months ago. I haven't returned, and I won't go back until they leave. The village is only a few miles from here, but I would recommend you avoid it when you leave."

Lieutenant Kelly nodded. "We'll do that."

Britta cleared off the long, heavy wooden kitchen table that had belonged to her mother's family for nearly as long as the farm had been in their possession. She spread an oilcloth over the top of the table, then pointed to the man the lieutenant referred to as Mr. Coleman. "Can you help me lift him up here? I'm not a doctor, but unless you want him to die, we need to dig out the bullets."

The lieutenant removed the bag he carried, set the stick Mr. Coleman still clutched in one hand by the door, and sat him up, removing the knapsack from his back. The wounded man was a dead weight in his unconscious state, but Britta and the lieutenant managed to get him up on the table.

"Remove his boots while I take off the splint," she ordered, picking up a pair of scissors and cutting through the fabric that held the sticks in place. More fabric was tied around the man's hard thigh. Blood had run down his leg and dried, plastering his pants to his skin. She poured hot water into a bowl and added a bit of cold water, dipped a rag into it, and set the cloth on his leg to loosen the material. She then noticed the burns on his arm and side with pieces of his shirt seared into the wounds.

"I'll be right back," she said, leaving the open, airy room that had a kitchen on one end and a sitting area on the other. She walked into her bedroom, the only other room in the small house. A medicine cabinet set in the wall provided a mirror, along with a place to keep necessary medical supplies. She gathered what she had on hand along with a pair of tweezers and a roll of gauze.

Back in the kitchen, she shoved a chair over to the high shelves on the wall opposite of the stove, climbed up and pulled down a bottle of whiskey Henri had kept for medicinal use.

She set the bottle on the table, took a small cup from a shelf, poured in a little, and handed it to the lieutenant. "You look like you could use that."

He shook his head. "Save it for him."

She nodded and set the cup aside, then checked to see if the wet rag had loosened the blood-caked cloth. With the lieutenant's help, she was able to remove Mr. Coleman's pants.

"How old are you miss?" the lieutenant asked as she bent closer to study the wounded man's thigh.

"Don't you know it's impolite to ask a lady her

age?" she glanced over at the soldier. "I'm twenty-five."

"Really? I would have pegged you for eighteen, maybe twenty."

Britta didn't know if that was a compliment or an insult. "Thank you, I think, Lieutenant Kelly."

"You're welcome, miss. Since we're gonna be working close together, you might as well call me David, and he's Bryce. Do you have a name? Or do you prefer I continue calling you miss, or ma'am?"

"My name is Britta Webster. You may call me Britta." As she spoke, she took her sharpest kitchen knife and set the blade inside the glowing heat of the fire in the stove. "Do you have any medical supplies in your gear, David?"

"I do." He opened the bag he'd set by the door and dug around inside, pulling out a small pack stamped with First Aid on the outside. David handed it to her.

Britta opened it to find bandages coated in a powder and a few other things she thought might be useful.

"Have you ever removed a bullet?" David asked as she set aside the pack.

"No, I haven't." Britta didn't want to think about Henri's bullet-riddled body or how feverishly she'd worked to save him. He'd lost too much blood by the time he'd made his way to her. She'd held him in her arms right there on the kitchen floor as his life ebbed away.

She was determined no one else would die in her home. Especially not these Americans. She'd encountered a few of them, and they all seemed the same to her: full of pride and good intentions, determined they could single-handedly win the war. But if that were so, the Germans would have been driven away months, if not years, ago.

She looked at David as she carefully removed Bryce's shirt, forcing herself not to notice his muscled chest. "Have you ever removed a bullet? Nursed a wound?"

"No. Not at all. I'm an engineer and spend most of my time drawing up plans and overseeing the construction of them."

Britta lifted an eyebrow and tipped her head toward the sink as she used the tweezers and hot water to pull the bits of fabric from the burns on Bryce's arm and side. "Roll up your sleeves and wash your hands. Together, we'll do the best we can for your friend."

"Oh, we aren't friends. We just met earlier today. Then again, after what we've been through, I owe Bryce my life. I'd say we're closer to brothers than friends."

"Good. Your brother is going to need all the help you can give." Britta smiled at him. "I have a little experience with injuries. A few times, when no one else was available, I've helped the local doctor. I'd go get him now, but he moved away six months ago and our village no longer has a doctor. From him, I learned the most important thing is to keep the wound clean. We help do that by keeping our hands and equipment clean."

"Makes sense to me," David said shaking his hands dry, then taking a place on the opposite side of the table. "Where do you want to start?"

"The worst part, I think, will be digging those bullets out." She threaded three needles and set them in a small pan to boil. When she finished that task, she pulled on a clean apron over her clothes, then washed her hands again, letting them dry in the air.

"Let's get it over with." Britta had no idea how to go about removing the bullets, but she drew in a breath, prayed for strength and guidance, then picked up the knife she'd heated to sterilize it and began the task. David proved to be a good assistant. Between the two of them, they managed to dig out the bullets.

"He's lucky he has such thick thigh muscles, or those bullets may have shattered the bone," she said as she poured whiskey on the wounds. Bryce's eyes flew open, and he started to yelp in pain, but Britta clapped a hand over his mouth to keep him silent.

"You must, must be quiet, Mr. Coleman. Do you understand me?" she asked, keeping her hand firmly pressed to his face. If a German passing by heard him yell, it would be tragic. She feared even the neighbors finding out she harbored Americans in her home.

He nodded, then his eyes rolled back in his head and he lost consciousness again.

"That's probably for the best," David said, lifting a clean rag and wiping away the blood she'd left on Bryce's face. Britta quickly stitched up the bullet wounds on his leg, then turned her attention to a bullet wound on his side. It appeared the bullet had barely grazed him, cutting the skin, but not becoming embedded in his body. The man was lucky he wasn't dead from the severity of his wounds.

"Grab that wooden spoon from the crock by the sink," she directed David as she stood poised with the whiskey over the wound on Bryce's side.

David picked it up and held it out to her.

"Stick it in his mouth for him to bite down on. He'll need it."

David nodded in understanding and set the handle of the spoon in Bryce's mouth. When Britta poured the alcohol on the wound, Bryce's eyes once again opened, but he clenched his teeth on the spoon. The veins in his neck stood out until they looked as though they might pop before she stopped.

"Almost finished, Mr. Coleman," she said as she spread ointment on his burns, wrapped his leg with the powdered bandages from David's supplies, then had David help her set the break in Bryce's lower leg. She ignored the grunting sounds the man made as she worked, surprised he hadn't once again fainted from the pain.

When she completed her work, assured she'd done all she could, she quickly cleaned up the kitchen, stowing all the bloody rags and her ruined apron in a bucket to burn later.

"We can't leave him on the table," Britta said, looking to David. "He's not going to be able to leave with you tomorrow. You know that, don't you?"

"I do, but I'm not sure what to do about it. I can't just leave him," David said, wearily sinking into a chair he'd pulled near the table.

"If I allow him to stay here, do you promise to come back for him?" Britta asked, wondering if she'd regret the offer. If the Germans discovered she harbored an American … she didn't even want to consider what they'd do to her.

"I promise, Britta. On the lives of my children, I promise I'll come back for him as soon as I can."

"How many children do you have?" she asked as she crossed the room and pushed aside a low table on an old, worn rug in front of a lumpy sofa.

"Two. A boy and a girl, Ryan and Camille. I'm not sure Camille even remembers who I am. She was so tiny when America entered the war."

"I can't imagine being away from your children for so long. Have you been able to go home on …" Britta searched for the right word. Although she had an excellent command of the English language, she occasionally struggled to find the appropriate term. "What is it when you go home for a visit?"

"Leave. Soldiers get leave. I haven't seen my wife or kids in two years. Two long years."

"I'm sorry." Britta glanced at him as she rolled the rug back and lifted a trapdoor in the floor.

David's eyes widened as he hurried over to stand beside her. "What's that?"

"Mr. Coleman's accommodations until you return. If anyone does come, he'll be hidden here." Britta lit a lamp and carried it down the narrow steps. The room had been used in World War I to hide three French soldiers while they healed from their wounds. They'd stayed in the tiny room for two months before they were well enough to leave.

Britta used the space to store food. She'd

learned early on in the war anything in the kitchen was apt to be taken by soldiers who happened upon her home, be they French, British, or German. She'd raised a big garden and had worked hard to preserve all she could. The shelves lining the walls were filled with jars of beans, beets, and peas. She'd also canned cherries and peaches and made two dozen jars of berry jam. She had no more sugar left, but she did have a large jar of honey she'd acquired by trading six loaves of bread to an old bachelor who lived alone in the woods a few miles away.

In another month, she'd add bins of potatoes and onions to her winter stores along with tomatoes and squash. She might not have much meat, but she had managed to keep her milk cow and a few chickens hidden.

Britta set the lamp on an empty spot on a shelf, then moved to a corner where three cots were stacked together. She lifted a cot, brushing away cobwebs that clung to it with the hem of her shirt. The room was cooler than upstairs, which would be good for her patient, but it held a dank, musty smell that came from the floor and walls being made of earth.

David looked like he wanted to protest bringing Bryce down to the cellar, but Britta didn't see that they had many choices. Not if they all wanted to stay safe.

"I'll bring down blankets and pillows. We'll make him as comfortable as possible," she said, trying to reassure David as much as herself. She would have hated to be trapped in the tiny room without any windows or light.

Before she changed her mind and put the wounded man in her bed, she rushed upstairs, gathered blankets and pillows, and even a set of sheets, carrying everything down the stairs. David helped her pad a cot with two old blankets. They tucked sheets over it, added a pillow at the head, and folded a blanket at the foot, then returned upstairs.

"Maybe we better clean him up a bit before we settle him on the clean sheets," David suggested.

Britta had hoped David would volunteer to do the job, but he stood back as she used the warm water that was on the stove to give Bryce a sponge bath. She refused to remove the cotton underwear he still wore. If David thought he needed a clean pair, he could see to that task.

"Are you sure you're up to helping move him?" Britta asked as she took a position at the foot of the table.

"Nope. But, as you said, we can't leave him here."

It took all her strength, and then some, to help David carry Bryce down the steps. By the time they had him settled on the cot, all three of them were coated in sweat.

"I'll bring down some water for him to drink, and more for bathing," Britta said when she and David started up the steps. She heard the sound of voices and the creak of the yard gate outside.

David shot her a panicked look as the two of them bounded up the remaining stairs. David grabbed his bag and Bryce's, along with Bryce's bloody clothes and Britta's rifle. He took everything with him as he rushed down to the cellar. Britta closed the trapdoor, jerked the rug over it, then slid the table into place just as the door opened and her neighbor appeared.

"Hello, Mrs. Bassett. Did you enjoy your afternoon?" Britta asked, forcing herself to smile as she went to the sink and washed her hands. Covertly, she glanced around to make sure nothing looked out of place and spied the bucket of bloody rags sitting out where anyone could see them. With her toe, she quietly slid the bucket beneath the curtain that hid the pipes beneath the sink.

Thankfully, Mrs. Bassett was too busy talking about her afternoon adventures with Britta's son to notice anything.

"Did you have fun, sweetheart?" Britta asked, drying her hands and lifting her toddler into her arms.

"Happy, Mama. Me happy!" Joshua said, patting his hands on her cheeks while smiling broadly, showing off his pearly baby teeth. At two, he was already saying many words and making short sentences. Britta only wished Henri had lived long enough to see their beautiful boy.

"Happy, are you? Hmm? Did you play outside this afternoon?" she asked, kissing his rosy cheek. He smelled of sunshine and strawberries. Mrs. Bassett had a huge strawberry patch, which was where Britta had picked the berries for the jam she'd made earlier in the summer. She breathed in his baby scent, resting her chin on top of his blond curls, then looked at her neighbor. "I hope he wasn't any trouble."

"None at all. I was happy to watch him while you weeded my garden and yours. Thank you for doing that for me, dear girl."

"You're welcome, Mrs. Bassett. I'm glad I was able to get that task completed today. It was such a help to have you watch Joshua for me."

"Anytime I can keep an eye on this little one, you let me know. He's such a good boy." The elderly woman leaned forward and kissed Joshua's cheek. He reached his arms out and hugged her, then said "mwah!" as he made a kissing sound.

The two women laughed and walked to the door. Britta snagged a basket that held grapes she'd picked from a vineyard that connected with the back side of her property. The farm had been abandoned for a few years, so Britta didn't feel any guilt in picking all the grapes she wanted. She'd gathered enough of them yesterday to put up several quarts of juice and jelly if she could get more sugar.

"Thank you, dear. The grapes look lovely, don't they?"

"They do, Mrs. Bassett. I hope you enjoy them."

"I will, Britta. Now, don't you work too hard. You and Joshua should enjoy this lovely weather we're having."

"Yes, ma'am. Thank you again for watching him for me today. I'm so thankful for you. Shall I plan to stop by the day after tomorrow to see if you need help with anything?"

"No, don't bother. I must go into the village to pick up several things, then my sister is coming to stay for a few days. Why don't you plan on coming over a week from today?"

Britta nodded, doing her best to hide the relief she felt at not trying to care for a wounded soldier and help her widowed neighbor who lived a quarter mile up the road. "That will be fine, Mrs. Bassett. If you need anything from me between now and then, let me know."

"Likewise, dear." Mrs. Bassett strolled outside and waved as she left through the open gate.

Britta helped Joshua wave goodbye to the kind woman, then rushed outside to lock the gate. At least if anyone else came, it would make a racket as they attempted to open the gate, letting her know they had unexpected visitors.

How had she gone from having an afternoon free to catch up on work to harboring two wounded Americans?

As she thought of wounds, she realized she hadn't given more than a glance to David's injuries. She really should check them before they did anything else.

After closing the door, she set Joshua on his feet, then hurried to move the table and rug.

"Mama, mama," her son chanted as he tried to cling to her legs.

"What, Joshua? What do you need?" she asked, picking him up and holding him on one arm as she lifted the trapdoor with the other.

"It's safe," she called down the stairs. She could see David had left the lamp lit, and couldn't blame him. It was so dark down there without it.

He hurried up the stairs and drew in a deep breath, followed by another. "I'm not great in small, cramped spaces."

"I'm sorry," she said, and she was. She knew what it was like to be forced into a tiny space, fearful of being discovered. "If you like, you can sleep on the sofa tonight."

"Thank you, but I feel like I should sit up with Bryce." David glanced back toward the stairs and shuddered.

"I can check on him. I have a feeling he'll sleep through the night." Britta shifted Joshua so he faced David.

The soldier smiled warmly. "Is he your son?"

"Yes," Britta said. "This is Joshua. He's two."

David made a silly face that brought out Joshua's smile. "He looks like his mama."

Britta nodded. "He does. I sometimes wish he looked more like his father, but he definitely takes after me. Henri had dark hair and brown eyes."

"What happened to your husband, if you don't mind my asking?"

Britta preferred not to discuss Henri's death, but she didn't want to be rude to David. "The Germans killed him almost three years ago. Henri never even knew we were going to have a baby."

"I'm sorry for your loss, Britta. I'm sure your husband was a good, brave man."

"He was. Henri was the very best of men," Britta said, feeling maudlin and emotional as she returned to the kitchen. Preparing a meal would take her mind off the heaviness in her heart, at least for a while. "I realized I never looked at your wounds, David. Would you like me to treat any of them?"

"If you don't mind, I think I'll clean up and see

if they're as superficial as I think they are. Is there somewhere I can take a bath?"

"There's a stream at the back of the pasture behind the barn. Just be mindful of soldiers. You never know when they'll pop up."

David grinned at her. "Like the two that arrived on your doorstep earlier."

"Exactly." Britta offered him a cheeky grin. While he retrieved a change of clothes from his bag, Britta set out a clean towel and soap with a cloth for scrubbing.

"Thank you, Britta. If I'm not back in twenty minutes, assume something has happened and I'm not returning."

"You'll be fine. There are plenty of trees to hide behind. Just climb over the fence behind the barn and stay in the pasture." Britta tried to set Joshua down, but he clung to her, sucking on his thumb, which he rarely did.

David noticed the little one's fear. "Maybe when I get back, he'll be more inclined to be friends."

Britta realized David had dried blood on his face and streaks of it on his clothes. He was dirty and sweaty, and no doubt Joshua had noticed these things even if she hadn't as they'd worked to help Bryce.

"He's generally cautious around strangers."

David gave her a knowing look. "That's a good thing. My daughter thinks everyone is her friend, and I mean everyone. Natalie said she runs up to complete strangers at the grocer's and wants to tell them all about her life."

Britta laughed. "Perhaps you have a photo of your family you will show me when you return."

"Sure, I will." David stepped outside, quietly closing the door behind him.

As soon as he was gone, Joshua wiggled to be set down. He ran over to the gaping hole in the sitting room floor and pointed to the steps. "Down. Me down."

"No, Joshua. You stay up here with me. Do you want to help me with dinner? You can be mama's helper."

"Me hep!" The little one raced back to her, giggling as he crashed against her legs. Britta picked him up, holding him tight before she rained kisses over his face, drawing out his laughter.

"No mo, Mama," he said, squirming against her.

"No more kisses? What is the world coming to?" Britta asked in a teasing tone, then set Joshua in a highchair that had been hers when she was a baby. She placed a handful of green beans on the tray. "Can you snap the beans for me, like a big boy?"

"Me, big! Me do beans."

Britta left him playing with the beans as she added more wood to the stove. She'd stewed an old hen yesterday until the meat was tender. If she added some vegetables to it, it would suffice for the meal, along with slices of bread, wedges of cheese, and grapes. She would strain off the broth to give to the wounded man in the cellar, sure it would be a while before he could eat solid food.

David returned fifteen minutes later, looking

clean and much better than he had before he'd washed off the blood and grime covering him from head to toe.

"If you'd dump this bucket," Britta toed the bucket of rags from under the sink, "into the barrel out by the garden shed, you can fill it with water and set your uniform in it. I'll give it a good scrubbing after we eat."

"Thank you, Britta. Do you want me to burn the rags while I'm at it?"

"I'll burn them tomorrow," she said, watching as David carried the bucket outside. From the window over the sink, she watched as he emptied it into the barrel, set his uniform inside, then filled it with water from the hand pump by the shed.

By the time they'd eaten the simple meal, Joshua was smiling at David and sharing with him the grapes she'd cut in half.

"You're good with children," Britta said as she cleared the table.

"I miss my kids," David said as he hid a grape in his hand, then made it appear by Joshua's ear. The little one squealed with joy at the game and banged his feet on the chair. "He seems big for his age. Didn't you say he's just two?"

"Yes. He had a growth spurt about six weeks ago. It was like he shot up overnight. Mrs. Bassett, my neighbor who watched him this afternoon, thinks he'll be a tall man, like his father."

"Likely so," David said, lifting Joshua from the highchair when the baby held up his hands.

Britta smiled at them as she started washing the dishes. "If you can keep him occupied, this chore will take far less time."

"My pleasure. Does he play horsey?"

"Hosee?" Joshua repeated.

"I'm not sure we know that game," Britta said, observing as David settled her son on one leg and proceeded to bounce him up and down and back and forth, like he rode a wild horse.

Joshua giggled and laughed and waved his hands in the air in excitement. When David stopped, Joshua patted his arm and spoke in French.

"He would like you to do it again." Britta translated.

David obliged, then looked to Britta. "Did he speak in French or German?"

"French. Once he is a little older, I plan to teach him English and German."

"That's a good plan. Can't hurt a fella to know more than one language." David bounced his leg and tipped it to one side. "Whoa, horse!"

"Hosee!" Joshua exclaimed. "Mine hosee!"

"Your horse, is that right?" David asked, lifting the boy and giving him a gentle toss in the air.

At first, Joshua looked frightened, but when he realized David was going to catch him, he clapped his hands and giggled. The two of them continued that game while Britta hurried to scrub David's uniform and hung it to dry on hooks near the stove.

"Thank you for doing that. And thank you, Britta, for everything. You didn't have to take us in, but I'm grateful you did, and Bryce will be too."

"Of course. It was the right thing to do."

She and David spoke throughout the evening, checking on Bryce several times. Britta sponged his face which felt hot but not feverish and spooned sips of cool water between his parched lips.

That night, after she'd tucked Joshua into bed and settled David on the sofa, she sat beside Bryce for a while, praying he would recover. The sooner he was well, the sooner he'd leave. She needed him to be gone not just because of the possibility of Germans finding him there, but because something about the man left her disconcerted in a way she didn't like at all.

Early the next morning, she awoke to find she'd fallen asleep in the chair next to Bryce. After checking to make sure he didn't have a fever, she spooned a few more sips of water into his mouth, then made her way upstairs. David snored softly on the sofa, and Joshua slept soundly in his little trundle bed. Britta gathered her things and stepped outside into the early morning light. It wasn't yet dawn, but the darkness of night had lifted enough she could make her way to the stream with no trouble. There, she bathed and washed her hair, then dressed in a clean pair of mended trousers and an old shirt that had belonged to Henri. She left her hair hanging loose to dry, the curls thick and heavy on her neck in the heat that hadn't lessened overnight.

When she returned to the house, she found the sitting room empty but could see in the lamplight David was in the cellar checking on Bryce. She went to her room and draped her damp towel over the footboard of her bed to dry, then quickly fashioned her hair into two long braids before she hastened to the kitchen. David's uniform was dry, so she neatly folded it and left it sitting on a corner of the table before she grabbed a basket for the eggs and a bucket for the milk.

She'd only taken two steps outside when David rushed out to join her.

"Did you sit up with him all night?" he asked, taking the egg basket from her.

"Not intentionally. The last time I checked on him, I fell asleep in the chair."

"Thank you for taking such good care of him, of us." David held up the basket. "I'm a city boy, but if you tell me what to do, I'll see if I can find the eggs."

Britta grinned. "Gently slide your hand into the nest and pull out the egg. Nothing to it. Keep an eye on the rooster, though. Don't turn your back to him."

David eyed her warily, then headed off in the direction of the chicken coop. She smiled as she heard him talking to the chickens.

"Whichever one of you is the rooster, mind your business. I just want eggs and no trouble."

Amused by his warning, she went to milk the cow. She fed Minerva and the chickens, then entered the house to find David sitting at the table, a few chicken feathers in his hair, holding Joshua on his lap. Her son was playing with what appeared to be David's identification tags.

"How'd it go with the chickens?" Britta asked, trying to keep a straight face as David glanced at her, scowling.

"Great. Ever thought about making a whole bunch of fried chicken?"

"No. What is fried chicken?" she asked, setting the milk bucket on the counter, then plucking the feathers out of his hair.

David expelled a flustered breath and rubbed a hand over his head. "They're killers, your chickens. Out for eyeballs, if not blood."

Britta laughed. "Surely not that evil, David. Did you find any eggs?"

"A dozen," he said, pointing to the basket he'd left on the table.

"Wonderful. We'll have eggs for breakfast." She strained the milk, washed the bucket, then glanced at David as Joshua continued to play with the tags, waving them around in his hands. "Fried chicken? What is it?"

"One of the best ways to cook a chicken. It's covered in … well, I'm not sure what, exactly. But it's coated with something and fried, and it's so good on a summer picnic."

Britta could hear the wistful note in his voice and see the homesickness on his face as he spoke.

"May this war be over soon so you can have fried chicken at a picnic with your family, Lieutenant Kelly."

He offered her a gentle smile. "May it be so, Britta. May it soon be so."

They had a quiet breakfast of eggs, cheese, milk, and strawberries.

As soon as they finished, David packed his things and checked on Bryce, who continued to sleep.

"Tell him I'll be back as soon as I can get some help. I won't leave him stranded."

"I know you won't, David. Be careful, and be safe." Britta held Joshua to keep her son from trailing after the soldier as he stepped outside. She grabbed a napkin-wrapped bundle and handed it to David. "Just some bread, cheese, and fruit for later."

"Thank you, Britta. Is there anything you need? I'd happily bring whatever it is when I come back for Bryce."

"I wouldn't turn down sugar. I've been out for a while."

"Sugar it is!" David walked through the gate, then waved. "Be safe!"

"You do the same!" Britta called, then hurried back inside, closing the door. She set Joshua on the floor in the kitchen with a few wooden blocks, then went to check on Bryce. His brow felt hot, and his skin was clammy.

"Let David return soon," Britta prayed as she bathed the man's feverish skin. If the soldier returned tomorrow, it wouldn't be too soon to suit her.

Chapter Three

Bryce kept having the same nightmare over and over. He was in a car with two soldiers being shot at by Germans. The car crashed, the driver was killed, and he felt flames licking at his flesh. Then he'd see a blue-eyed angel and a blond-haired cherub. Cool hands would touch him reassuringly, and a soothing voice would assure him all was well.

He'd wake up in the dark, alone and disoriented. Pain more excruciating than any he'd ever experienced would engulf the entire left side of his body. Unable to bear it, he'd sink back into the dreams again.

After one particularly vivid dream, he awakened to find what surely had to be a heavenly creature bending over him, brushing a cool cloth over his brow. Her eyes were the biggest and bluest he'd ever seen, and her hair frothed around her in a tangle of golden curls. Behind her, a light glowed, highlighting the white cotton gown she wore.

Convinced he was hallucinating, he squeezed his eyes shut and forced himself to relax. He soon fell asleep.

The next time he awakened, he heard what sounded like whispers; then he felt a tiny hand touch his cheek. He opened one eye and looked into the smiling face of a cherub. Golden curls, bright blue eyes, and a delightful grin filled his vision, along with a scent that put him in mind of his nieces and nephew when they were babies. Did cherubs smell like talcum powder?

He sucked in a deep breath and felt a sharp, piercing pain in his side. Wincing, he closed his eyes and let himself drift into the painless void of sleep.

Eventually, Bryce left the land of slumber. When he tried to stretch his limbs, it caused a reaction of pain from his left shoulder all the way down to the toes of his left foot. He opened his eyes and glanced around, realizing he was someplace dark and dank, possibly a cave.

As his eyes adjusted to the dim light cast by a single oil lamp burning across the room, he could see shelves lined with jars full of vegetables and fruit. He turned his head and noticed a narrow set of stairs leading upward and daylight spilling down them from above. He was certain he was in a cellar, but whose cellar was the question.

He recalled riding with Lieutenant Kelly out to a project Colonel Thompson wanted them to look over. They'd been shot at, the car crashed, and the driver died. Bryce remembered helping David from the car before he'd shot the gas tank and blown it up. Vaguely, he recalled burns from the exhaust pipe and radiator water and being shot at a few times. He thought he and David had walked quite a distance, and there may have been splints on his leg, but he wasn't certain.

He glanced down to see a sheet covering him from the waist down. He lifted it and studied the splints that went from the top of his thigh down to his ankle. So, his leg was broken. He glanced at the puckered flesh of his side and his left arm and decided the burns hadn't been imagined either. Even feeling the slight air current caused by the movement of the sheet made them hurt. He assumed the discomfort created when he drew in a deep breath was from cracked ribs.

Had he imagined stumbling into a woman's home with David, or was that real?

Bryce was still trying to sort out his thoughts when the stairs creaked and he watched a young woman with hair the color of sunshine tread quietly down the steps. He gaped at her, realizing she was the angel of his dreams, even if she was dressed in worn trousers with her hair braided like a child's.

"Hello," he said but found it hard to speak when his mouth felt as though it had been stuffed with cotton.

"You're awake. That's wonderful," she said in English, surprising him. She lifted a glass from a crate being used as a makeshift table by his bed and held it to his lips.

Bryce took a few sips of the liquid, then settled his head back against the pillow. That small bit of effort had sapped his energy and he felt his eyes drifting shut. When he next awakened, light still spilled in from above, and he heard footsteps on the floor over him. He cleared his throat and it wasn't long until the angelic woman rushed down the steps and over to his side.

"Drink this," she said, holding the glass to his lips. Bryce drank half of it before he tipped his head away from the glass.

"Where am I?" he managed to ask.

"France, or Germany, depending on whom you ask." She smiled at him and pressed the back of her hand to his forehead. "Your fever broke in the night. I think you'll be fine now."

"Good. How long?" he asked, still finding it hard to talk.

"How long have you been here?" she asked.

"Yes."

She frowned. "You and Lieutenant Kelly arrived on my doorstep eight days ago."

"Eight days!" Bryce shouted, but it came out in a whisper. "David?"

She adjusted the sheet covering him and fluffed his pillow, avoiding his gaze. He reached up with his right hand and gripped her arm with a strength that surprised both of them. "David?"

"He went for help a week ago. I haven't seen him or anyone else since then. He promised to return as soon as possible. If he's able, I'm sure he will."

Bryce had visions of the man captured by the Germans and tortured. Or shot on the roadside. Or lost in the forest, wandering alone so long he starved to death.

"I'll find him," he said, trying to sit up, but lacking the power to do more than raise his head.

The woman laughed at him and easily pushed

him back down. “You aren’t fit to do more than stay right here in this bed. When you can climb up those stairs without help, then you can discuss going to play hero, but for now, you must rest. If you bring back your fever and delirium by doing something stupid, I’ll shoot you myself. You nearly died, Mr. Coleman, and I have no interest in keeping you here a day longer than necessary.”

With that, she turned and stormed up the stairs. He could hear pans clanging and banging in what he assumed was the kitchen. A short while later, she appeared with a mug of steaming liquid.

“Drink,” she said, holding it to his lips. The chicken broth was hot and tasted wonderful, seasoned with bits of herbs and spices. Greedily, Bryce drained the mug, then fell asleep.

The next day, he was able to stay awake for longer stretches of time. The woman appeared with more broth, then informed him she had to go check on her neighbor. Before she left, she closed the trapdoor, leaving Bryce in the cellar. He listened as she slid something heavy across the floor, no doubt to hide the entrance.

If she was so cautious, so careful, to keep him hidden, he had to question where they were. When he asked about their location, she always answered France or Germany. He didn’t understand what that meant any more than he understood how she spoke such fluent English. He knew she wasn’t English. Truthfully, she looked German more so than French and reminded him so much of Mamie, his beloved grandmother. His great-grandparents had come to America from Germany and started a cobbler business. Mamie still had some of her father's tools and could repair a pair of boots better than the shoe store in Holiday.

Bryce wished he'd asked Mamie to teach him the skill. Not that he couldn't buy any pair of shoes or boots he wanted, but there was something about preserving old traditions that seemed far more important to him than they had a few years ago. He supposed it was because he'd seen so much loss and death and destruction in the past two years.

The woman had been gone about an hour, or so the small clock on the crate by his bed said when the wick of the oil lamp sputtered and went out. Encased in complete darkness, Bryce tried not to panic. He'd never liked the dark—not as a child, and not as an adult. He knew there was nothing in the room that hadn't been there before the light went out, but he imagined spiders crawling on his leg and getting into the bandages beneath his splint, or a rat coming out of hiding and nibbling on the burned skin of his arm.

Repulsed by the thought, he pulled the sheet up over himself, then nearly cried out at the pain it caused when the cloth touched his seared flesh.

Tossing back the sheet, Bryce closed his eyes and forced himself to relax. He'd trained himself to sleep whenever or wherever, so he attempted to convince himself now was a good time to slumber. Only, he was tired of sleeping. If the woman was to be believed, he'd done nothing but sleep for more than a week.

As he remained in the darkness, he tried to sort out what he would do if David never returned.

Bryce couldn't stay with this woman indefinitely. By now, Colonel Thompson would be aware he was missing. Perhaps Lee would have sent troops out searching for him and David when they never arrived at the rail line project.

But if they were behind German lines, they'd be impossible to find. He couldn't blame the colonel for not risking the lives of others to track him down. No, if Bryce was going to be rescued, he'd have to do it himself. Just as soon as he had the strength to get up out of bed.

Unable to rest or relax, he began reciting poems, then Psalms. He hummed every tune he could remember and had started on Christmas carols when he heard what sounded like the hinges squeak on a door and footsteps entering the house. He held his breath, remaining silent as two sets of footsteps crossed the floor. He listened as the furniture upstairs was shoved aside; then the door opened and blessed, beautiful light spilled inside.

"Mr. Coleman? Are you awake?" the woman asked, sticking her head inside the opening above the stairs.

"I am. The lamp went out, though. If it isn't too much trouble, would you mind filling it, please?"

The woman hurried down the stairs. "I'm so sorry. I should have checked that before I left. Are you well?"

"Yes," he said, although he was anything but well. He'd been so fixated on staring at the light flooding into the space from upstairs that he didn't notice the woman carried a little one with her until she stood beside his bed.

"Mr. Coleman, this is my son, Joshua." She jiggled the boy slightly as he shyly tucked his head against her neck. "Joshua, you remember Mr. Coleman."

"Byce," the boy said, smiling up at his mother.

"Bryce. That's right," Bryce said, working up a smile for the child. "How old are you, Joshua?"

The boy looked to his mother.

"He's only two, but he's tall for his age."

Bryce would have guessed the child to be closer to four from his size. "His father must be proud of having such a fine son."

The woman shrugged. "He would be if he were still with us."

Before Bryce could ask any questions or offer his condolences for her loss, she rushed up the stairs. It wasn't long until she returned with the lamp.

She lit it and set it on a shelf closer to his bed. "I do apologize, sir. I know how frightening it can be to be stuck down here in the dark."

"You sound like you speak from experience."

She shrugged. "We hid here a few times when the German army was passing through."

"So, you are French?"

She nodded. "Yes. And we would be in France, if the Germans hadn't taken over this area again. They did the same thing in the Great War."

At least Bryce had a better idea of where they were now. "Can you please tell me your name again?"

"Britta. I'm Britta Webster."

"Britta," Bryce repeated, thinking the name fit

her well. With the right clothes and a hairstyle that didn't look like it belonged on a twelve-year-old, he thought she might be unbelievably beautiful, not that it mattered to him.

In the long hours, he'd had nothing more to do than rest in this bed and examine every aspect of his life, he'd decided if he ever made it back to Holiday, he would beg Kate to marry him and settle down to raise a family. Life was too short to waste even a day of it. He might not be wildly, passionately in love with her, but they'd always gotten along well and there were worse ways to start a marriage, or so he concluded.

A crash from upstairs drew him from his musings and sent Britta racing up the steps, taking them two and three at a time. Impressed by the speed with which she moved, he could see why she preferred pants to dresses.

"Is he okay?" Bryce called, hoping the baby hadn't hurt himself.

"He's fine. Just tipped over a stack of books."

"Books? Could I read one?" Bryce asked, hopeful for anything to break up the boredom he experienced, trapped as he was in the cellar.

"I'd happily bring them to you, but they're written in French."

"That's fine. I can read French and German."

Her head appeared in the opening again. "You can?"

"Yes, ma'am. My grandmother's parents came from Germany and she taught me the German language. My mother hired a French tutor and insisted my sisters and I learn not only to speak it but also read and write the language."

"Your grandmother is German?" Britta asked as she came downstairs with two books in her hand. She set them on the bed next to Bryce.

He nodded and looked at the titles. A copy of a William Faulkner book that had been translated into French held more appeal than an academic book on French poets of the seventeenth century.

"What's your grandmother like?" Britta asked, holding a glass to his lips.

Bryce drank deeply of the grape juice that still held a taste of sunshine in its tart sweetness. "That's good. Thank you."

Britta gave him a begrudging smile and set the glass on the crate by his bed. "Is your grandmother still alive?"

"Yes, at least last I heard. We call her Mamie, but her name is Cora Lee. She's kind and caring, loving and sweet. She's a wonderful baker and cook. Whenever I had a problem and needed someone to help me work through it, she was always willing to listen. Mamie is one of the nicest people I know."

"I'm glad you have her in your life." Britta edged toward the stairs acting fidgety, like she wanted to share something with him, but wasn't certain she should.

"Are you German?" Bryce asked, wondering if he'd offended her when her blue eyes widened.

"I'm …" she sighed. "My father was born and raised in Germany. He was a fine man, with a keen mind, and he was a good papa, but I am *not* German. I was born in France, and if there is any hope for justice in this world, I shall die in France."

Before he could say anything, she charged up the stairs. He heard her footsteps, Joshua babbling, and then silence after what sounded like the door slamming.

At least he knew Britta wasn't a German spy. Not even the world's finest actor could have summoned such a raw, vehement reaction to being asked if they were German.

A few hours later, she brought him more broth for dinner, along with two soft-boiled eggs and another glass of juice.

Bryce fed himself and felt quite triumphant when he got through the meal without spilling anything or falling asleep.

He rested for a while; then Britta returned with a tray holding medical supplies. "I thought we should change your bandages. I haven't disturbed them for a few days."

"Thank you," he said, holding still as she removed bandages, washed the areas with a clean, warm rag, then applied salve and rebandaged him. When she finished she ran a warm cloth up his good leg, along his chest, and over his arm and neck. It felt so good and refreshing, Bryce thought he might have moaned in pleasure but didn't open his eyes in case he had.

Embarrassed at the intimate contact with this woman who was a stranger, and a somewhat prickly one at that, he just prayed David would return soon.

The following morning, Bryce was awakened by a light touch on his cheek. He opened his eyes and turned to see Joshua standing next to his bed, holding what looked to be a crudely carved wooden horse.

"Hosee!" the boy said, shoving the toy at Bryce. He took it from the little one with his right hand and galloped it along the edge of the mattress, making neighing sounds. Joshua clapped his hands in delight and leaned closer. "Go mo!"

"Yes, little man," Bryce said, grinning at the child. Joshua wore a long nightshirt. His curls sprang up in every direction, and his feet were bare, making Bryce wonder if he'd left his bed when he was supposed to be sleeping.

Muted light barely filtered into the opening of the stairs from the open trapdoor, so he assumed it was still early out. Either that, or it was a cloudy day. If more than a week had passed since his arrival, it meant it had to now be September.

"Go mo, pease?"

Bryce galloped the horse around on the bed, then made the horse buck and jump. "Now that's how a wild bronc in from the range does it, Josh."

"Josh?" the boy asked, staring at him. The little boy patted his chest. "Me Josh?"

"Yep. That's you. Josh, the cowpoke."

The little one giggled. "Poke. Poke! Me a poke!" The youngster jumped and kicked out his legs, jostling Bryce and the bed in the process, but he didn't mind. It was too much fun to see the child so happy.

"That's right, Josh." Bryce reached out and tweaked his little nose. "A regular ol' cowpoke."

"Me Josh!" the boy proclaimed; then he touched Bryce's chest with his tiny fingers. "Byce."

"Yep. I'm Bryce. You said that well, Josh."

"Josh. Josh. Josh," the toddler chanted. "Me Josh!"

"Joshua!" Britta's frantic voice carried down to them. "Joshua, answer me!"

"Mama!" Josh called and ambled to the stairs. "Mama! Me an Byce!"

Britta appeared on the stairs, raced down them, and swooped her son into her arms. She held him so tight he whimpered. She loosened her grip on him and kissed his cheeks. "I'm sorry, baby, but I couldn't find you when I woke up. You scared me half to death."

"He's been down here for a while," Bryce said, trying not to notice the way the light filtering in the opening highlighted the transparency of Britta's white nightgown. Her hair looked lush and thick as the curls cascaded over her shoulders and midway down her back. Bryce had a sudden urge to bury his fingers in the tangled tresses.

Caught off guard by the unwanted notion, he forced himself to think of Kate with her brown hair, brown eyes, and entrancing smile. She was nothing like this reserved, often cool woman who barely tolerated Bryce's presence in her home. He could never imagine Kate leaving a wounded man in a dark hole in the ground for weeks on end. No, his Kate would have given up her own bed before she'd done that. At least he liked to think she would. Then again, Kate was nearly as particular about everything as his sister Ardith was.

Besides, Kate was safely tucked away in Holiday where the most exciting thing to happen in the last ten years was when an engine exploded at Milton's garage and knocked a wide hole in the back wall of the building. Thankfully, no one was hurt, but it had been all anyone talked about for a month.

He thought Britta wrapped a tough shell around herself as a form of protection. Honestly, Bryce couldn't imagine living in enemy territory, trying to raise a child, and fearing every unusual noise might be someone coming to do them harm. No wonder she was short-tempered and sometimes cross with him.

He knew it was beyond dangerous for him to be there. If the Germans found her harboring an enemy … he hated to think of what they'd do to her and the baby.

"I'm sorry he bothered you, Mr. Coleman." Britta glanced over at him as she turned toward the stairs.

"He wasn't any bother, ma'am. We were just playing with his horse." Bryce held up the wooden horse.

"Still, he shouldn't come down here like that. I've tried to warn him, but he's just so little, it's hard for him to understand." Britta started up the steps.

Bryce grinned at the toddler. "Josh can come anytime he wants. I don't mind a bit. It was nice having his company."

Her spine stiffened and her voice took on an icy tone. "His name is Joshua, not Josh. Don't you dare try to Americanize my son."

She marched out of the cellar and by the sound

of her footsteps, she was good and angry. He figured it had more to do with Josh scaring her than anything he'd said.

Despite her efforts to keep her son out of the cellar, Josh often appeared by Bryce's bed. The toddler had dragged a blanket, a set of plain wooden blocks, and a cloth ball made of scraps down to the cellar.

Britta finally gave up on keeping the child out of the cellar and allowed her son to spend time with him.

Bryce couldn't explain it, but the hours spent with Josh were the happiest he'd known for a long while. Something about the little one just reached into his heart and grabbed onto it with both hands. Even after he left this place, he planned to keep in touch with Britta solely for the purpose of providing assistance with Josh's care.

Bryce had been around enough youngsters, thanks to his sisters' offspring and those of his cousins, to know Josh was smart and bright and seemed ahead of other youngsters of the same age. He took delight in teaching the boy English words, along with his colors and even a few numbers.

One afternoon, Bryce tossed the ball to the far side of the small, cramped room while Josh chased after it, giggling each time he retrieved it. Britta had gone outside to work in the garden.

The door squealed in protest as she barreled into the house and raced across the floor. Listening, Bryce was certain he could hear the sound of a motor, like a vehicle approaching.

"What is it?" he called, but Britta didn't

answer. Instead, her hasty steps dashed around the house; then her head appeared in the opening to the cellar.

"There's a car with three German soldiers pulling up outside," she said in a shaky voice. Her eyes were wide and filled with fear. "Keep Josh quiet, please."

"Of course." Bryce set a protective arm around the toddler, then looked at Britta. "Take a calming breath, Britta. Don't show any fear. You've done nothing wrong, so act that way."

She nodded as she set a box full of Joshua's things on a step, then shut the door. The familiar scrape of what he'd learned was a table let him know she'd hidden the entry to the cellar.

Bryce prayed for the soldiers to continue on their way without causing any trouble, then glanced down at Josh. The boy looked like he was about to cry, picking up on Britta's terror and his own nervousness.

As he'd instructed Britta to do, Bryce drew in a calming breath, then another. He managed to work himself into a sitting position on the bed, grateful for the lamp that dispelled the consuming darkness.

Awkwardly, he lifted Josh up beside him. The little one bounced on the bed a few times and would have giggled, but Bryce gently tapped his mouth. Confused, Josh stared at him. Bryce held his index finger against his own lips and made a soft "shh" noise.

Josh mimicked him, holding his finger to his little lips and saying "shhh."

"That's right," Bryce whispered, picking up the

boy and ignoring the pain the movement created. He patted Josh's back as the toddler rested his head on his shoulder. Bryce rocked from side to side and prayed the child would fall asleep. In the thick silence around him, he strained to hear what was said but couldn't even pick up the rumble of voices through the thick cellar walls.

Footsteps thudded across the floor and Bryce held his breath. Soothingly, he continued to rock Josh and rub his back, hoping the little one would fall asleep.

It might have been minutes, but it seemed like hours before he heard the table being shoved aside and light spilled into the dank space once again. Bryce would die fighting to keep the baby safe if it came to that.

Protectively holding Josh against his chest with his right hand, he released a relieved breath when Britta rushed down the steps, nearly tripping over the box of toys she'd set on the fourth step. When she reached the floor, tears dripped down her cheeks and she looked like a person who had stared into the face of great evil.

Although it made him want to yelp in pain, Bryce lifted his left arm to her. Without a word, she ran over to the bed, collapsed against him, and cried.

"It's over now. It's over. They're gone. All is well," Bryce assured her in a tender voice. "Don't cry, Britta. You did well."

Finally, her sobs lessened and she leaned away from him, eyes darting to Josh.

"He slept the whole time?" she asked, brushing

a gentle hand over her son's golden head.

"Yep. It's a good thing he was ready for his nap. Otherwise, I don't know how I would have kept him quiet," Bryce said, thinking God's timing was always so perfect.

"You did a good job, Mr. Coleman." Britta wiped her tears away with the palms of her hands, sniffled twice, then stood. "I apologize for my outburst. It won't happen again."

Bryce had a feeling Britta Webster was a woman who rarely indulged in the luxury of tears and probably needed to cry far more often than she did. "Anytime you need a shoulder to cry on, feel free."

"That won't be necessary, but thank you."

She reached for Josh, but Bryce shook his head. "Leave him be. He's fine. In fact, I might join him for a nap. Before I do, tell me what happened."

Britta gave him an exasperated look as he tried to return to a resting position while still holding Josh. He managed without wincing in pain too many times. When he was settled on his side with Josh cradled against him, Britta sat on the floor next to the bed and trailed her fingers through Josh's hair.

Bryce wondered what it would feel like to have her feather her slender fingers through his hair, then decided the excitement of the Germans arriving must have pushed him into a state of near-delirium.

"There were three of them. I saw the car coming down the road and got the chickens and cow hidden before I ran inside here. The soldiers said they'd heard there were Americans in the area and wanted to know if I'd seen any. I assured them I hadn't, but they insisted on coming inside to search the house. I'd managed to shove Joshua's little trundle bed beneath mine, so it appeared that I was here alone. It didn't take long for them to look through the house, then I gave them juice and bread. They looked around outside and left. I wonder if there is a troop moving through here or if they heard about you and David escaping."

"Could be either or neither." Bryce felt his eyes growing heavy with exhaustion. "You did well, Britta. I'm proud of you. Most women wouldn't have handled themselves even half that well."

"Thank you," he heard her say before he fell asleep.

Chapter Four

Britta could hardly bear to let Joshua out of her sight after the Germans had stopped by the house. Their visit had terrified her, and it wasn't just the thought of what would happen if they realized she harbored an American. She feared for her son.

What if the Allies lost the war? What would happen to her? To Joshua? The idea of her son being forced to grow up and become a Nazi almost made her physically ill. It was against everything she and Henri had stood for. She couldn't bear the thought of it.

While the American in her cellar made slow but steady progress in his healing, she tried to formulate plans. It pained her heart so greatly to think of leaving behind the land that had been in her mother's family for centuries, but she would if that's what it took to keep Joshua safe and give him a chance for a better future than she could offer him there.

It had been more than a month since David had left for help, and they'd heard not a word from him. Bryce seemed to be losing hope that his friend would rescue him, and Britta couldn't help think David had never made it to the American camp. There were a hundred ways he could have been caught, captured, or killed in the miles between here and there.

Regardless of his circumstances, she had to focus on hers and what was best for Joshua. She hadn't missed the way Bryce's incredible pale green eyes lit with joy each time her son scooted down the steps of the cellar to play with him. In fact, it seemed Joshua preferred the American to her most of the time.

He'd never had a man in his life, and she could see now how her son relished the attention and affection Bryce lavished on him.

Was Bryce merely being kind because he had nothing better to do, or was he truly a good man? David had told her Bryce had saved his life. And he'd been nothing but honorable and gentle in his actions since he'd been in her care. He'd even let her cry all over him the day the Germans had scared her nearly witless. It wasn't until later that evening she realized she'd rested against Bryce's injured side. It had to have caused him great pain to hold her as he had, but he'd not uttered one word of complaint.

If her heart hadn't still been so riddled with grief over the loss of Henri, she might have even looked at Bryce with interest. As it was, she'd decided she wouldn't fall in love again. She couldn't go through losing another man she loved, and it would be hard for anyone to measure up to her husband. Henri had been a good provider and a dear friend, and she missed him every single day.

She quietly peeked into the cellar to find Joshua curled up next to Bryce on the narrow cot, both of them sleeping. Britta smiled in spite of herself, then went outside. She pulled the sweater she wore together in the front, wondering when the air had gone from hot to cooler temperatures. How would she keep Bryce warm and fed through the winter? Her dwindling supplies were almost gone and she'd soon need to make a trip to the village to restock. The thought of going and leaving Bryce alone in the cellar made her stomach ache with worry. What if Germans came while she was gone? What if he tried to get up and injured himself? What if …?

The sigh she expelled seemed to come all the way from her soul as she walked behind the house and up a slight hill to where she'd buried Henri next to her parents beneath the wide branches of an old oak tree.

Britta dropped to her knees next to the simple wooden cross that marked Henri's resting place.

Like one of the movie shows she'd heard about but never seen, her life with Henri played through her mind, one image—one memory—at a time. They'd been so happy together, so in love. And then he was gone far too soon.

Grief that she'd tamped down deep as she'd gone about the business of surviving in a war-torn world suddenly, abruptly, spilled free. Britta fell onto her face on the grass over Henri's grave and wept. She wept for the loss of her husband. She cried for the loss of her dreams. She railed against the Germans for all the destruction they'd brought to her country, her family, and her friends.

She couldn't bring herself to lambast God for allowing it all to happen. Not when He'd kept her and Joshua safe, warm, and fed. There were days when her faith had been the only thing that had sustained her.

Britta had no idea how much time passed as she at last allowed herself to fully grieve the loss of her parents and husband.

Depleted of both tears and energy, she finally sat up and wiped her eyes and nose on a handkerchief she pulled from her pocket.

"I'll love you forever and always, Henri Webster. Always." Britta brushed her fingers through the still-green grass, then rose to her feet and walked with heavy steps back to the house. She stepped inside to see Joshua's golden head as he climbed the last few steps of the cellar.

"Mama!" he said, rushing to her with a happy smile.

Britta picked him up and held him close, kissing his cheeks and breathing in his baby scent. She hated to think of him growing up too fast, but he'd changed so much in recent weeks. His vocabulary increased by the day, thanks in great part to Bryce. That wretched man had been teaching him to speak in English, though, and Joshua had all but abandoned most of the French words he'd learned. She supposed, if she truly intended to leave the farm behind and go somewhere they wouldn't have to worry about living in a war zone, it would be a good thing for her son to speak English along with French. She wasn't sure she could bring herself to teach him German, even if it was part of her father's heritage.

"Hungy."

"You're hungry?" she asked, wondering when her son had developed such an appetite. He seemed to always be hungry the past few days. Then again, they were mostly existing on milk, cheese, and eggs. She'd killed a chicken and roasted it yesterday, and between Bryce and Joshua, it was already all gone. And Bryce couldn't seem to get enough of fresh milk, claiming he'd been craving it since he'd left home two years ago.

"Hungy! Me an Byce hungy!"

"You men need food, do you?" she asked, carrying Joshua on her hip over to the sink. She set him on the counter while she washed her hands.

He climbed onto his knees and leaned forward, looking at the window. "Vwoom!" he yelled, pressing a hand to the glass. "Go, vwoom!"

Britta's heart fell to her feet as she saw three vehicles approaching the house. Two cars held soldiers and a small truck drove behind them.

She grabbed Joshua and raced for the cellar. Much to her surprise, Bryce stood near the stairs, reaching up with his good arm. "I heard the rumble. How many are there?"

"Two cars and a truck," she said, handing her son to him.

Bryce nodded and took a hobbling step back as she slammed the trapdoor shut, flipped the rug over it and shoved the table into place.

Heart racing, she rushed through the house

gathering anything that might hint she had a child and dropped it onto Joshua's bed before she shoved his trundle beneath her bed out of sight.

A sharp rap at the door made her want to run in fear, but she took calming breaths like Bryce had taught her and plastered a smile on her face as she answered the door.

Her smile rapidly changed from fake to genuine as David tipped his head to her in greeting, grinning broadly. "I'm back!"

"Oh, David! It's so good to see you," Britta gave him an impulsive hug, then stepped back. "Come in. Please, come in!"

David had one arm in a cast and a bandage wrapped around his head. He looked far thinner than he had those weeks ago when he'd left, but he seemed to be in good spirits as he moved back and allowed a distinguished-looking man to precede him inside.

"Mrs. Webster, this is Colonel Lee Thompson. We've come to get Bryce," David announced.

"Colonel Thompson," Britta said, feeling like she should curtsey in the man's presence. He possessed a regal bearing and commanding presence, but when she dared look in his face, she saw a twinkle in his eye and kindness in his smile.

"Mrs. Webster, it's a pleasure to meet you. Lieutenant Kelly has sung your praises until we were convinced you had a halo and wings," the colonel said as he looked around her humble home.

Britta couldn't help but laugh. "Far from it, sir. Mr. Coleman would tell you I more likely have horns holding up the halo and a pitchfork hidden beneath the wings."

The colonel chuckled then sobered. "Bryce is here? He's well?"

"Not well, yet, but he's getting better. He's here." She hurried to push aside the table, roll back the rug and lift the trapdoor. "Mr. Coleman, you have visitors."

The colonel leaned over, peering into the cellar. She watched as Bryce stepped into the light spilling in from the open trapdoor. He held Joshua on his good arm. The moment he saw the elderly man, he let out a whoop and smiled broadly.

"Sir! Are you ever a sight for sore eyes!"

Colonel Thompson grinned. "I could say the same for you, son. We'll have you out of there in a jiffy."

Britta reached down for Joshua, but he clung to Bryce, burying his face against the man's neck. Hurt by her son's preference for him and overwhelmed by the Americans who filled her house, she moved back until she bumped against the wall.

"Everything will be fine now, Britta," David said as he leaned against the wall beside her.

Mutely, she nodded. "Thank you for keeping your word."

"How could I do any less? You promised to take care of Bryce, and I promised to come back. Looks like we both did what we said." David smiled at her, then stepped forward as two men bearing a stretcher carried Bryce up out of the cellar, with Joshua clinging to him, eyes wide and uncertain.

"David!" Bryce's smile widened as he saw his

friend. They exchanged handshakes and Britta could almost feel the relief that both of them experienced at realizing the other had survived.

"Help him into that chair," the colonel said, pointing to an armchair that had belonged to Britta's father.

When Bryce was seated in it, Joshua cuddled up against his right side, Britta felt a sense of panic. Even though Bryce was basically helpless, his presence in her home had been reassuring. Comforting. If he left, who would be there to encourage and support her the next time the Germans came to call?

What if the Germans discovered he'd been there, along with a dozen other Americans?

About to be sucked into her fears, she forced herself to sound pleasant as she looked at the colonel. "Would you gentlemen care for refreshment? I have bread and jam, cheese, and fresh grape juice."

"That would be lovely, ma'am, but we can't tarry. I fear we must leave quickly before the Germans become aware of our presence," the colonel said as he looked over Bryce.

Since he couldn't stand to have anything touch his burns, she'd taken a few old pairs of Henri's pants, cut them off above the knee, and given them to Bryce to wear. That's all he had on at the moment.

It had been distracting enough seeing him in the dark cellar with hardly any clothes on, but in the broad daylight, she couldn't help but admire his finely formed physique. She'd not been aware he possessed the ability to stand, but she had an idea he'd been exercising and keeping his muscles functioning when she wasn't looking. And right now, she was looking plenty.

David nudged her with his elbow and waggled his eyebrows, causing heat to flood her cheeks as she forced herself to glance away.

"We'll give you a few minutes to say your goodbyes; then we need to leave, Bryce," the colonel said, herding all the men out the door.

Britta waited until they were outside before she let her gaze meet Bryce's. He truly had the most unusual eyes. They were green, but pale, almost like frost that had stolen in overnight and coated a deep forest glen.

"Britta, I can't thank you enough for all you've done for me. I'd be dead right now if it weren't for you. If there's anything I can ever do for you and Josh, let me know."

It was on her tongue to correct him again for calling her son Josh, but she didn't. Instead, she fell to her knees in front of his chair and took his right hand between hers.

"If you meant what you just said, then take me with you. Please. Take me with you to America. I can't bear to raise my son here. If Germany keeps control, then his future will be …" Her voice choked and she couldn't finish her thought. She cleared her throat and looked at Bryce. "Please? I'm not asking for me. I'm asking for my son."

Bryce appeared shocked by her request. "I can't take you with me, Britta. They'll never allow you to accompany me, even if I do get sent home.

You live in what is now occupied-Germany and everything about you looks German. Even if you were English, I couldn't take you with me. We'd have to be married for that to happen, and even then, I'm not sure they'd grant approval."

"Then marry me. If you get me to America, I'll disappear. You'll never hear from me again, but at least Joshua will be safe."

"No. It would never work, and living life on the run is no better than staying here. That's no way to raise Josh. He deserves far better than that."

Britta squeezed his hand tighter, so desperate she was ready to prostrate herself before him and beg. "Please, Bryce. Please, please don't leave us here. I will do anything to keep Joshua safe from harm. I'll be your maid, your slave, whatever you want, just please take us with you."

Bryce shook his head. "I'm not doing any of that. Even if I went along with this crazy scheme to marry you, I can't guarantee they'd let my wife travel with me."

"I can," the colonel said from behind them.

"Sir?" Bryce gave Colonel Thompson a questioning look.

"I heard more of that than you probably wanted me to. It's obvious you need to go home, Bryce. I can make the arrangements for you and Mrs. Webster, if she becomes Mrs. Coleman, to travel to America," the man said. His gaze settled on Britta. "Are you German?"

"No, sir. My father came to France from Germany years ago. He was a professor and was threatened to either join a particular political group or die, so he left in the middle of the night with nothing except what he could carry on his back. He eventually found his way to the nearby village, met my mother, and fell in love. This is the home where I was raised. Where my husband and I intended to live out our days until the Germans killed him. Henri was a French soldier home for a brief visit. He'd gone to the village to purchase supplies. A group of Germans stopped him and started asking questions. Without warning, they opened fire on him. Four innocent bystanders were also killed that day."

"I see," the colonel said, looking from her to Bryce. "Son, are you willing to marry this woman?"

"Well, I ..." Bryce hesitated. He looked down at the child on his lap. Joshua grinned and reached up a hand, patting Bryce's bearded cheek. "I suppose I am."

"Splendid," the colonel said, practically bouncing on his feet in glee. "Mrs. Webster, if you'll quickly pack your things, we'll all be on our way. You and Bryce can have a simple ceremony when we return to the base."

"Oh, sir. Thank you, sir!" Britta hopped up and gave the colonel a hug, then bent over and kissed Bryce on the lips.

Something unexpected happened when her mouth touched his. The contact sizzled on her lips and left them tingling even after she moved back from him and ran into her bedroom.

Britta yanked off her clothes, changed into one of the two nice dresses she had, and tugged a battered suitcase from the back of the big wooden cupboard she used as a closet. It didn't take long to pack the scant decent clothes she and Joshua owned, along with her son's blankets and toys that were in the room. She took Henri's uniform from the drawer where she'd carefully packed it away and added it to the suitcase, along with the few things that had belonged to him. Someday, they'd be important to Joshua. After securing the family heirlooms she owned in the suitcase, she closed the lid.

She realized her hair was still in braids and quickly unwound them, then tied her hair back at the nape of her neck with a faded ribbon and pinned her hat on her head.

Her fingers trembled as she picked up her handbag, stuffed in the envelope of money she'd kept hidden for an emergency, and tugged on the one pair of gloves she owned. Before she could change her mind and tell Bryce to leave without her, she snatched up her coat and Joshua's, then opened the door.

Soldiers carried a crate full of books outside, along with the knapsack that belonged to Bryce.

"What should we do with the food, sir?" One soldier asked as his head stuck up from the cellar.

The colonel looked to Britta as she made her way over to him. "My neighbor could use it, along with the cow and chickens. She's older and doesn't have much. I was supposed to visit her in the morning. If I don't arrive, she'll come looking for me."

"Leave her a note, a short one," the colonel said, motioning for the men with the stretcher to load Bryce on it. He still wore nothing but her husband's old pants, and Joshua continued to cling to him as though he were a growth attached to Bryce's neck.

"It's okay, cowpoke," she heard Bryce assure her son. "We're just going on a little trip. Everything is okay."

"Josh a poke?" Joshua asked in a small, frightened voice.

"That's right. Josh is a cowpoke. When we get settled in the truck out there, maybe you can show David your horse." Bryce rubbed Joshua's back and held him tenderly.

In spite of herself, Britta's heart melted at the way Bryce so gently comforted her son. She might barely tolerate his presence, but Joshua adored him.

"Hosee! David, hosee!"

"That's right, your horse," Bryce said, smiling at Britta as the men carried him and Joshua from the room.

"Everything will be well, Mrs. Webster. Do you have paper to write that note to your neighbor?" the colonel asked.

"Yes, sir." Britta rushed to write a few lines to Mrs. Bassett, letting her know they had to leave, but not saying why, and inviting the woman to take the cow, the chickens, the food, and anything else she could use. Hopefully, someday Joshua could come back and claim the home that was part of his heritage.

Britta looked around, surprised to see her books and anything of sentimental value had been packed and carried out to the waiting vehicles. She had no idea how the men had done it so quickly, but they had. She ran down to the basement and hefted a small green trunk that had belonged to her great-great-grandmother then rushed into the kitchen and grabbed a few tools that had been handmade by her great-grandfather. With one last glance at the only home she'd known, she stepped outside into the autumn light.

As she closed the door behind her, she let her hand rest on the knob a minute, praying for guidance in the days ahead. She had a feeling the next chapter of her life was going to be far different than the ones she was leaving behind.

Chapter Five

Loaded into the back of a truck fitted with all the equipment of a mobile medic station, Bryce relaxed on the comfortable cot as David settled onto a bench next to him. Britta had finally been able to pry Josh away from him, despite the youngster's howls of protest. He'd been told she would ride with Colonel Thompson in his car and knew Lee would take good care of her.

He couldn't believe he'd just promised to marry her, but he couldn't bear to leave them behind. Not when Josh had become so precious to him. He couldn't have loved the little one more if he'd been his own son.

Rather than dwell on what the future would bring, he reached out a hand to David and patted the man's shoulder. "Thank you, my friend, for coming to the rescue. What happened after you left Britta's house?"

"I went in the direction she said, trying to find the bridge to cross over the river. Germans were guarding the bridge, so I had to keep walking. I almost got caught and ended up hiding in a cave for three days. When I finally resumed my journey, I happened upon a camp of Germans and had to do some fast footwork to keep from being captured. In my haste to escape, I fell down a ravine and busted my arm, conked my head, and sprained my ankle. I limped to an abandoned farmhouse and stayed there until the swelling in my ankle went down enough I could walk again. The next time I set out, I headed north and walked all the way back to Colonel Thompson. By then, I couldn't remember how to find you, and he made me stay in the hospital until the doctor declared me fit to travel."

Bryce couldn't believe all his friend had gone through. "I'm sure glad you made it back to base camp in one piece."

"You're not the only one. Colonel Thompson was fit to be tied when I arrived. He started sending out scouts looking for the car we blew up and trying to find you. As soon as the doc gave me my walking papers, I spent every waking moment studying maps, trying to figure out exactly where I'd left you. Thank goodness, I finally remembered the name of the village Britta mentioned was nearby. After we located it, I had no trouble finding my way back to her place. But this part of the country is crawling with Germans. The quicker we are back at the base, the happier I'll be," David said, leaning back and studying him. He smirked and shook his head. "You ol' dog. Seems to me you and Britta got real cozy while I was gone."

"What?" Bryce asked, halfway sitting up, then lying back down as a bump in the road jolted him. "It's not like that. The woman is reserved and standoffish, and I'm not even sure she likes me."

David grinned. "I can see that from the way she couldn't keep her eyes off you."

Bryce scowled. "Maybe you should have the doc check your eyes. I think they're malfunctioning."

A laugh rolled out of David. "Not at all, my friend. She likes you, even if she might not know it yet. Joshua sure took to you, though."

Bryce nodded. "He did. I love that kid. He's smart for his age and full of life. If it hadn't been for him, I might have gone mad down in that dark hole in the ground."

"I hated to leave you there, but Britta seemed concerned about German soldiers finding you if you stayed upstairs."

"She wasn't wrong to worry. One day, three of them showed up and went through the house with a fine-tooth comb." Bryce glanced at David. "I had Josh with me in the cellar. I don't think I've ever been as afraid of anything in my whole life as I was right then of being discovered, and the fear wasn't for myself but for the boy."

"That's what happens when you grow up to be an adult and take on the responsibility of a child." David gave him a knowing look. "I think you care about Josh and his pretty mother."

"Pretty?" Bryce scoffed. "Britta dresses like an adolescent without any fashion sense."

David scowled. "Don't you sound uppity, Mr. Coleman?"

Bryce sighed and ran his hand through his hair that was in need of a trim. "I didn't mean it like that. I just meant that today is the first time I've seen her wear anything other than worn-out trousers and too-big shirts with her hair in two braids. I didn't even know she owned a dress or had a figure beneath her loose-fitting clothes."

A vision of Britta in a thin cotton gown, backlit by the lamp infiltrated his thoughts. Oh, he knew about her fantastic figure even if he'd attempted to block it from his mind.

"Well, she does own a dress, obviously, and she looks nice in it too. You might mention that to her later. If I heard the colonel correctly, you intend to marry her."

"I told her I would, but the thing is, David, I have a girl back home. What's she going to think if I come home with a wife?"

"That circumstances changed, and so have you." David leaned forward. "If I remember correctly, you said you weren't convinced marrying her was the right thing to do. If you weren't willing to marry her before the war, she probably knows you aren't planning on marrying her when you go home."

"Maybe, but I'm not ready to marry anyone. I don't know anything about being a husband or a father. It's not just Britta I'm marrying. I'm taking on another man's family."

David nodded. "True, but that other man never even knew about Josh because the Germans killed him before Britta had a chance to tell him she was expecting. Would you leave that innocent child there to be forced to become a Nazi? You know, I've heard they have boys as young as twelve in their army. Is that what you want for Josh?"

Bryce glowered at him. "Of course not! I want him to grow up somewhere he can play in the sunshine and laugh and run through the grass without fear of soldiers shooting at him or kidnapping him. I want him to be a normal child with a normal life. But to do that, I have to marry a woman I barely know and I'm not even sure I like, even if she did save my life."

"Well, there is that. If she hadn't been willing to take you in, and then spend hours digging out bullets and gently removing every last thread of cloth that was embedded in your burns, you'd probably have died of an infection weeks ago. Let's not even take into consideration the great debt you owe that woman for giving you care and shelter all these weeks." David gave Bryce a hard look. "Would you honestly leave her there for the Germans to use?"

Bryce stiffened. The thought of anyone laying a finger on Britta made protective instincts swell inside him until he felt the fury of a rampaging cavedweller. "No. I wouldn't want that."

David continued studying him, then finally sat back with a smug grin. "I predict everything will work out just like it's supposed to. I heard the colonel say something about getting you on board a ship that's leaving soon. If he can do that, you'll be home before you know it. I'm sure once you are back in your little town in Oregon, things will seem much different."

"I hope you're right. And I hope I'm not making the biggest mistake of my life by agreeing to marry that woman."

"You know the important things about her," David said. "She's kind and good. She can cook and keep a home. She's a wonderful mother. She's courageous and brave and stronger than most men I know. When it matters, she's someone you can count on and trust. That's more than most people have as a background when they wed."

Everything David said was true. Bryce couldn't imagine many other women who would invite three Germans into their home, feed them, and get them out the door again without losing their composure, but Britta had done that very thing. It wasn't until after the soldiers were gone that she had given in to her fears and tears.

Bryce pointed to the boxes of Britta's belongings that had been loaded into the truck. There were only four, and one of those was stuffed full of books. "It was good of Colonel Thompson to have the men pack her things. I doubt she expected to be able to bring any of it with her."

"A woman needs the things she holds dear to her heart. My wife has a box full of special treasures she would walk through fire to keep safe. In that box are the first corsage I gave her, Ryan's first tooth, and my daughter's baby shoes. Now that you aren't trapped in a cellar, you might think about ways to court Britta. If she's going to be your wife, make sure you treat her like one, instead of a polite stranger."

"Enough with the advice, David. Tell me about the project that we never reached. Did they figure out the problem?"

The rest of the way to the base they discussed rail lines and engines. When the truck braked to a stop outside the hospital tent, Bryce was relieved to have finally arrived. Before they parted ways, he dug money out of his knapsack and asked David to see to a few matters for him.

Colonel Thompson personally oversaw his delivery into the hospital and waited as the doctor looked him over. The splint on his leg was removed and his leg X-rayed.

"Whoever stitched you up did a good job. The break is healing well. I'm going to put a cast on it, just to keep it protected on your trip home, but it should be ready to come off when you get to America." The doctor carefully examined his burns. "They did a good job of treating the burns, too. You'll have scars, but it could have been much worse. You've cracked four ribs, but they appear to be healing nicely. Overall, I think another month or so of rest and you'll be well on the road to recovery."

"Thanks, Doc." Bryce was glad he would eventually mend, although he was tired of resting in bed. He was a man of action and always had been. Sitting still had never come easily to him. But since he felt as weak as a kitten, he supposed more rest was exactly what he needed. He'd get plenty of it on the ship home.

"How soon can he leave?" the colonel asked when the doctor finished his exam. "I've got a spot reserved for him on a ship that leaves tomorrow."

"As long as it's on a hospital ship heading home, then I don't see why not."

"That's good." The colonel watched as Bryce was settled into a bed in the infirmary. "I'm going to go make arrangements for you Bryce. I'll have the chaplain stop by for a visit later. If you aren't opposed, I'll see to it you and Britta exchange vows before you leave in the morning."

"Yes, sir." Bryce looked at the man he considered an honorary uncle. "Thank you, sir, for coming to get me. I thought I might spend the last days of my life in that horrid cellar."

The colonel's eyes shone with emotion. "If I let that happen, your mother would row a boat all the way over here just to slug me in the eye."

Bryce chuckled. "She would at that, sir. Thank you, though, for everything."

"My pleasure, son. Now, get some rest. You've got a big day ahead of you tomorrow."

Bryce fell asleep within minutes of Lee leaving his bedside. He awoke long enough to eat the filling but somewhat bland meal he was served. He'd just finished the last bite of bread when a chaplain walked in and made his way over to him.

"Bryce Coleman?" the man asked, reaching out to shake his hand.

"That's me, sir." Bryce shook his hand and liked his friendly countenance.

"I'm Chaplain Peters. Colonel Thompson asked me to check on you. He indicated you and Mrs. Webster would like to wed in the morning. Is that still your intention?"

Bryce thought about saying no—that he'd changed his mind. But he didn't. He'd given her his word and intended to keep it. Britta had been honorable with him, and he would do no less for her. Besides, David was right. If she hadn't given him her best, he would have died weeks ago.

"That is my intention, sir. If possible, I intend to take her home with me when I leave tomorrow."

The chaplain nodded. "The colonel explained that to me. I just want to make certain you're prepared to be a husband and father. Her son is a lively little fellow."

Bryce grinned. "That he is. And smart as can be. He already knows how to count to five, and he knows several colors."

"Spoken like a proud papa," the chaplain said with a grin. "What about Mrs. Webster?"

Bryce wasn't sure what the chaplain was getting at. "What about her?"

"Are you as enthralled with her as you are her son? Will you honor, cherish, and protect her no matter what comes?"

"I will, sir. At least I'll try my best to do those things."

The chaplain studied him for a moment before he again spoke. "Tell me, son, one thing about her that you admire."

Bryce's mind went blank. One thing about Britta he admired? One thing? There wasn't just one thing, but a hundred things. He pictured her humming a song he didn't recognize and dancing around the cellar with Joshua in her arms. He envisioned her kissing her son and comforting him when he'd tripped and scraped his knee. He recalled the gentle feel of her hands as she tended to his wounds. The nourishing, delicious food she prepared. The care and concern she'd showered on him even when she had no idea if they'd both be captured or killed for his presence in her home.

"Britta is selfless. She does things, not in hopes she'll gain something from them, but because she's a good person and truly wants to help." Even as she'd begged him to take her with him, it wasn't for herself that she asked, but to create a better future for her son.

The chaplain made a humming noise and took a step back, looking pleased by his answer. "I'll see you in the morning at eight sharp."

"Yes, sir. Thank you, sir," Bryce said, uncertain if the chaplain intended to marry him then or lecture him on the finer points of being a fit husband. He could have told the chaplain he admired Britta's intelligence, or courage, or even how utterly tantalizing she looked when her hair was down and she wore nothing but a plain cotton gown, but he was glad he'd kept those thoughts to himself.

Bryce might have tossed and turned all night in worry, but the journey to the base had left him exhausted. He fell asleep dreaming of Britta pressing her lips to his, and the tingle that lingered long after the kiss ended.

He awoke before dawn the next morning. With a bit of begging, he was given a bath, then his dressings changed. A nurse found a pair of trousers that would fit him and split them up the left leg to go over his cast. Wearing a shirt was going to be torturous, but he refused to get married bare-chested. Two nurses slathered his burns with salve, wrapped gauze over them, then slid a thin white undershirt over his head. By the time they finished, he felt lightheaded but ignored it as they helped him finish dressing.

David appeared just as a nurse finished helping him on with a sock and shoe; since the cast on his leg went from the top of his thigh all the way down to his toes. "You look ready for inspection, Bryce."

"I'll take that as a compliment." He grinned at his friend. "Were you able to locate the items I requested?"

"I got everything on your list. It wasn't easy, and I had to enlist the help of three nurses, but I think everything is ready."

Bryce reached out his hand. "Thank you, David, for everything. I know you saved my life, and I'm grateful every day for all you've done for me."

David scoffed. "Are you kidding? If you hadn't climbed up that tree and pulled me from the car, I'd have died right then. I owe you for my life, Bryce."

"No more than I owe you for mine." Bryce sat up as the colonel entered the tent and the men who were able, saluted him, David included.

"At ease, men. At ease." The colonel walked over to Bryce and placed a hand on his shoulder. "You ready to do this, son?"

"Yes, sir, I believe I am. Is Britta ready?"

"She is ready and waiting, and so is Josh."

Bryce nodded. "Then let's get to it."

A nurse pushed over a wheelchair, and the colonel helped Bryce get settled into it. David carried the crutches another nurse held. Bryce had vehemently refused to get married sitting down. Even if he had to lean on a crutch, it was better than being stuck in the wheelchair.

The colonel pushed the chair into a small tent. The inside had been draped with red and white crepe paper streamers and paper bells. Bryce had no doubt they were meant to be Christmas decorations, but they looked nice with the autumn flowers someone had arranged in two big bouquets near where Chaplain Peters waited on the far end of the tent. A small table set to one side was covered by what looked to be a white sheet and held a single layer cake covered with white frosting.

"This is great, David. Thank you so much," Bryce said, smiling at the man who had become more than a friend to him. He was like a brother, which was precisely the reason Bryce had asked David to do what he could to provide a decent wedding ceremony for Britta. He'd given him money to purchase whatever he could find, like a cake and flowers.

"My pleasure. When the nurses heard a wedding was being planned, they were excited to help. One of them even sold us a dress she bought in Paris when she was on leave, and another who had the day off went to the nearby village to get flowers and a few other things."

"Then I owe them all a great deal of thanks." Bryce looked from David to Lee. "Where's Britta?"

"She's in my tent. I've been given the great honor of walking the bride down the aisle. And Josh is being brought in by a few of the nurses. He's been eating up the attention from the pretty girls."

Bryce chuckled. "That sounds about right."

David handed the crutches to the chaplain, then managed one-handed to push Bryce's chair up next to the man. A group of nurses entered the tent and stood at the back with Josh. The toddler was dressed in a new shirt and pair of pants. His unruly curls had been combed into something resembling a style, and he held a little stuffed bear in his hands. When he saw Bryce, he squealed with delight.

"You stay right there, cowpoke. It'll just be a minute; then you and your mama and I will head out on a big adventure."

Josh gave him a curious look, but when a nurse handed him a cookie, he forgot all about wanting to come to Bryce.

Four of the nurses began to hum the "Bridal Chorus" from *Lohengrin*, an opera composed by Richard Wagner. Bryce had attended enough weddings to recognize the song as one often performed as the bride walked down the aisle.

Colonel Thompson appeared at the door of the tent with a woman Bryce scarcely recognized on his arm. Britta wore a gown the same shade of blue as her bright eyes. From growing up with two sisters obsessed with fashion, he knew the neckline was a sweetheart style, and it had a ruffled drape across the front of the skirt that fell just below her knees. Shirred sleeves came to her elbows and gathers added a softening touch to the shoulders. The gown appeared to have been made for her as it accentuated her generous curves. Her hair had been pinned on top of her head with a few curls escaping, and a smart little hat that matched the gown perched almost over her right eye with fine black netting draping over her face. She wore a pair of black heels and silk stockings.

Considering how hard stockings were to come by, Bryce had to assume David had paid a pretty penny for them. Every single cent was worth it to see Britta looking so lovely. He had no idea when she was attired in a nice dress and had her hair styled she'd look like she belonged on a movie screen in Hollywood.

As she took a step nearer, he noticed she carried a bouquet of red roses and wore a brooch that appeared old.

When her gaze met his, Bryce smiled and she blushed. With David's help, Bryce rose to his feet and leaned on the crutches for balance as Lee placed Britta's hand in his. He repeated his vows flawlessly, then listened as she did the same, feeling like he was outside himself observing the proceedings instead of actively participating in the ceremony that would tie his life to Britta's for the remainder of his days on earth.

When Chaplain Peters asked for the rings, David pulled two from his pocket and handed them to Bryce. He slid a solid gold band onto Britta's left ring finger, holding his breath until he realized it fit perfectly. She nudged a plain gold ring onto his finger, and the ceremony soon ended. Bryce gave her a brief, chaste kiss, although he found himself wanting to prolong it, deepen it.

The nurse holding Josh set him down and the little boy raced over to them, babbling so fast, Bryce could only pick out a few words like mama,

Byce, poke, and boat. Apparently, someone had informed Josh he was going to ride on a boat.

Although Bryce hadn't been aware of it, a soldier had been taking photos of the ceremony. The young man snapped several photos as Bryce and Britta cut the cake and fed each other a thin slice. Josh wanted in on the action, so Britta picked him up and held him while Bryce fed him a few small bites, trying to keep the active boy from smearing frosting all over his clothes.

In a whirlwind, they were hugged and congratulated, then escorted out to a waiting car. Bryce saw Britta press something into the hands of one of the nurses and give her a hug.

"Your things have already been loaded on the ship, but you'd better hurry up. It wouldn't do for you to miss it. When you get there, give the captain this," Lee said, handing Bryce an envelope and drawing his attention away from Britta. "Send a telegram as soon as you reach the States. The ship will dock in Charleston. I sent a telegram to your father, so he's aware you have been located and are on your way home. I want you checked out by a doc as soon as you put into port. If all is well, you'll be released to travel to Holiday."

"Yes, sir. Thank you, sir." Bryce felt emotion well within him as he shook the colonel's hand. He knew he was fortunate the colonel had taken such a personal interest in him and his welfare, otherwise he might have been left to try to find his own way back to camp or been captured and killed.

Then there was David. Not only had he kept his promise to come back for Bryce, but, with the help of the nurses, he'd made the wedding seem like a real ceremony, not just a rushed legality.

Bryce looked over the group. "Thank you all, for everything."

"Just go have a happy life, son," Lee said, squeezing his good shoulder. He gave Britta a parting hug, tweaked Josh's nose, then stepped back. "I expect to hear from you both from time to time."

"Yes, sir," Britta said, looking like she was about to burst into tears.

"Come on, wife. We'd better get going," Bryce said, waiting as she tossed the bouquet over her head to the group of nurses, then slid into the car. David handed Josh to her; then Bryce shook hands with both David and Lee again before he climbed in next to her. Once his crutches were stowed in the trunk, they drove away from camp.

"How far is it to the ship?" Bryce asked, looking at Britta as she stared out the window, no doubt trying to gain control of her emotions.

Without looking at him, she spoke, but her voice sounded quivery. "I'm not certain. No one said."

"It's about two hours, sir," the driver said from the front seat.

"Thank you," Bryce said, then turned to the woman who was now his wife. A woman he hardly knew, yet to whom he felt so oddly connected. "You look lovely, Britta."

She turned to him, her eyes luminous with unshed tears. "You don't have to say things you don't mean, Bryce. We may not love each other, but we can at least be honest."

"I am being honest. You do look lovely. In fact, only a blind man would fail to notice you're absolutely beautiful." He offered her a charming, teasing grin. "I had no idea you were such a sweet dish. Here I thought I was marrying a tomboy and instead got a pin-up girl."

"I'm not even certain of half of what you said, but I suppose it was meant as a compliment." She glared at him in mock affront, then offered him a look of sincerity. "Thank you, Bryce, for doing this and for the wedding. David said you paid for everything. Everyone has been so kind."

"You are most welcome. Every woman should have a nice wedding." He offered her an encouraging look. "What did I see you giving to one of the nurses?"

"Oh, it was a charm that belonged to her great-grandmother. She said the family legend is that if a bride carries it on her wedding day, she'll have a long, happy life with her husband."

"That was a swell thing for her to share with you." Bryce suddenly recalled the things his sisters carried on their wedding days. "Did they tell you about that something borrowed, something blue rhyme?"

Britta smiled. "They did. The dress was something blue. One of the nurses bought it last month in Paris. It's the finest thing I've ever owned. And one gave me a shiny new penny to put in my shoe for something new. The charm was something borrowed. The something old is this." She touched the brooch pinned to her shoulder. "It belonged to

Henri's grandmother."

Bryce leaned a little closer and admired the finely crafted piece of jewelry that held a ruby set in a gold filigree oval. "It's very nice, Britta, and I'm glad you have something like that to pass on to Josh. It will be a treasure for him someday."

She nodded and glanced out the window.

Bryce touched her hand, drawing her attention back to him. "You really and truly do look lovely."

"Thank you, Bryce, for everything." Britta dropped her gaze to her lap. "I'll do my best to not be a burden to you."

"Isn't that what every husband longs to hear on his wedding day?" Bryce muttered half under his breath. He expelled a sigh, then took Britta's hand in his, holding it lightly, getting used to the feel of her much smaller hand pressed to his.

Although it would have never entered his mind before today, right now Britta seemed so fragile and delicate instead of the paragon of strength he'd depended on the past weeks. "You are not a burden, Britta, and if I didn't want to marry you, I wouldn't have."

"I know, but I just …"

He placed a finger on her lips to silence her, then realized the folly of his actions. Touching her soft lips only made him yearn to kiss her, really kiss her. He sighed again, then settled back in his seat. "All this excitement has worn me out. I'm gonna rest a while. You and Josh might want to take a nap too."

A glance down assured him Josh had already fallen asleep with a few lingering cake crumbs on his mouth and cheeks. Bryce brushed them away and looked at Britta. The smile she turned on him held such warmth, such depth of affection, he had to force himself to face the back of the driver's head and close his eyes. "Rest," he said, then pretended to sleep.

Although he'd intended only to feign a need to rest, he quickly fell asleep and didn't awaken until they arrived at the dock. The driver knew where to go. Bryce observed a ship painted bright white with red crosses on it. It looked like Lee had arranged for him to travel home on a hospital ship. He hated to take space on it that could be used by a soldier who needed to go home, but he was eager to leave and return to Holiday. He needed to be in a place he could heal without glancing over his shoulder, waiting for someone to shoot at him.

The car stopped and the driver ran around to open Britta's door. She got out and picked up Josh, settling him on her hip. The little boy excitedly pointed to the ship.

"Boat. Go, Mama. Go on boat!"

"Yes, baby. We're going on the boat," she said, looking to Bryce as a sailor in a neatly pressed white uniform pushed a wheelchair toward them.

Britta stayed close beside Bryce as he was helped into the chair and then pushed onto the ship. The driver carried their overnight bags and Bryce's crutches as he trailed after them.

"I'm to give this letter to the captain," Bryce said, handing the envelope Lee had given him to a petty officer who looked like he knew what he was doing.

"I'll see he gets it right away," the man said, then rushed off, leaving them to wait. Bryce took the bags and the crutches from their driver and thanked him for his help, then sent him on his way.

Josh whined to get down, but Britta kept a tight hold on him lest he get into trouble, get hurt, or fall into the water. Bryce hadn't given a thought to how challenging it would be to keep the child safe and entertained during the voyage. His only focus had been on getting home.

"Hey, cowpoke, it won't be long before we're in our room; then your mama can set you down." Bryce smiled at the toddler and Josh turned his attention from wiggling to holding out his hands.

With a look at Britta, Bryce set the bags beside the wheelchair, handed her the crutches, then took Josh. The little boy settled against him and released a sigh. When Josh reached up and patted Bryce's cheek, he felt like his heart turned to syrup. Perhaps he and Britta would never be more than reserved acquaintances, but Josh had already laid claim to Bryce's heart. He could hardly wait to show the child Elk Creek Ranch or take him for a ride in the engine of a train. His family would love the boy, and he could envision Mamie rocking him to sleep in her chair by the big fireplace in the house at the ranch.

The only question was how Britta would fit into his world and life. At the moment, she looked frightened and uncertain and so young. He still wasn't sure how old she was. If she'd mentioned it, he didn't remember, and that irked him. A husband should know a few things about his wife, even if she intended for the arrangement to be in name only.

"Mr. Coleman?" the captain asked as he approached them with hurried steps.

"Yes, sir," Bryce said, holding out a hand in greeting. The captain took it in his and shook it.

"Colonel Thompson made arrangements for your passage. It's highly unusual, but he mentioned you two are newly wed."

Bryce nodded and tipped his head to Britta. "As a matter of fact, we exchanged vows just a few hours ago."

"The colonel stated as much in his note. If you'll follow Petty Officer Sutherland, he'll get you settled. Should you need anything during the voyage, please let us know. Congratulations on your nuptials." The captain offered them a curt nod and rushed off.

"This way, please," said the petty officer, picking up their bags and taking the crutches from Britta, freeing her hands to push Bryce's chair.

Although Bryce expected to be given accommodations in one of the medical wards on the ship where he envisioned rows of beds filled with wounded men, they were taken to a small, private room that held two narrow beds.

"Here we are," the petty officer said as he set the bags and crutches inside the room, then stepped back.

"Who had to give up their space for us?" Bryce asked as Britta wheeled him inside. There was just barely room between the two beds fastened to the walls for the wheelchair. At the far end of the narrow space were a sink and a toilet. A closet near the door offered a bit of storage space for their belongings. The accommodations didn't look as comfortable as a prison cell, but they were far better than Bryce expected.

"Two officers, sir, and they were glad to do it. It's not often we get newlyweds on our ship or little ones. We all extend a warm welcome. Please let us know if you need anything. Meals will be delivered at eight, noon, and six. If you require anything else, just ask. And if you need medical assistance or supplies, you'll find the ship's head doctor at the end of this corridor on the left."

"Thank you," Bryce said, nodding with appreciation to the young man. "Please extend our thanks to the captain, and the officers who so kindly gave up their room."

Britta looked like she was about to cry. She offered the petty officer a watery smile. "Yes. Please give them all our thanks."

"Of course. Lunch will be up as soon as we set sail." The petty officer checked his watch. "In about an hour. Enjoy your day, folks. And if you need help with the little one, there are several nurses who would gladly watch him for a while. When they heard a toddler was coming on board, they grew quite excited. Most of them are located down one deck."

"That's great. Thank you." Bryce waited until the man left and closed the door behind him before he set Josh down and took Britta's hand in his, rubbing his thumb over her knuckles. "What's wrong?"

"Nothing," she whispered, struggling to hold herself together.

Bryce somehow managed to turn the wheelchair around in the cramped space using his good hand and foot. He backed it between the beds to keep Josh from playing in the toilet; then he caressed Britta's hand again. "Something's wrong. Tell me."

She shook her head, but her chin quivered and tears welled in her eyes until one big drop rolled down her cheek.

Bryce had never been able to bear the sight of tears, and it pinched his heart to see her struggling with them now. "What upset you, Britta? Is it staying in the same room with me? I promise I'm too weak and wounded to give you anything to worry about."

"It's not that," she said, sinking onto one of the neatly made beds. "It's this. All of this." She waved her hand around the room, but he had an idea the gesture was meant to encompass all the changes that had taken place in her life in the past twenty-four hours. "Everyone has been so kind and gracious. I don't feel as though I deserve any of it. I forced you into agreeing to marry me, and I … I …" She burst into tears, burying her face in her hands.

Josh stared at her with wide eyes, then hurried over to her, patting her knee. He looked at Bryce expectantly. "Mama owie. Mama owie, Byce!"

"I know, cowpoke," Bryce said, picking up the child and setting him on his lap. When Josh was settled, he reached out and handed Britta a handkerchief. She took it, holding it to her face as she continued to cry.

"Mama?" Josh asked, his little voice filled with concern.

"It's okay, Josh. Your mama will be just fine." Bryce assured the child, but he hoped it comforted the woman too. "Mamie says sometimes the best thing in the world for a girl is a good cry."

Josh just looked at him like he should have already fixed Britta's tears. They did begin to lessen; then she sniffled and glanced at him as she wiped at her nose and dabbed at her tears. "She sounds like a smart woman."

"She is, and I'm looking forward to introducing you and Josh to her." Bryce didn't know what to do to help Britta. He had a feeling she needed to work through some things on her own. "I may not be the husband you want or one you even like, but I'm here if you ever need to talk. I have two older sisters, so I'm not scared of girls."

A small smile lifted the corners of her mouth. A mouth he was coming to realize was entirely kissable. "Tell me about your family."

Bryce settled more comfortably in the chair, then pulled Josh closer to his chest. "My sister Ardith is the oldest. She's married to Emil Johnson and they live about an hour from Holiday, that's the town where we grew up. Her husband is a banker. They have two children, both girls. Cheri is seven and Josephine is five. Ardith can be a little … um ..." Bryce searched for a polite way to describe his bossy, unyielding sister. "Ardith is exacting."

"Exacting?" Britta asked, as though she tried to understand the description.

"She likes things done a certain way and things to be a certain way—most often her way."

"Ah, I see." Britta dabbed her nose and leaned back, setting her handbag on the bed behind her. She unpinned the hat she wore, setting it aside.

Bryce was so distracted by her hair, pinned in a mass of curls on her head with tendrils framing her face, he stared at her for a long moment before he returned to the conversation.

"Carrie is the middle child. She's two years older than me and is married to Cliff Emmett. He runs a lumber mill. They have a girl, Olivia—she's four—and a boy, Gavin. He just turned three last month. Carrie is full of fun and laughs. I think you'll like her, and I know she'll like you. If you have questions about anything, she'd be happy to help you."

"That's good to know. I'm already learning you Americans are a different lot than the people I'm accustomed to being around." Nervously, Britta twisted her hands together, keeping her head down. "I hope your family won't despise me."

Bryce lifted her chin with his hand and forced her to meet his gaze. "They'll love you and Josh. I guarantee it. I've already told you about my grandmother. She and Gramps live out at the ranch with my cousin Hayes and his family."

"Do you have many cousins?"

Bryce shook his head. "No. At least very few that are related by blood. My grandparents have been friends with the Milton family for years, so we've always considered all of them to be cousins and aunts and uncles. As for blood relatives, my uncle Jonah has two daughters. They all live in Idaho, so we don't see them often. Uncle Noah lived on the ranch with his wife and two children—a boy and a girl. He survived World War I but died of pneumonia two months after he returned home. His wife remarried two years later and moved to Portland, but their son, Hayes, refused to go. Mamie and Gramps finished raising him, and he owns the ranch now. My dad goes out to help often. As for my mother, she's an only child of two only children, so there are no other relatives. Her mother passed before she moved to Holiday, and my Grandfather Lennox died last year."

"I'm so sorry. Were you close to him?"

Bryce thought of his relationship with his grandfather. Close had never been a word he'd use to describe it. While the man had spoiled all three of his grandchildren, it was Bryce that he'd doted on, because he was a boy. That and his mother had given him the middle name of Lennox. Bryce wasn't overly fond of it, but he supposed it did pay tribute to his grandfather.

He was convinced his ties to a man who had been one of the richest in America was part of the reason he and Britta had a private room on an overcrowded hospital ship and were able to get immediate transport to America instead of waiting months. He felt bad about what he viewed as cutting in line, but he was more than ready to be at home with the people he loved.

When Britta continued to look at him expectantly, he realized he'd failed to answer her question. "We weren't particularly close. My grandfather was a complicated man, one who wasn't easy to know. In fact, I was so angry with him the last time I saw him, I refused to speak to him, and now he's gone. I've felt guilty about that ever since the day I received news of his passing."

"I'm sorry, Bryce. It's hard to lose a loved one under any circumstance. You don't seem like the type of person to harbor bad feelings toward someone. What did he do that upset you?"

Bryce considered making light of the truth or not telling Britta, but she was his wife and now that the vows had been made, he intended to honor them as long as they both were alive. As her husband, he knew he needed to open up to her, to share his life with her, even if it wasn't something he felt comfortable doing.

"I was in my last year of college when the Japanese bombed Pearl Harbor. I wanted to leave school and enlist right then, but my parents assured me the war would still be there when I graduated. The day I had my diploma in hand, I went to enlist, only to find my name on the list of men exempted from service. Convinced it was a mistake, I went to two more enlistment offices, and they both turned me away. Angry, I made the trip home from Portland and went straight to my father, demanding to know what had been done. Dad was as upset as I was when I told him what had happened. It wasn't that he was eager for me to serve, but the Colemans are an honorable bunch, and he felt it was my right to make the choice to serve. Mother was relieved I'd been exempted but had no idea how it had happened. We were still discussing it at dinner that night when Grandfather arrived from one of his many trips. He chuckled and said he'd had his attorney file the necessary paperwork to have me listed with a reserved occupation."

"What does that mean?" Britta asked, appearing as though she tried to understand a term she didn't know.

"It means there are certain occupations in our country that are deemed important enough that a man in that position is not only exempt from serving in the military but is then forbidden from military service. My grandfather had made a case that I was to be the sole heir of his vast business interests and therefore, I couldn't be spared to serve."

"Are you really the sole heir?"

Bryce nodded. "He provided a sizeable dowry for my sisters and left funds for each of their children, but I own all of his business assets. My mother has taken charge of them until I'm ready to step into the role of president of my grandfather's company. She's a crackerjack when it comes to business matters."

Britta gaped at him, as though she was trying to understand all he'd shared. "How did you end up in France?" she finally asked.

"I found out a battalion was being formed that was specifically for dealing with railroads. Although I was prohibited from enlisting, I was able to sign on as an independent, civilian contractor. Because of my background and knowledge, I was sent straight to Africa. From there, I was moved to Sicily, then Italy where I was stationed at Naples until they moved me to France. David and I were on our way to a new project when the Germans shot our driver and we ran off the road, and you know the rest."

"I do, but I don't understand about the railroad part. How does that relate to your grandfather? How do you know about trains?"

"Grandpa Coleman was a train engineer. He worked his way up to it, doing everything from running the telegraph to serving as a brakeman. He shared his love of trains with my father. Dad worked as a mechanic for many years and still helps out sometimes, although Grandfather Lennox hated that he did. Dad was, and still is, one of the best mechanics in the world when it comes to repairing trains. Grandfather Lennox owned several rail lines and trains, among other enterprises."

Britta looked like she wanted to say something as she opened her mouth, then closed it again.

"I'm sure this is a lot for you to take in." Bryce didn't know how to tell her he had enough money in his bank account to build her a castle, a hundred castles, if that's what she wanted. He had the distinct idea money wasn't something that would impress his wife.

"Are you saying your grandfather was a rich man and left you his rail lines, and trains, and other enterprises, as you call them?"

"Yep. That's about right." He glanced down at Josh. The toddler entertained himself with the little stuffed bear he'd carried all morning. Bryce discovered David had acquired it for him. Hopefully, one of the trunks in the closet would contain some of the child's toys. Otherwise, it would be a long, long trip indeed.

Bryce looked back at Britta and could see she struggled to put the pieces of his story together. He knew it was hard to understand. There were times his family didn't make a lot of sense to him either.

"You said your father was a professor," he said, hoping to draw her attention away from thinking about his family. "What did he teach?"

"Languages. Papa taught French, English, Italian, and a handful of other languages, along with a few literature courses. When he was a young man, he spent two years traveling the world, studying languages and cultures before he settled down to teach at one of the oldest universities in Germany. He came from a wealthy family. Like your mother, he was an only child, doted on, spoiled. Because of his skill with so many languages, he was approached to join a certain political party. When he refused, they began to threaten him, threaten to do harm to his parents."

Britta sighed and was silent for so long Bryce wasn't sure she would continue.

After a deep breath, she went on with the story. "Not long after that, my grandparents were in an automobile accident that killed them both. Papa was convinced it was not an accident. He packed a bag with the things that meant the most to him and fled into the night. He left behind everything to be able to follow his heart and do what he believed to be right instead of what the Nazi party declared to be true. He was shot as he escaped but managed to make his way to a farmhouse in the country where an elderly couple offered him assistance and care as he healed. Once he was able to leave, he made his way to France. He stopped in a small village to purchase a few supplies and happened upon my mother who was also gathering supplies that day. They fell in love in an instant, wed a week later, and lived very happily in the house that has belonged in my mother's family for generations. Mère was always independent and strong, while my father tended to be more of the dreamer. When Germans took our land away from France, Papa wanted to leave, but Mère insisted we stay. Her family has always stayed, regardless of what might rage in the world around them. Germans raided our home not long after the war began. Papa was shot and my mother simply could not or would not live without him. She died a few weeks later. I buried them on the hill behind the house, and Henri is there beside them."

Everything in Bryce wanted to pull Britta into his arms, to comfort her for her devastating losses, but he didn't. Instead, he brushed his fingers along the line of her jaw and tucked a wayward curl behind her ear. She closed her eyes as though she appreciated the touch—the gesture.

A knock at the door made her jump. Bryce leaned back and tightened his hold on Josh as Britta hurried to open the door.

One of the young sailors stood at the portal, smiling. "Ma'am, the captain wanted me to let you know we are ready to set sail. He thought you might like to watch from the railing."

"You go on, Britta. Josh and I can wait here."

Bryce held no sentiment in sailing away from France, but he was sure Britta would need a few minutes to say goodbye to the place that had always been her home.

"Are you sure?" she asked, even as she grabbed her hat and handbag.

"I'm sure. Josh will keep me out of trouble until you return."

"Thank you," Britta bent and kissed his cheek, then Josh's, before she rushed to follow the sailor.

Bryce wondered how he and Britta would manage to stay out of each other's way in the tight quarters. Part of him admitted he hoped they couldn't. Before he lost himself in thoughts of Britta's smile, he dredged up a vision of Kate, but her brown eyes kept changing to blue, and her sleek brown hair became a tousle of blonde curls.

Chapter Six

"We are what?" Britta asked, sure she'd misunderstood Bryce.

"Sharing the bed." Bryce pointed to the enormous bed in the hotel where he'd made arrangements to spend the night. "Unless you think you'll be able to fit in Josh's crib, this is it."

"I'll sleep on the couch," she said, grabbing a pillow from the bed.

She had no idea how Bryce was able to move so quickly while hobbling on crutches, but he blocked her between the bed and the wall before she could march into the other room of their suite and claim the couch as hers.

"You'll be fine," Bryce said reassuringly. "The bed is big enough we can each take a side and have three feet in between us. I'm too tired to argue with you, but I'd rest better knowing you were in the same room with me. After our voyage, I've gotten used to listening to you obliterate the peaceful night air with your outrageous snores."

Britta swung the pillow and hit him in the face with it, making him laugh.

They'd arrived in America yesterday morning

and made it off the ship with no trouble. Bryce had been taken to a military hospital where he was given a thorough examination while she and Joshua waited and waited. Bryce was kept overnight just to observe him, while Britta and Joshua were given accommodations nearby. She'd felt fearful of being on her own, but a car had arrived the next morning and taken her back to the hospital. She watched as the doctor removed Bryce's cast and officially released him from his duties. When they finally left the hospital, they took a taxi to the luxurious hotel that had left Britta fighting the urge to gape at the splendor of the ornate lobby.

Exhaustion nearly overtook her as they made their way upstairs in an elevator to their room. She'd never ridden in an elevator until they arrived at the hospital yesterday. It left her feeling like her stomach was floating in the wrong place, but Joshua had laughed and clapped his hands, enjoying the ride.

During the voyage to America, Britta had spent a good part of the journey taking care of wounded men. When the nurses had discovered she wasn't squeamish and that Bryce wasn't on the verge of dying, they had asked if she'd mind helping with a few simple nursing tasks.

Much to her surprise, Bryce had taken over Joshua's care without a qualm. He'd become a big playmate for her son, but he'd also stepped into the role of father. The first time Bryce had disciplined Joshua for misbehaving, Britta had started to tell him he had no right to say anything to her precious boy. Then she glanced at the gold band on her finger and reminded herself Bryce had every right as her husband. For the first time in Joshua's life, she was having to learn to share him, and she didn't particularly like it.

It did strange, unexpected, unwanted things to her heart to walk into their room and see Bryce's dark head bent over Joshua's golden curls. Bryce was loving and kind, tender and sweet, but he didn't allow Joshua to get away with being spoiled or indulged either.

Bryce was fair.

He was fair with Joshua and with her, and everyone he came in contact with, which was few people since he remained in their tiny room most of the time on the ship. It was challenging for him to walk on the unsteady deck on his crutches, although he tried to get some exercise every day.

The first few days of their journey, he'd been exhausted and had slept long hours. While he slept, Britta had taken Joshua outside to explore the decks. Soon, off-duty sailors and nurses had eagerly watched for their strolls so they could play with her jovial son. Joshua had a way of laughing that brought out everyone's smiles. She'd thought about taking him below decks to visit the wounded men but feared the sight of some of them might cause Joshua to scream in terror. She couldn't do that to her son or the men.

Once Bryce had recovered from his fatigued state, he was more than willing to keep Joshua with him while Britta did what she could to help the nurses. She had thought her contributions offered little, but her efforts seemed to be appreciated. As she'd worked, she'd asked the nurses about American homes and customs. The more they shared, the more confused she became, and the more she dreaded arriving in America.

Yet here she was, spending the night in a hotel that was far nicer than any place she'd seen. Their suite was nearly twice the size of her house. Even so, she was not prepared for Bryce to announce they'd share a bed when she suggested they retire early after they ate dinner in the room.

"You are sleeping in this bed, with me, Britta. That's all we're going to do is sleep. Josh will be right here in his crib." Bryce motioned to the crib that had been set up just a few steps from the end of the bed. In truth, her son was too big for a crib, but he seemed to be entertained with it and had wanted to sit inside it after she'd bathed him and dressed him in his pajamas.

Reluctantly, she readied for bed in the bathroom, then stepped into the room. Bryce sat propped against the headboard, shirtless, with Josh resting in the curve of his arm as they read a bedtime story. She had no idea where Bryce had acquired the book since the few children's books she'd brought along were in French, but this was an American picture book about a little train engine that could do great things.

Despite her misgivings about the night ahead, she smiled that Bryce was reading a train book to her son. The man was completely enthralled with trains. She wondered if he'd been as singularly focused on them and as intense about them as a child. Somehow, she thought he probably had always held a fascination for them.

When Joshua yawned and rubbed his eyes, Bryce closed the book and kissed the top of the baby's head, further melting her already soft heart. It would be so easy to love this kind, good man, but she wanted no part of loving another. Not when it caused such heartache. Henri's death had ripped such a gaping hole in her life, nothing could ever fill it or fix it.

She took Joshua from Bryce, tucked him in, and hummed the lullaby her mother had sung to her when she was a child. Once Joshua's eyes drifted shut, Britta turned to face her husband. On the ship, it had been easy enough to forget they were married. She'd told herself they were merely bunkmates. Besides, she'd kept Joshua in bed with her since there had been no other place for him to sleep. Several mornings, though, she'd awakened to find her son had climbed into bed with Bryce and sprawled on the man's broad chest as they'd both slept.

Bryce cleared his throat, drawing her back to the moment. He motioned to the far side of the bed. "I hope you don't mind that I took this side. If I need to get up, it will be easier to get at my crutches from here."

"Of course. Whatever you want," she said, hurrying around the bed to climb in, then realized the lights were still on in both rooms of their suite. Britta checked to make sure the door was locked, turned off the electric lights, another convenience she had yet to adjust to, and returned to the bed. Bryce had slid down and rested on his right side, facing her, with the covers pushed back on his left. Even though it was now nearing the end of October and the nights were cool, he still could hardly bear to have anything touch his burns. They had healed a great deal, but the scars would always be there. That morning, the doctor had told him he might always have some sensitivity with the burns.

Britta hoped he would one day be able to forget they were there. And she shouldn't even think it, but she was deeply grateful he hadn't burned his face. Bryce Coleman was an incredibly handsome man, from his thick black hair to his intriguing green eyes. His nose was a little broad, but short and straight. His lips were exceptionally formed and tantalizing. He had a chiseled jaw, a thick neck set on broad shoulders, and a wide chest.

In truth, she'd thought about how nice it would be to rest against his strength and warmth, but she wouldn't. Not now, maybe not ever. And certainly not when her gaze kept flicking to his bare chest and the dark swirls of hair covering it.

His hair needed to be trimmed, and the beard he'd allowed to grow looked scraggly, but she knew beneath it was a face that turned women's heads, hers included.

Rather than surrender to the sudden urge to scoot close to her husband, kiss those tempting lips, and allow herself to care in a way she hadn't since Henri died, she rolled to face the wall, turned off the lamp by her bed and closed her eyes.

"Have sweet dreams, Britta," she heard Bryce say, then felt the mattress shift as he rolled onto his back.

"You too," she whispered before she fell into an exhausted slumber. She awoke the next morning to the sound of Joshua's giggles. She found him and Bryce sitting on the couch, reading a newspaper. Or, more accurately, Bryce was attempting to read while Joshua stole pages of it and raced around the room, laughing.

She'd barely said good morning to them when their breakfast arrived. As she spread jam on Joshua's toast, Bryce glanced at her over his cup of coffee. "By the way, Colonel Thompson's daughter Susie will be here at ten to take you shopping."

"Wha… what?" Britta asked, wondering when had Bryce had time to organize a shopping trip without her knowledge, and why he'd do such a thing.

"Susie and her husband live here in town. She knows the best places to shop. I figured you and Josh could use a few things before we head to Holiday. You'll both need clothes for winter. It gets cold at home."

"I'm sure the clothes we already have will suffice," she said, trying to hold onto her temper. She wasn't sure if Bryce was being generous or if he was embarrassed by her. Other than her wedding dress, her dresses looked dated and worn, and the material was mediocre in quality. Joshua had outgrown half of the things she'd packed for him. She wasn't even sure what she'd need to purchase for him or what sizes to buy since American sizes were different from those in France.

As though he sensed her turmoil, Bryce laid his hand on top of hers and squeezed it gently. "Susie will know what you need. I think you'll find she's heaps of fun, as my niece Cheri likes to say."

Every argument she offered to stay in the hotel was countered with a reason why she must go, most of them involving Joshua's welfare. Bryce knew she'd do anything for her son. He was the sole reason she'd married a man who was a stranger and left behind everything familiar to travel to a new country and a fresh beginning.

Unable to come up with more arguments, she finally gave up trying and rushed to get ready. While she attempted to fashion her hair to imitate the rolled styles so popular with American women, she'd heard Bryce on the telephone although she couldn't figure out with whom he conversed. She also heard two knocks on the hotel door and him answer, but was unable to listen to the conversations as she struggled with her hair.

Britta didn't want to wear her wedding dress on a shopping excursion, so she'd donned her next nicest gown. It looked more like something a servant would wear compared to the clothes of the women she'd seen in the hotel. The hat she pinned on was brown and plain, as was her coat.

She felt like a dowdy country bird when Susie Thompson Howard arrived a few minutes later in a military-style gown of dark maroon trimmed with black braid. A black hat with maroon ribbons perched on the fashionable young woman's head, and she wore the cutest pair of heels Britta had ever seen.

"Bryce!" Susie had rushed inside and given him a hug as he balanced on one crutch. As she pulled back from him, she talked so fast, Britta had trouble keeping up with her.

"We had a telegram from Dad. He gave us the scoop. I'm so glad you look as peachy as you do. In fact, you look pretty swell for a fella who's been rolling in misery for a while. You always were the cat's pajamas." The petite, beautiful woman turned to Britta and held out her hand. "I'm Susie Thompson Howard. Dad just raved about you and your son. I'm so pleased to meet you. He's right in saying Josh looks just like you. Oh! What I'd give for that hair or those blue eyes!"

Britta shook the woman's hand, offered a polite reply, and wondered what would happen if she locked herself in the bedroom and refused to go. Bryce took a seat on the couch and pulled Joshua onto his lap. Her son stared at Bryce with admiration before turning to Susie with an enchanting grin.

"He's so adorable, exactly like Dad said," Susie said as she cupped Joshua's chin and offered him a warm smile. "He's just a cutie pie."

Numbly, Britta nodded. She felt Bryce take her hand and place something in it. She glanced down to see it was a wad of cash. She had no idea where he'd acquired it, but had no intention of keeping it. She'd already tucked some of the money she'd brought with her from home into her handbag and hoped it would be enough to purchase a few things for her son. Then she realized she'd have to get the money converted into American dollars. Oh, why was everything so complicated?

With a headache beginning to pound behind her

temples, she just wanted to crawl back into the incredibly comfortable bed, yank the covers over her head, and sleep the day away. Not that she'd ever done such a thing, but the temptation beckoned her to race into the bedroom and lock the door.

As though she sensed her turmoil, Susie took the money from Britta's hand, slipped it into Britta's old handbag, then nudged her toward the door. "I'll have her back in time for dinner, Bryce. You men have a fun day."

"We will, Suze. Do you want to have dinner with us? I can order a meal for you."

"I promised Billy's folks …" Susie looked to Britta. "Billy is my husband. He's serving in the Pacific," she explained, then turned back to Bryce. "I promised his folks I'd dine with them this evening, but thank you for the offer."

"You girls have fun and shop all you like. If you run out of money, call, and I'll get more to you."

"I'll do that, Daddy Warbucks." Susie winked at him, waggled her fingers at Josh, then tugged Britta out the door.

From that moment until they returned to the hotel at four that afternoon, Britta felt as though she'd been caught up in a whirlwind. Susie was outgoing and fun, and half the time Britta had no idea what her Americanisms meant, but in spite of herself, she had a wonderful time. Susie kept encouraging her to buy more things, but Britta felt like she was wasting money when she'd already acquired two serviceable dresses, a new pair of shoes, a winter coat and hat, two pairs of gloves, and a scarf.

Susie insisted she'd need dresses for church, dresses and suits for shopping and traveling in, dresses for parties, dresses of heavy wool for cold winter days, and lighter weight dresses for warmer months. There were skirts and sweaters, blouses, and even a few pairs of trousers and jeans. They purchased winter boots and shoes, heels nearly as cute as the pair Susie wore, and flats that looked comfortable. By far, Britta's favorite pair was a black wedge heel with thin straps that fastened around her ankle and a toe cap fashioned from scallops of leather.

The shopping spree included new nightgowns, a heavy robe as well as a light one for summer, a vast array of undergarments, stockings, hats, gloves, handbags, and trunks to pack it all in.

After lunch at a tea room where they ate delicate sandwiches and salads followed by decadent sponge cakes and little tarts with berries, Susie led the way to a children's store where they bought clothes for Joshua. Britta didn't feel nearly as guilty spending Bryce's money on things for her son as she did for herself.

By the time they finished shopping Britta had learned all about American money and that Susie was a delightful woman who'd quickly become an ally and friend.

They returned to the hotel, both of them laden with packages. The big department store where they'd purchased Britta's clothes had delivered the trunks of clothes earlier in the afternoon and they sat just inside the door.

The two women entered the suite to find Joshua and Bryce asleep on the couch. The little boy was curled into Bryce's side. The big man slept with his hand protectively holding the toddler to him.

"Now that's a picture," Susie said in a whisper as she backed toward the door. "I won't wake them, but tell Bryce I appreciate the new outfit, and I'll see you both the next time you're in town."

"It was wonderful to spend the day with you, Susie. Thank you for everything," Britta said, giving her a hug.

"You're welcome. Just remember what I shared, and you'll do fine." Susie winked at her, then rushed out the door.

Britta hated to disturb her two men, so she carried the packages she held into the bedroom, opened them, and spread the things across the bed, feeling like a princess from a magical story.

The next morning, Bryce oversaw the transfer of their belongings by the hotel porters to a truck that would deliver them to the train station. He'd given Britta suggestions about what to wear and pack in their traveling bags, then spent the better part of an hour on the telephone making arrangements for she knew not what.

While she styled her hair and fussed with her new clothes, she could hear Bryce speaking to someone in the suite. When she walked into the room, she couldn't help but stare at Bryce, now that she could see his face again. He'd had a barber come to the room to cut his hair and shave the thick beard from his face.

With all that hair gone, there was no hiding the

fact she was married to an incredibly attractive man.

Still unsettled by Bryce's gorgeous appearance, she wasn't prepared for more surprises when they boarded the train a few minutes before ten. While she'd expected to sit in a seat with Joshua, her legs cramped to one side while Bryce took up the majority of the space, she bit her lip to keep her mouth from falling open in surprise when they were led into a private train car. It had a spacious sitting area, a comfortable bedroom, and a private bathroom.

"Isn't this a little extravagant?" she asked, just loud enough for Bryce to hear.

He made a dismissive, growling noise. "I'm not riding from here to Oregon on those hard seats with my legs jammed up around my ears." He yanked off his tie, tossed his hat onto a hook by the door, and sank onto what appeared to be a comfortable sofa. After he shoved his crutches into a corner behind an armchair, he leaned back with a weary sigh.

"Please let me know if you need anything, Mr. Coleman," the porter said, tipped his head politely to Britta, and closed the door behind him.

"Turn Josh loose. If you close the door to the bathroom and bedroom, there's not much he can get into. I had a few toys and his favorite blanket brought in." Bryce turned so his leg was propped on the sofa.

Britta set Joshua on his feet, removed the cap he wore, unbuttoned his coat, and set her handbag on a side table that looked to have cost more than the entire contents of her home in France. She slid an extra throw pillow beneath Bryce's leg, earning a grateful look from him before she removed her hat and gloves, then ventured down the short hallway to the bedroom. After removing her coat and Joshua's and hanging them in the closet, she carried a few of her son's toys into the sitting room. She'd barely taken a seat in the armchair when the train lurched ahead. Joshua rolled to his side, giggling as the train began chugging along the tracks.

"Attaboy!" Bryce grinned at Joshua, winked at him, then settled back with a sigh that sounded weary. "Wake me up when you two get hungry," he said and closed his eyes. From his even breathing, Britta knew he fell asleep almost immediately.

She took advantage of his slumber and Joshua's fascination with the new toys Bryce had somehow managed to procure for him to stare out the window as they traveled through a country that was so new and foreign to her.

Days later, when they reached Baker City, Oregon, Britta felt frazzled and fatigued. Bryce had been like a different person on the trip. At each stop, he'd gotten off and hobbled on his crutches inside the depot. She twice saw him sending telegrams, and once she noticed he used the telephone. She wondered if he was conducting business or staying in touch with his family.

When possible, she got off the train at the stops and walked with Joshua, trying to burn off some of her son's energy. She couldn't begin to imagine how hard the trip would have been if he'd been confined to a small seat. At least in the luxurious car, he had room to run, spread out his toys, and nap. Much like on the ship, their meals were delivered to them at a set time each day.

Despite the brave front Bryce projected, Britta could tell he was in pain. The doctor had given her a list of exercises Bryce should do every day, and she'd forced him to do them, whether he liked it or not. She was sure his body was protesting the unfamiliar movements.

Now that they were nearly to Holiday, she felt overwhelmingly nervous and Bryce appeared to be on edge. Joshua reacted to the strained atmosphere by growing cranky and fussy.

"This is where we switch trains," Bryce said, pulling on his coat and straightening his tie as the train rolled to a stop. "We'll have an hour and a half before we need to board. If you'd like to explore around town, there's a dress shop my mother and sisters frequent, and you'll find a nice general store with a variety of items just a few blocks from it. If you're hungry, the hotel on the main street has a comfortable dining room, or there's a bakery."

"There's nothing I need, but I might take Joshua for a walk to see if it improves his disposition."

Bryce pushed himself up from the sofa when the train stopped moving, grabbed his crutches, then tickled Joshua beneath his chin. "You be good for your mama. It's less than an hour trip once we leave Baker City until we'll be home."

Home.

Britta certainly didn't feel like she was heading home. Everything was so … different. Even the vegetation looked like something from an alien planet. Bryce had told her the pale, scraggly plants were called sagebrush and assured her there was no better scent in the world than sagebrush after a spring rainstorm. She'd have to take his word for it because right now the unfamiliar landscape disturbed her. There were towering mountains covered in trees and snow and rolling hills dotted with brush and rock. Out the train window she'd watched cowboys herding cows through a pasture, and Bryce had mentioned something about knowing the Jordan family.

Britta hastily pinned on her hat, picked up her handbag, then lifted Joshua in her arms. He squirmed against her and whined, but she ignored his fussing and stepped off the train as soon as Bryce opened the door to their car. She waited to make sure he made it to the platform with his crutches, then set Joshua on his feet, took his hand, and walked toward the heart of town.

Baker City was small compared to many of the towns and cities they'd gone through on their journey west, but it held a certain charm. She found herself peering in store windows and stopping to admire interesting displays. Josh would want a snack soon, so she found the bakery and selected half a dozen cookies, then wondered if she should have purchased a gift to present to Bryce's family when she met them. She had no idea what was appropriate or expected.

Worry made her stomach tighten in painful knots as she left the bakery and crossed the street to a park. Since it was a weekday, the park was empty for the most part. Joshua ran over to a swing and leaned his midsection across the seat. Britta picked him up and set him on the seat, showed him how to hold onto the ropes attached to it, and gave him a small push. His happy giggles made her smile and her anxiety lessened.

She allowed Joshua to run around the park for almost thirty minutes before she took his hand and they headed back toward the depot. She glanced inside the depot office and saw Bryce deep in conversation with a man she assumed was probably the stationmaster.

Rather than disturb him, she took a seat on an empty bench near the door, settled Joshua on her lap, and hoped her son would fall asleep.

Instead, Joshua stiffened his body and threw himself backward so fast, she had to work to keep from dropping him. He whimpered and whined as he wiggled against her, growing crankier by the minute. Britta knew youngsters sometimes had tantrums, and from the way Joshua was behaving, she was sure she was about to experience a full-fledged fit.

Desperate to keep his temper from erupting, she was at her wit's end to entertain him when a pair of hands reached for him.

"May I?" a man asked, holding out his hands for Joshua.

Much to Britta's surprise, her son practically leaped onto the man's lap, then settled down with a contented sigh.

The man was older, his hair and beard white, but his eyes twinkled with mirth and joy. He wore a dark green coat with a red vest and a pair of black and gray trousers. If it hadn't been the beginning of

November, she would have thought he was dressed for a Christmas party. With his round cheeks and ready smile, his features were the jolliest Britta had ever seen.

Something about the man made her feel lighthearted and happy, feelings she'd known far too little of since her childhood.

"Thank you," she said, nodding toward Joshua as he stared at the man with wide, inquisitive eyes.

"You're welcome, my dear. Traveling is hard on the little ones, isn't it? Cooped up on the train for days is wearying for anybody, but especially for them. They can't even properly voice their concerns or discomforts." The man jiggled his leg and Joshua giggled, clapping his hands together; then the gentleman looked at Britta. "Oh, dear. I've completely forgotten my manners. My name is Nick."

"It's lovely to meet you, Nick. I don't know what magical spell you cast over Joshua, but I'm glad you happened along when you did. I was certain he was about to have a tantrum, and it's not something anyone would find endearing. He's usually such a good boy, but we've journeyed all the way from France. I believe he is as tired of traveling as I am."

Nick chuckled. "I can't blame the boy. He's just ready to be home, aren't you, son?"

Joshua nodded and babbled something about pokes. Britta wished Bryce had never started calling him a cowpoke. Her son had nearly driven her mad repeating the word over and over.

When she'd pointed out the window to the

cowboys moving the cattle, Joshua had squealed so loudly, she thought her ears might start to bleed. Bryce had made things worse when he told Joshua they were cowpokes on a cattle drive. Joshua had been trying to say cattle drive all morning without success. It came out sounding more like waddle dive.

"Heading to Holiday?" Nick asked as he took a gold pocket watch from his vest and dangled the chain in front of Joshua. The boy took the watch and began playing with it, trying to figure out how to get it open.

Britta hoped he didn't break it because the watch looked old and expensive. "We are heading to Holiday."

"Is that where you live?" Nick inquired.

"No. I mean, we will be living there, but this is our first time to see the town, to be in America. My husband grew up there."

"And you're from France? I can detect an accent, although you have an excellent command of the English language."

"Thank you. My father was a language professor. I grew up in France, but our home is now under German control. Two Americans were injured and showed up on my doorstep. One went for help since the other was too wounded to move, so the injured one stayed with me for several weeks, waiting to be rescued. When his friend returned with troops to transport him to their base, I begged him to take us along. I can't bear the thought of what might happen to my son if Germany wins the war. He agreed, and we married the morning we left

France." Britta had no idea why she was spilling her life's details to this stranger, other than he seemed so approachable, friendly, and sincere.

"It was a brave thing you did, leaving behind your life there to try to give Joshua a better future. Is your husband a good man?" Nick asked, making a silly face at Joshua when her son held up the watch to him. Nick took the watch, opened it, and a song began to play, one that made Britta think of happy Christmas memories from her past.

Joshua held the watch to his ear and wiggled his head back and forth to the music.

"My husband is generous, thoughtful, kind, and so wonderful with Joshua. I couldn't ask for a better spouse when it comes to how he treats my son. As for me, though, I have no interest in falling in love again. I did that once, and all the love I'm capable of giving to a man disappeared the day I held my Henri in my arms as he died. I can't endure that kind of pain again. I just can't. I know it isn't fair to Bryce, but I refuse to allow myself to love again. Due to his wounds, Bryce has been sent home to recover. So, I'm on my way to meet the family of a man who married me out of pity, a man who could do far better than a girl like me."

"I do believe you are discrediting yourself and your husband. If he hadn't wanted to marry you, I'm sure he would have found a reason not to. Instead of seeing yourself as a burden to him, perhaps you should think of the blessings you've brought to him. Most men would be thrilled to have a beautiful, intelligent, tender-hearted wife as well as an adorable son."

Britta shook her head. "I'm none of those things, Nick. I'm just a country girl who'd never even been somewhere with electricity until we boarded the hospital ship in France. Bryce deserves a cultured, elegant woman who can throw fabulous dinner parties and knows the difference between a morning dress and one you wear to an afternoon tea."

"Your husband knows what he's doing. If you'd allow yourself to love again, you might just be surprised by the miracles that take place."

"I don't think I have any love left in me, not the love Bryce deserves. I just wish …"

Nick smiled at her and she felt as though she was suddenly basking in the warmth of summer sunshine. "What do you wish? What is the deepest, dearest wish of your heart?"

"That Bryce would love me, and I would love him in return, and we'd have a long, happy life together." Britta had no idea where the words came from, but she realized they were true. She longed to love and be loved, and not just by anybody, but by Bryce. In the time she'd known him, she'd seen him at his worst, overcome with unendurable pain.

Yet all the while he had suffered, all the days he'd spent in her cellar, he'd never complained. He'd remained a good, solid, dependable, brave man. One who made her son feel special and loved. One who did his best to encourage and support her. One who would be so easy to love, if she felt worthy of loving him.

A hand on hers drew her back to the present. The man beside her patted her hand, then smiled.

"Then may your wishes come true," Nick said in a voice laced with what she could only think of as humor. It was as if he knew some secret and couldn't wait for her to discover it for herself.

She tamped down a wistful sigh as Nick took the watch from Joshua and tucked it into his vest pocket, then handed her son a small candy cane. It seemed an odd thing to have in his pocket at the beginning of November, but the sight of it made her smile. She could count on one hand the number of times she'd savored one of the peppermint-flavored striped sticks, but she had no objection to her son enjoying the treat.

"Mama!" Joshua said, climbing off Nick's lap and holding the candy out to her. She took a lick and gave it back to him with a smile, brushing her fingers through his unruly curls. She would need to comb his hair before they arrived in Holiday. It was important to her to make a good first impression on Bryce's family.

"Thank you, Nick. It was so kind of you to give him the treat. He's never had a candy cane before," she said as she helped Joshua hold the candy so he didn't smear it all over her coat. "And I appreciate you listening to me go on and on. I've never shared so much with a complete stranger before. I should apologize for …"

"Who are you talking to?" Bryce asked from above her. She tipped her head back and looked into his handsome face as he gave her a curious look. She whipped her head around to see the bench beside her was empty. Even though she held Joshua, she hopped up and took a few steps forward, her gaze scanning the platform for Nick, but he was nowhere to be seen.

"There was a man, an older man, with a red vest and green coat. He made me think of your American Santa Claus. He was so kind and jolly, and he gave Joshua the candy stick, and …" Britta realized she sounded delirious, but the man had been real. Hadn't he? Of course, he had been because Joshua was joyfully sucking on the candy, getting sticky sweetness all over his face, hands, and shirt.

"You don't say. Was his name Nick by any chance?" Bryce questioned, his face impassive.

"Yes. Do you know him?"

Bryce shook his head, and then chuckled. "Nope, but you ought to ask Mamie and my mother about him sometime."

Britta glared at him wondering if he was serious or teasing. Before she could figure it out, Bryce motioned to a train car. "We'll be in that one, Britta. I'll load your things if you want to take Joshua inside and wash up. There's no private bathroom on this car."

"I'll see to it right away," she said, rushing inside the depot and to the restroom. She did her best to clean up her son but refused to take away the candy that had kept him quiet. Instead, she dampened the two handkerchiefs she had with her and hurried to board the train. If Bryce's family objected to a little boy with candy-sticky fingers, then they would certainly object to her.

She found Bryce seated in the last seat of the car with his injured leg stretched out in the aisle.

She had to step over it to take a place next to him. In the close quarters, she held Joshua on her lap.

When her son held his candy out to Bryce, the man grinned and licked the rapidly-disappearing stick. "Thanks, cowpoke. It's been a long time since I had a candy cane. Tastes as good as I remember."

He looked at Britta. "I don't know your favorite candy, wife. Do you have one?"

Britta had enjoyed so few indulgences purchased from a store in her life, she couldn't say that she did have a favorite. "My mother used to make a few treats during the holidays, but I've never had many pieces of candy from a store. My father once brought home a box of chocolate bars that were divine. And I do love anything peppermint-flavored."

"What about licorice or butterscotch discs, or even Life Savers or jelly beans?"

Britta shook her head.

"Gum? Do you have a favorite gum?"

"I've only tasted a few, and none were to my liking."

Bryce pulled a packet of gum from his pocket and held it out to her. "Give that one a try."

Britta had seen him chewing gum a few times but hadn't thought to ask for a piece. Not when her experience with chewing gum was a rubbery, fruity substance she disliked. She accepted a piece and stuck it in her mouth while Joshua was busy with the remnants of his candy cane; otherwise, he would have wanted one too.

A burst of fresh mint filled her mouth and she smiled.

Bryce chuckled as he gave her the package of gum. "Keep it. I can tell by the look on your face you're enjoying it."

"Thank you." She tucked the gum into her handbag and then looked at Bryce. "I truly do appreciate everything you've done for me, for both of us, Bryce. There is nothing in the world I can do to ever repay you."

He shrugged. "There's no debt to pay, Britta. You saved my life. You gave me shelter when I needed it most. You nursed me and fed me, bathed me, and took care of me when I couldn't care for myself. If it weren't for you, I'd be dead." He offered her a charming smile. "Maybe you don't think so, but I happen to be of the opinion my life is worth something."

"Of course, I think it is," she said, placing her hand over his, then jerking it back when she felt something electric race up her arm. Ever since they'd been cooped up together on the ship, she'd discovered each time she touched Bryce, whether intentionally or by accident, something zinged from the point of contact to her head and through her extremities. It was a most unsettling feeling but not altogether unwelcome.

"I'm glad to hear that, wife." Bryce adjusted his position in the seat, then held out his hands. Joshua leaned forward with a smile, then settled against the big man with a contented sigh. "All this time we've spent together, there are things about you I still don't know, Britta. What's your favorite color? Favorite song? Favorite meal? How old are you?"

"I thought you knew my age, Bryce. I'm twenty-five. And you're twenty-four, correct?"

"I am twenty-four, but I had no idea I'd married an older woman. Oh, won't Mama be properly scandalized."

At the mention of his mother, Britta felt her face blanch. What if the woman hated her? What if his family refused to accept her and Joshua and sent them packing?

Bryce dropped his hand on Britta's leg and gave it a gentle pat. "I'm just tying a knot in your rope. Mama won't care if you're ten years older than me, although she might frown on things if you were ten years younger. That would classify as robbing a cradle, I do believe."

Britta felt warmth seep into her from Bryce's hand, and she nodded her head, hardly able to keep her wits about her.

"What about my other questions?" he asked.

"My favorite meal was the one my mother always served on Christmas Day. It was herbed roast with sautéed vegetables, brie toast, roasted potatoes, and a bûche de Noël for dessert."

Bryce frowned. "A butch de what?"

Britta laughed softly. "A bûche de Noël is basically a cake with a filling, rolled together, and frosted to resemble a log. The tradition goes back to medieval times when a log of wood, often from a fruit tree to ensure a successful harvest in the year to come, would be carried into the home and placed in the hearth. Other things, like salt or wine, may have been sprinkled on top before the log was lit aflame. This generally took place on Christmas Eve, and the log had to burn three days for luck, although ideally, it would last into the New Year. The ash was fabled to protect against lightning strikes and the coals were used for medicinal purposes. As more homes had stoves instead of hearths, the tradition shifted, and eventually, an edible version of the log was introduced. My mother's creations were beautiful and delicious."

Suddenly awash in memories, nostalgia, and an acute feeling of homesickness for a place that hadn't existed in years, Britta stared out the window as she worked to control her emotions.

Bryce's breath stirred the hair by her ear that had escaped the carefully fashioned roll she'd pinned at the back of her head. The minty scent of it along with the warmth of his presence tantalized her senses. "I'm sorry you lost your parents, but I'm glad you have memories of special meals and times with them. If you'd like to make the cake this year, we'd all be happy to try it."

Britta nodded and drew in a deep breath to calm herself. Instead, she filled her lungs with Bryce's unique masculine scent. The musky, spicy fragrance made her think of winter woods draped in snow, much like his eyes put her in mind of frosted trees.

She turned and found his lips so near to hers, she felt an overwhelming urge to kiss them, to taste them, but she refused to give in. Not when she couldn't bear the misery of loving anyone again.

Unsettled by her unwanted feelings for Bryce, she leaned back from him and cleared her throat. "If no one objects and the supplies are available, I'll bake one. My favorite color is red, deep Christmas red, and a close second would be bright blue. My favorite song, I suppose, is a hymn we used to sing in church. We've never had a radio, so I don't know any of the modern music."

"No radio. No candy." Bryce shook his head and made a sad face. "That's tragic. Terrible, even. We will set out to fix that right away."

Uncertain if he was serious or not, when he winked at her she knew he was being silly again. He was such a lighthearted man, given to teasing. She'd been aware of his flirting with her several times in recent days, but had tried to feign ignorance to his efforts. At first, she thought it was part of the way he acted with everyone, which would have been disturbing, but it wasn't. The only one he'd flirted with was her, as it should be, since she was his wife.

How could she expect a virile man like Bryce to remain wed to her in name only? Would he respect their vows? Would he respect her? Would he, at some point, demand his husbandly rights? She couldn't imagine Bryce doing such a thing, but the niggling thought that he did have rights as her husband wouldn't let her relax.

Growing more distressed by the minute, Britta felt as though she'd swallowed a rock by the time the train arrived in Holiday. She glanced out the window, studying the pasture on the other side of the tracks where horses grazed in the distance in front of a big barn. Outside the other window, she caught a few glimpses of what appeared to be a quaint and welcoming little town.

"You'll be fine. They're going to love you and

Josh," Bryce said quietly, as though he could sense her turmoil. "Shall we get him cleaned up so we can go?"

"I'm sorry. I should have taken care of that before he fell asleep." Britta's fingers shook as she took out the damp handkerchiefs and attempted to clean the candy from her son's face and fingers. A sink and soap would have done a much better job, but she did what she could with what she had.

"Oh, stop fussing. We'll give him a bath when we get home." Bryce stood, still holding Joshua as the little one resisted waking.

Grateful her son had fallen asleep, Britta knew it had made the last leg of their journey peaceful. Britta reached for Joshua, aware Bryce couldn't navigate the steps without his crutches.

Once she'd taken her son from him, he motioned for her to precede him off the train. She accepted the hand of the porter as she stepped off the train, then turned back to watch as Bryce edged down the steps. Even leaning on crutches, he cut an imposing, handsome figure. One that turned heads as they made their way across the platform.

Before they reached the end of it, an older man, who looked so much like Bryce there was no doubt in her mind the two men were related, rushed toward them, his face wreathed in a smile.

"Bryce! Oh, son! It's so, so good to see you," the man said. He enfolded Bryce in a tight hug, knocking one crutch to the ground.

Britta bent to the side and retrieved the crutch, holding it as Bryce returned his father's hug then hopped back one step on his good leg. He took the crutch from her with a grin, then tipped his head toward her.

"Dad, I want you to meet my wife, Britta, and our son, Josh. Britta, this is my father, Zach Coleman."

"It's a pleasure to meet you, sir." Britta dipped her head, at a loss for what else to say. Bryce had caught her off guard when he introduced Joshua not as her son, but their son. *Our son.* She felt baffled beyond belief by this man she had married, who was proving to be nothing like she'd anticipated. That lone gesture, those two little words, meant the world to her.

Zach gaped at her a long moment before his confused look gave way to a smile. "Welcome, welcome. Britta, is it?" he asked. He gave her a light hug, careful not to disturb Joshua, then kissed her cheek. He turned to Bryce and thumped him on the shoulder. "When you said you had a surprise, you could have mentioned you were married with a child."

"I could have, but then where would the surprise be?"

Zach laughed and pointed to a pile of trunks and bags behind them. "All of these yours?"

Bryce glanced over his shoulder. "Yep. Ought to be two more trunks."

"I'll send Daniel to collect them as soon as we get to the house." Zach glanced back at Britta. "I hope you'll enjoy living in Holiday. I assume Bryce met you somewhere in Europe?"

Britta nodded. "In France, although right now, the region has been taken over by Germany."

"Well, welcome to America and our little town. You speak English so well," Zach said as they made their way out to a big four-door sedan.

Britta had yet to learn the various auto manufacturers in America, but the deep blue color of the car and the shiny chrome accents made her look at the vehicle in admiration. "Thank you, sir."

"How about you call me Zach, or Pops, or Dad. Sir and Mr. Coleman are too formal, especially for my new daughter to use."

Britta gaped at the man. Just like that, he'd accepted her into his family. No questions. No judgment. Just ready acceptance. She could have wept with relief. Instead, she smiled with a heart full of gratitude and slid into the back seat.

"Bryce, you sit back there with your family. Today, I'll play chauffeur."

"Hot diggity," Bryce said with a grin, climbing in beside Britta. "This might be a first."

Zach chuckled, the sound so like Bryce's laughter, Britta felt more at ease as the car pulled away from the curb. They headed down a wide street and past a park where a large gazebo stood.

She waited until they drove past a huge feed store across the street from a garage with a sign that read "Milton's" before she faced her husband.

"You didn't tell your family about me?" Britta whispered to Bryce, wondering if he was embarrassed by her. What other reason would he have for not telling his parents he was bringing a wife and child home with him?

"No. I wanted to surprise them. I sent Dad a telegram to meet us, but I didn't mention you or

Josh. I knew he'd love you the minute he clapped eyes on you both. Mom doesn't even know I'm coming home. She thinks I'll be in Charleston for another week. She's going to be so excited when she realizes I'm here." Bryce looked like a mischievous boy as he grinned in anticipation. "Wait until Mama meets you. I predict you'll not have a chance to hold Josh the rest of the day. She loves babies."

Before Britta could digest this bit of news, they'd turned onto a private lane lined with neatly trimmed hedges and shaded by towering trees. Zach circled in front of a house that looked closer to a castle than a home, then drove the car around to a side entrance.

"I think it will be easier for you to navigate getting into the house over here, son," Zach said, as he got out and opened Britta's door.

She managed to stand, holding her sleeping son against her shoulder. Joshua had started to awaken, but she knew it would take him a few minutes before he was ready to open his eyes and interact with the world around him. She prayed Bryce's family wouldn't reject him. Wouldn't reject a child that didn't belong to them but was now part of their family.

"Go on in while I send Daniel to get your things. Your mother was in the library reading when I left." When Zach grinned at Britta, a strong similarity to Bryce was evident in his smile. The main difference she could see in the two men were the color of their eyes and the shape of their noses.

Bryce led the way to the door and pulled it

open, holding it as Britta hesitantly stepped inside, uncertain what to expect. She assumed they were about to step into a room, but it was an entry with white marble floors and walls. The ceiling had a skylight surrounded by plaster tiles of flowers and vines. The chandelier also featured vines and flowers and the woodwork surrounding the doorway in front of her looked to have been carved from oak.

"Oh, my," Britta uttered when she finally found her voice.

"Ostentatious, isn't it?" Bryce said, grinning at her. "You ought to see the front entry. It's a doozy."

He led the way through the entry and into a sweeping curved hallway that was wider than Britta's house in France. From her position just inside the doorway, she could see stairs that swept both up and down and a home filled with such grandeur, she feared Joshua might break or disturb something if she set him down.

"Come on," Bryce whispered, tipping his head toward a doorway to the left.

Through the wide portal, she could see walls paneled with carved wood and wooden floors covered with an Oriental rug. Floor-to-ceiling shelves held books and assorted pieces of art, like bronze statues, and even what appeared to be colorful geodes. A huge fireplace cast off warmth and light, and sunshine spilled in the windows behind a broad desk.

As quietly as possible, Bryce made his way into the room, looked back at Britta, and winked.

Britta moved behind him, trying to absorb the richness of her surroundings, unable to take it all in.

Bryce had told her his grandfather had money and owned many businesses, but she had no idea of the level of wealth the Coleman family possessed. She felt so out of place, she could envision being asked to work as a servant to the housemaids.

"Zach, where did you disappear to? I thought I saw the car outside," a beautiful middle-aged woman spoke as she sat at a desk with a pen in one hand and papers spread in front of her. An abundance of chestnut hair was piled on top of her head in an old-fashioned style that suited her. She wore a dark green dress that looked to have been tailored specifically for her. Even from her distance across the room, Britta could see the material was of the finest quality. "I'm working on the invitation list for the Christmas party. I wanted to get some of the details out of the way before Bryce comes home next week. I can hardly…"

The woman looked up, dropped her pen, and let out a strangled noise. Britta couldn't tell if it was a laugh or a sob.

"Oh, my baby is home!" Bryce's mother hopped to her feet and rushed around the desk, flinging her arms around his waist, squeezing him tight.

Britta knew it had to hurt his still-healing burns, but he laughed and handed her one of his crutches so he had a hand free to wrap around his mother. He kissed the top of her head and rested his cheek against the pile of hair. "Hi, Mama. Did I surprise you?"

"Surprise me? Goodness sakes, son, you're fortunate I have a strong constitution, or I might be in the throes of death on the floor."

He chuckled and Britta heard his mother's soft laugh.

"I'm so, so happy you're home, Bryce. Oh, but I've worried and fretted and prayed and hoped, and here you are, not looking too much worse for wear." She stepped back to get a better look at him and noticed Britta. "Oh, hello," her voice sounded pleasant, inviting.

"Mama ..." Bryce moved aside and settled his hand on Britta's back, nudging her forward. "This is Britta, my wife, and our son, Joshua. Britta, this is my mother, Lorna Coleman."

It was a good thing his mother had been standing in front of the sofa, because she fell back against it, her mouth hanging open, eyes darting from Bryce to Britta to Joshua.

As though he sensed the unease in the room, Joshua whimpered and buried his face against her neck.

"You're married. With a son," Lorna said. To her credit, the woman seemed to quickly gather her wits. She stood, smiled, and reached out a hand, rubbing it gently on Joshua's back. "I apologize. Bryce has always possessed a talent for shocking me speechless."

Britta smiled in spite of her worries, picturing Bryce as a rascally boy, contriving ways to leave his mother floundering at his antics. She wondered if Joshua would do the same to her. If he'd grow up to be so confident and carefree.

"I understand, Mrs. Coleman," Britta said, watching as Joshua slowly shifted his head so he could see the woman. When she smiled at him, he grinned in return.

"Please, call me Lorna, or Mom, or Mother. I hope we can be friends as we get to know one another, Britta." Lorna offered her a studying look, one that made Britta glad she'd taken time to change into one of the suits Susie had helped her purchase. In truth, Britta had never felt so pretty, so well-groomed, as she had since she'd arrived in America. She'd never worn cosmetics, but Susie had helped her choose colors that complemented her fair skin. The woman had even given her a lesson in how to apply lipstick and mascara.

Britta just hoped Bryce's mother wouldn't take one look at her and declare her unfit to associate with the Coleman family. Lorna had the look of someone who had always had the best in life. How would Britta ever fit into the woman's luxurious world?

"You are just beautiful, Britta. And Josh looks just like you." Lorna gave her son a sly smile. "Why, with that glorious golden hair, those big blue eyes, and that curvy figure, you're lucky someone didn't try to steal her away from you, son."

Bryce scowled at his mother, surprising Britta. "They'll have a fight on their hands if they try. I'd clobber them with a crutch."

She wondered if he was putting on a show of affection for the benefit of his family. He certainly didn't need to do it for her. She knew he didn't care for her, not the way a husband should, but he had acted as though he'd like to be friends and had done so many thoughtful things for her. Things she still didn't understand. Like purchasing a new wardrobe for her. Then again, maybe it was to keep from being embarrassed by her appearance.

Confused, Britta did her best to smile and answer Lorna's questions about where she came from and Joshua's age. Within five minutes, the woman had managed to get Joshua to come to her, ordered tea to be served in the sitting room, and divested Britta of her coat.

Bryce waggled his eyebrows at Britta and motioned toward his mother who was holding Joshua up to look out the window at a pasture behind the house where four horses grazed.

"Hosee! Me poke! Go hosee, Mama! Hosee, Byce!" he bounced excitedly in Lorna's arms.

Britta watched as Bryce hobbled over to where his mother held Joshua. Lorna Coleman was tall, but even she looked small when Bryce settled an arm around her shoulders and kissed Joshua's cheek.

They'd just turned back toward her when a woman raced into the room, flung her arms around Bryce, and pressed her lips to his in a kiss that made it clear she was not a relative.

To his credit, Bryce tried to extract the woman's hold on him while keeping balanced on his crutches. Finally, she stopped kissing him and stepped back. Britta didn't think she'd ever seen a woman any prettier than the brown-haired, doe-eyed female gazing at Bryce. Her lips were plump and red, her skin smooth and clear, and her tall, willowy figure made her appear graceful and elegant. She was everything Britta was not, and in that moment she realized Bryce had sacrificed much more for her than she'd ever considered.

"You're back!" the woman said in a breathy voice. "Mrs. Dale called Mrs. Humbert, and she told Mrs. Warrington who passed the information on to me that she was sure she saw you and your father at the train station. I had to rush right over and see if it was true. Oh, my love! I'm so happy you're home. Now, we can finally plan our wedding. It's short notice, but we could perhaps have a Christmas wedding. Wouldn't that be ..." Her voice trailed off as she noticed Lorna holding Joshua.

She turned around and glowered at Britta. Eyes that had been soft and full of warmth when she'd gushed over Bryce turned hard and cold as she flicked a dismissive glance over Britta.

"Who is that?" the woman asked in a contemptuous tone.

"Kate Kingston, I'd like to introduce you to my wife, Britta, and our son, Joshua. Britta, Kate is ..."

Kate's lovely features twisted into a mask of hate as she swung back her hand and slapped Bryce across the cheek.

"Kate!" Lorna admonished, but before she could do more than take a step toward her, the woman flounced out of the room. Britta heard the door they'd come in earlier slam as she left.

"Well, that went better than I expected," Bryce said dryly, rubbing his cheek, then taking a seat on the sofa.

Britta knew it was ridiculous, but she had the urge to rush after the girl and smack her as hard as she'd just hit Bryce. And maybe pull out a handful of that sleek brown hair. If anyone ought to do the slapping, it was Britta, since the woman had locked her lips to Bryce's. After all, he was her husband.

But, from what she'd just witnessed, he was promised to another. One who was not going to graciously accept Britta's presence in his life.

Lorna gave Britta a sympathetic look, then patted a spot on the long sofa. "Please don't take offense to Kate. She's always been a bit high-strung. Frankly, I'm relieved beyond words that Bryce is not going to marry her. We have enough dramatic flair in the family with Ardith."

Bryce chuckled while Britta nervously took a seat between him and his mother.

She looked at Bryce, then Lorna. "I had no idea Bryce was engaged to wed."

"I'm not!" he growled, leaning back with a sigh. "I never once asked Kate to marry me, and I have no idea where she came up with plans for us to marry at Christmas. That was never discussed. In fact, I haven't even written her a letter since March."

Britta kept her thoughts to herself, but she kept picturing Kate pressed against Bryce. It appeared things in Holiday were going to be far more complicated than she'd imagined.

Chapter Seven

"Britta?" Bryce called, wondering where he'd find his wife. He'd looked all over the main floor of the house, and she was nowhere to be seen, not even in the kitchen where she seemed to prefer to spend time with Maude and Dodi, the cook and his mother's former nanny. The two women and Maude's husband, Marcus, had been employed by the Lennox family for years.

It seemed the more time he spent in Holiday, the more Britta retreated from him. Not that he could blame her. His well-intentioned family was sometimes overwhelming, and there were days a constant parade of people passed through the house.

Then there was the matter of Kate not taking his marriage with any degree of grace or civility. In fact, she'd practically shouted from the rooftops it was a sham marriage and should be annulled.

Regardless of what his marriage was, sham or not, it was none of her business or anyone else's. The more trouble Kate tried to cause for Britta, the more grateful Bryce felt that he'd been saved from marrying such a mean-spirited, shallow woman.

He'd been an idiot to ever think Kate was more than a spoiled, selfish girl. She'd obviously only shown him her best side, even as she'd attempted to manipulate him into doing her will. His sister Carrie had told him a few stories about things Kate had done to girls who'd shown an interest in Bryce when they were younger, making him cringe. How could he have been so stupid, and why hadn't his mother or Carrie mentioned their dislike of Kate sooner?

Even if marrying Britta hadn't been something he'd planned to do, and even if he'd agreed to their union out of a sense of duty for saving his life, he didn't regret it. Britta was the type of woman who would make any man an excellent wife. She was caring and giving, thoughtful and kind. The more he got to know her, the more she intrigued and fascinated him.

They'd been in Holiday for six weeks. In that time, he'd been able to gain a lot of ground physically, but he felt as though he took four steps back in his relationship with his wife for every step he took forward. Britta had even offered to have the marriage annulled, but he'd adamantly refused.

It didn't help any that his sister Ardith was good friends with Kate and continually made disparaging, hurtful commentary about his choice of a spouse.

Unlike Ardith, who looked down her nose at both Britta and Josh, Carrie had been warm and welcoming. Almost too welcoming as she involved Britta in various committees and organizations.

The truth was that Bryce missed his wife and

son, missed spending time with them. He missed cuddling Josh and listening to Britta's soothing, pleasant voice. He missed teaching the little boy new words and helping him explore the world around him every bit as much as he missed watching the tender way Britta interacted with their son.

From the moment he was able to be aware of his surroundings after being injured, he'd been with Britta and Josh constantly. Now, if he was home, they were not, and vice versa. There were days it seemed the only time he spent with Britta and Josh was in the hour they bathed and tucked the toddler into bed. Then they'd turn in for the night, each of them quietly settling onto their side of the big bed in the room they shared.

He didn't know when it had happened, but he'd gone from viewing Britta and Josh as an obligation to seeing them as a blessing. The problem was that Britta kept him at arm's length, making it clear she was still in love with her deceased husband. Bryce had no idea how to compete with a ghost, especially when his wife was struggling to adjust to life in America.

In her little country home, nothing had been easy, but it was simple and quiet. Unless there was fighting nearby, it had been mostly peaceful. Here in Holiday, it seemed as though it was constant noise and distractions with hardly a chance to relax and draw in a deep breath.

Which was why Bryce had endured all he could of being at Lennox Manor. He needed time away from the hustle and bustle of his parents' home to clear his mind and regain a sense of balance. Neighbors, friends, and even acquaintances Bryce didn't particularly like were constantly dropping in, wanting to hear every detail about his time away in the war. He had no interest in telling what he'd seen or experienced.

He'd gained a clear understanding of why his father always seemed so hesitant to talk about his experiences in France during the Great War. It was better to leave those memories behind than drag them forward into the future.

Then there was the hovering.

His family, the household staff, and close friends hovered over him as though he had one foot in the grave and might perish at any moment, which was far from happening.

He just wanted a place he could breathe deeply, sit quietly, and figure out his plans for the future. When he'd gone off to college, he'd been cocky and confident, knowing his grandfather would one day leave all his vast holdings to Bryce to manage. He'd majored in business management, focusing on the classes that would help him successfully run Lennox Enterprises.

Then Pearl Harbor changed everything. All those things he'd been planning and working toward seemed so unimportant.

Bryce knew he was no longer the same person he was before he left for Africa. He'd changed in ways he couldn't even fully fathom. The biggest change of all was falling in love with a woman who didn't return his love. A woman he'd so brashly wed out of a sense of indebtedness to her for saving his life.

Not that Bryce would change a thing.

He couldn't imagine a life without Britta or Josh in it. A part of him felt like he'd known them forever. But he longed for the day when he and Britta would be truly united in marriage, in friendship, and in life. United in heart and mind, body and spirit. It had been just a few months ago when he'd considered marrying Kate even though he knew he wasn't in love with her. He'd never loved her the way a man should love the woman with whom he intends to spend the rest of his life.

That love—that all-consuming fiery love—was what he felt for Britta. He loved his wife deeply, enduringly, and longed to be wildly and passionately in love together.

However, if things continued as they were, he doubted they would ever experience a happily ever after. Which was why he was determined to find Britta and immediately implement much-needed changes.

"Britta?" he called again, making his way upstairs. The house had an elevator, but taking the stairs helped exercise his leg and improve his mobility. After weeks in a splint, and then the cast, for a while, Bryce felt as though his leg might never be anything but stiff. Slowly but surely, it was starting to feel better, though. "Britta!" he bellowed, wondering where she could be.

He topped the stairs and listened, hearing a voice from the room his mother had used as her office until she'd taken over his grandfather's desk in the library. Bryce had already talked to her about continuing to oversee Lennox Enterprises until after Christmas. Bryce just needed a few weeks to do nothing but enjoy the holiday season.

He hated to burden his mother with the work, but she thrived on it. His business savvy came from her, not his father who much preferred to work on trains or round up cattle at the ranch. Lorna had assured him it wasn't a burden at all to her, and she'd happily continue managing the business until he felt ready to take over.

Relieved, Bryce had talked at length with his cousin Hayes and made arrangements to stay in the house that had once belonged to his great-grandfather out at the ranch. Grant Coleman had built the house when he'd remarried a kind woman named Ava in his later years. His wife had become a much-loved member of the family, but after she and Grant had passed, the house had remained empty.

Bryce thought it would be the perfect place for him and Britta to escape and spend some time together. If he ever had any hope of winning over his wife, he needed to at least have an opportunity to get to know her better and for her to see him not as the wealthy grandson of a tycoon but the man who had fallen in love with her.

The last time Ardith and her husband Emil had come to visit, they sat around bragging about their growing bank accounts while Britta had gotten down on the floor and played games with the children. Bryce had wanted to join her, but Emil had insisted on going over several company investment accounts. It was in moments like that he realized how pleased he was he'd married Britta. Kate would no more have sat on the floor letting his niece and nephew crawl all over her than she would have danced the polka on the dining room table.

A vision of Kate's appalled look if he'd ever suggested such a thing made him smile as he stepped into the small office where Britta was on the telephone. She glanced up at him and nodded once in acknowledgment of his presence.

"I can do that, Carrie. Thank you for including me. Yes, I'll see you tomorrow afternoon." Britta hung up the phone, sighed, then turned to face him. "I had no idea American housewives had so little time to themselves. I'd say it was just your family, but from what I've observed, the Milton girls are equally as overburdened by social obligations."

Bryce took Britta's hands in his and pulled her to her feet close to him. "How would you like to escape from it all for a while?"

A curious look in her eyes gave him hope, even as she stepped back from him. He took a pack of spearmint gum from his pocket and held it out to her. He'd discovered Britta couldn't resist it, and he did his best to hide a grin when she eagerly snatched a piece and stuffed it in her mouth.

Ardith had gone on and on one evening, elaborating about the demise of proper etiquette when women engaged in the vulgar occupation of chewing gum. Carrie had shoved two pieces in her mouth and blown a bubble in their sister's face, making their father laugh, but he'd seen Britta unobtrusively throw out her gum and hadn't seen her chew a piece since.

Although she and Carrie got along well, it seemed to him Britta strived to live up to Ardith's ridiculous standards of the perfect woman. He knew part of what Ardith said was meant to remind him of what he'd missed out on by not marrying Kate. Her words, though, had the opposite result. The more she tried to illustrate how Kate would have made a better wife, the more grateful he was to be married to Britta.

Bryce had concluded Ardith was a snob and a stinker, and the less time spent with her, the better.

"I don't know how I could possibly escape even for an afternoon, Bryce. I'm supposed to meet the pastor's wife in an hour for a lesson in American Christmas songs so I can assist with the children's program. This evening, I'm to help the women's league with filling the monthly boxes they send to Britain for war relief. Tomorrow morning, the Milton women have invited me to join them in baking cookies for the school program. And Carrie asked me to come over to help her organize a coat and toy drive for the needy after lunch." Britta glanced at the watch she wore—one he knew his mother had given to her. Up until Britta had arrived in Holiday, she'd had no need for a way to tell time.

"As of this moment, you are no longer obligated to help with any of that. We are leaving." Bryce took her hand in his and led her out of the office toward the bedroom they shared that connected to the nursery. If he'd timed it right, Josh ought to be waking up from his nap any minute.

He did hate to take the little boy away from Lennox Manor, though. His parents and all the staff doted on him. There was never a lack of someone to hold the child, play with him, or feed him. He'd been rocked to sleep by everyone from the gardener to the housemaids. But, if things went as Bryce planned, Josh would get to know Mamie and Gramps better, as well as the cousins that lived at Elk Creek Ranch.

"Leaving? What are you talking about, Bryce? I can't leave. I have far too much to do." Britta tried to tug away from him, but he tightened his hold on her hand. "Grab your coat and hat, wife, while I get Josh. We're going to the ranch."

"The ranch?" Britta asked, her voice full of hope. He didn't miss the way interest sparkled in her eyes. They'd only been out to the ranch twice, but both times Britta had mentioned how much she'd enjoyed being there. And she and Mamie had connected like they were long-lost friends, which was another reason he thought staying out there for a while would be a grand idea.

Britta had been more relaxed and at ease around his grandmother than she'd been the entire time they'd been in Holiday. He knew Lennox Manor was not an average home, and he couldn't even begin to understand what it must be like for Britta to go from living in her humble dwelling in France to a four-story home with servants.

No, getting out to the ranch would be good for them all. He was sure of it.

"I've asked Mama to tell all interested parties that you are unavailable for any commitments, committees, organizations, and other involvement until after Christmas, or unless there is something you truly want to do. Otherwise, we're going to stay out at the ranch and enjoy a slower, quieter pace for a few weeks. Do you think you can stand to put up with me without a house full of people for a while?"

Rather than answer, Britta threw her arms around his neck, kissed both of his cheeks, then hurried into the nursery as Josh announced the end of his nap with several giggles.

Bryce changed into a pair of old jeans, a thick flannel shirt, and a pair of worn boots. He'd already had Dodi oversee packing suitcases for all of them and a trunk full of Josh's toys and favorite things, like his well-loved blanket. They'd been delivered out to the ranch right after lunch, along with enough groceries to keep them fed for a week or two. Even having to use ration coupons, he was able to get most of what he wanted.

Dodi had sent two of the maids out to clean the little house, make the beds, and put away the groceries. Everything should be ready and welcoming by the time they arrived.

Britta returned to the room with Josh toddling along beside her.

"Byce!" Josh shouted, running straight to him. Britta had already changed the boy into a pair of overalls and added a sweater. Josh carried the little stuffed bear David had given to him. It had become his favorite toy and he'd named the bear Dave.

Bryce had written to his friend a few times, letting him know they were doing well. He'd even sent a box of Christmas treats to David's family for the holidays and had received a kind letter from the man's wife. While he was mailing gifts, he'd sent a big box of gifts with a note to the family of Corporal Matthews. Bryce still felt guilty they hadn't been able to give the young man a proper burial, but he hoped the boy's parents would feel better knowing their son had been brave right up to the end.

Britta touched his arm, bringing him back to the moment. "If you'll keep Josh busy, I'll change and meet you downstairs. In the kitchen?"

"That'll be fine, Britta. If there are any books or magazines you want to bring along, feel free. I already had Dodi pack our clothes and Josh's things."

Britta shook her head. "I thought Josh's room looked a little empty, and I couldn't find his green sweater. When did you arrange all this?"

"This morning, after Ardith left."

Britta gave him an exasperated look. Although she hadn't said anything, he knew she held no fondness for his older sister and he couldn't blame her. Ardith was trying, exhausting, and someone he didn't particularly like or want to be around. To her credit, Britta had been nothing but polite, even when Ardith had been downright rude.

"The last place you'd ever find Ardith is at the ranch, which is another grand reason for us to spend the remainder of the holiday season there."

"I … it's …" Britta stammered, and Bryce grinned at her.

He playfully swatted her backside. "Hurry up and change. Josh and I are ready to go, aren't we, cowpoke?"

"Poke! Poke! Giddyap!" Josh skipped out of

the room, giggling, and Bryce hurried after him. They made their way to the kitchen where Maude gave them each a cookie, then handed Bryce a basket she'd packed with a cold supper.

"Thanks, Maude. I sure appreciate you doing this." He took the basket from her and set it near the door, then picked up Josh before the little boy could wander into the pantry. For whatever reason, the room full of food off the kitchen always seemed to fascinate him.

"We'll miss having you and your family here, Bryce, but I know how much you enjoy being at the ranch. Are Cora Lee and Jace excited about your visit?"

"They are. I phoned Mamie this morning, and she was thrilled about us coming to stay for a while. She and Britta get along like two peas in a pod."

"That's grand. Britta needs that," Maude said, lifting the lid on a pot and stirring the contents before she set the lid back on. "She tries so hard. It's not always easy being somewhere new."

"I know, which is one of the many reasons we're going to the ranch."

Maude grinned. "And here I thought it was the hovering and fussing and constant presence of friends and family that drove your need to escape."

Bryce chuckled. "Well, there is that little problem." He handed Josh another cookie when the little boy kept stretching to reach the cookie jar on the end of the counter. "We will still see everyone at church on Sundays."

"Yes, you will, unless you get snowed in at the ranch. Marcus claims his knee is telling him we're in for a big storm."

Bryce grinned. For years, Marcus had been the best weather gauge around based on arthritis in his knee acting up. If he said it was going to storm, then it would storm. Bryce didn't mind, though. Being snowed in with Britta in his great-grandfather's snug little home sounded like a dream about to come true.

"I'm ready," Britta said as she breezed into the kitchen, looking far younger and happier than she had that morning. Instead of the fashionable dresses she'd been wearing, she'd changed into one of the dresses she'd brought with her from France, and she wore her old brown coat with a pair of snow boots. Although Christmas was still two weeks away, there was half a foot of snow on the ground.

Bryce thought about the stories his parents had told of the year they had met when snow was piled head high along the sidewalks. He'd never seen that much snow and hoped they didn't get anywhere near that much this year, but he wouldn't complain if they had a white Christmas.

"Let's head out," Bryce said, opening the door and lifting the basket of food. Josh ran outside and Britta raced to catch him and pull on the stocking cap the little boy had tossed off on his way outside.

Bryce had left his car parked at the back entrance near the kitchen door. Josh rushed straight to it, trying to get the door open.

"Go, now, Byce! Go see hosees!"

"Yes, cowpoke," Bryce said indulgently, opening the door and watching as Josh scrambled inside and climbed onto the front seat. He set the basket in the back along with a few other things he wanted to take out to the ranch, then waited until Britta was seated to walk around the car and slide behind the wheel.

Josh leaned against his side as they drove out of town, standing with his hand on Bryce's shoulder, pointing to every cow and horse they passed.

"He's going to be a cowboy when he grows up," Bryce predicted.

"There are worse things to be," Britta said, smiling at him, then leaning back into the seat, seeming to relax more with each mile that distanced them from town.

By the time they reached the ranch, she seemed like a whole different person. Bryce waved to Hayes as they drove past the main house and made their way to the smaller house located just far enough away to maintain everyone's privacy.

Bryce parked by the back door under a shelter that had once held his great-grandfather's buggy but now served as a place to keep snow off the firewood that had been stacked there to stay dry.

"I haven't seen this house. Who does it belong to?" Britta asked as she looked up at the structure that appeared tiny compared to Lennox Manor.

"Technically, Hayes, but no one lives here. They haven't since my great-grandpa and his wife passed away."

"Oh. And we're going to stay here?"

"Yes. Just the three of us. No maids, no cooks. No other relatives. And it doesn't even have a telephone."

Britta beamed. "That's wonderful!"

Bryce laughed and got out of the car, then picked up Josh and carried him into the house and set him down.

Britta walked up behind him and before she could step into the house, Bryce swept her into his arms and carried her inside. At first, she was too caught off guard to do more than gasp and wrap her arms around his neck. Once they stood inside the sun-drenched kitchen, she swatted him on the shoulder.

"Bryce Coleman, you are going to injure yourself if you don't put me down this instant. What on earth possessed you to do such a thing?"

"Well, I don't know how you do things where you were raised, but here, it's a tradition to carry the bride over the threshold of her new home."

"But I … it isn't … we aren't …" She sighed. "Thank you. Now, would you please set me down? Joshua disappeared. I don't want him to get into something he shouldn't."

Reluctantly, he set her on her feet and watched as she hurried out of the kitchen into the living room. The house smelled clean but also held the scents of Christmas. He breathed deeply, relishing the scent of one of his grandmother's bayberry candles. They always made him think of Christmas and happy holiday memories.

After he retrieved the basket of food and the box of supplies he'd brought along, he made sure the wood box was stocked, then removed his coat and went in search of Britta. She and Josh were on the couch, Britta on her knees facing backward as she held Josh up. The two of them peered out the window that offered a grand view of a pasture full of fat cattle. With a blue sky overhead, snow on the ground, and one of the barns visible in the distance, it made a postcard-perfect scene. Especially with Britta in the center of the picture.

"What do you think, Josh? Do you like those cows? My great-grandpa started the herd when he had a bunch of Angus cattle sent over from Scotland," Bryce said as he moved behind them. He picked up Josh so he could get a better view of the animals.

"Cows! Me wide cows!" the little one said, bouncing in his arms.

Bryce laughed. "You can't ride the cows, but there's a pony around here you can ride."

"Me wide, Mama! Me wide!"

Britta smiled at him, then turned around and stood. When she did, Bryce had to resist the urge to bend down and kiss her. She looked so happy, he wished he'd thought to bring her out here weeks ago instead of staying trapped in town.

Trapped was a great word to describe how he'd felt with everyone fussing over him, wanting him to rest and stay close to the house. He loved to be outside, exploring and moving around, preferably near a train.

Right now, though, he felt anything but trapped. For the first time in a long time, he felt free. Free to be himself. Free to be with Britta. Free to explore the undeniable attraction that had been building between the two of them for weeks, even if she refused to admit it.

Moments like this, when he could see the

longing in her big blue eyes, gave him hope that someday she might learn to love him even a portion as much as he already loved her.

He gave Britta a tour of the house that had two bedrooms, a bathroom, a living room, and a kitchen. Electricity had been installed, even if no one had thought to add a telephone. Without that communication convenience available, Bryce hoped they'd enjoy plenty of peace and quiet.

After they ate the meal Maude had packed for them at the small table in the kitchen, Bryce added wood to the fire. He could envision greens on the mantel and stockings hanging from it on Christmas Eve. They needed to get a tree and maybe even purchase some decorations.

Josh seemed content to sit on the rug in front of the hearth and play with a set of blocks that had letters painted on the sides.

Bryce sat beside him, spelling out simple words. He knew the little one was too young to be able to fully understand, but it was fun to listen to Josh try to pronounce the words.

Britta sat in the rocking chair close to the fire, knitting what looked to be a scarf. Bryce had no idea she even knew how to knit, but as her fingers flew, he assumed she'd had plenty of practice in the art.

The following morning, they were eating a simple breakfast of toast and eggs when a knock sounded at the door.

Bryce hurried to open it and welcomed his cousin inside. "Hayes. Good morning. Come to check on us already?"

"Not exactly." Hayes tipped his head to Britta when she appeared in the living room with Josh on her hip. "Bonnie isn't feeling well this morning, so I'm going to take her in to see the doc. Mamie says she can keep an eye on the kids, but I'd feel better if you could drop in and check on them in an hour, just to make sure they aren't wearing her out."

"We'd be happy to," Britta said, stepping forward and offering Hayes a reassuring smile. "We can go over as soon as we finish breakfast. Tell Bonnie we hope nothing is wrong."

Bryce thought of his cousin's wife, who was seven months pregnant. They already had three youngsters. Chance just turned seven, and they had twin daughters, Pearl and Ruby, who were five. Josh had been quite taken with the identical twins. He knew the little boy would have fun playing with his cousins.

"If you need us to help in any way while we're here, Hayes, just say the word," Bryce said, reaching out to place a hand on his cousin's shoulder.

Hayes nodded in thanks. "I appreciate that. If you can just help Mamie with the kids, that would be much appreciated."

"We'll head right over," Bryce said, waving to Hayes before he closed the door. It was even colder outside than he anticipated, but the day looked like it would be clear and sunny.

Britta was still dressed in her robe and had a scarf tied around her head to keep her curls out of her face. "Can you finish feeding Josh? I'll change; then we can head over."

Bryce knew Hayes had to be worried to come over and ask them to go to the house. He made a shooing motion with his hand. "Go on and get ready. You don't have to wear a dress. Pants or jeans are fine here on the farm. I want you to be comfortable."

Britta nodded, then hurried out of the room. Bryce watched the slight sway to her hips as she left, thinking husbandly thoughts that would only get him into trouble.

Last night, he'd been sure Britta had planned to sleep in Josh's room, but there was only one small bed, so she'd finally crawled into the big bed with him, even if she left an acre of mattress between the two of them.

One of these nights, Bryce might just roll over in the dark and see if she was completely resistant to his kisses.

For now, though, he'd keep his hands, and lips, to himself.

Josh slapped his hands on the tray of his highchair and kicked his feet as he ate the last bite of his toast slathered with Maude's delicious huckleberry jam. Every summer, Maude and Marcus took a week off to spend time camping in the woods, and they always returned with gallons of huckleberries that Maude turned into pies, preserves, and jam.

Britta had mentioned how good they would taste on crepes. He recalled her making crepes a few times when they'd been at her home in France and looked forward to her making them again. She hadn't had the opportunity to cook since they'd been in America until this morning. Instead of expecting a huge breakfast, Bryce had assured her something simple would suffice for their first lazy day away from town.

Only now, it seemed they might be busy after all. Bryce didn't mind going to the main house. He adored his grandparents, especially Mamie. He looked forward to spending time with her and watching the way she and Britta interacted.

If anyone could get Britta to step out of the past and embrace the present, his grandmother was the woman for the job.

Chapter Eight

"That's it. We're finished," Hayes called as Bryce turned the team of draft horses toward the gate. In the week he'd been at Elk Creek Ranch, Bryce had taken on the task of helping Hayes with the feeding twice a day so Gramps, who usually drove the team, could stay inside where it was warm.

Britta spent nearly every waking moment at the ranch house. Poor Bonnie had been ordered to complete bed rest by the doctor for the remainder of her pregnancy, so help was needed in caring for the house and the children.

Mamie did what she could, and Gramps helped, too, but they were both in their eighties and not as spry as they'd once been.

Britta seemed to blossom as she spent her days in the kitchen, cooking beside Mamie, and caring for Hayes and Bonnie's three rambunctious youngsters as well as Josh.

The little boy thought he was in heaven with three cousins to entertain him. The twins treated him like a cuddly toy, while Chance gave Josh lessons in everything from how to wear a cowboy hat to how to twirl a rope. Of course, Josh's rope was a soft piece of string, but he loved slinging it around and around.

Bryce had purchased a little cowboy hat, boots, chaps, and a saddle for Josh for Christmas. There was already a pony on the place that no one rode often, so Bryce figured Josh could learn how to ride on old Elroy.

For Britta, he'd struggled to find just the right gift. He knew it had to be something from the heart, not something for her to wear or anything along those lines. He hoped she'd like what he'd landed on. Time would tell, he supposed.

He'd finished shopping for the rest of his family, and Britta had been busy making a few things in secret that he thought she was keeping hidden at the ranch house.

Bryce had always loved the ranch, but especially the big house. It had an open front room with a big dining area and kitchen behind it. A wing on each side of the house held three bedrooms. His grandparents had added two bathrooms and updated the kitchen several years ago, not long after they'd had electricity and a telephone installed. They'd continued living in the house, even after Hayes had married Bonnie. They stayed in one wing of the house while Hayes and his family took the rooms on the other.

Bonnie was the type of girl who preferred to be out riding on the ranch beside Hayes instead of inside working in the kitchen, and Mamie loved to cook and shared her love for her family through the delicious meals she created. The arrangement worked out well for everyone.

"What are your plans today?" Bryce asked as Hayes climbed over the back of the seat and sat beside him.

"Bonnie made a list of gifts I'm to go into town and purchase today. Last week, we'd planned to leave the kids with Carrie and take the train into Baker City for an overnight trip, but our plans got derailed."

"Only slightly," Bryce said, grinning at his cousin. The two of them looked enough alike to be brothers, although Hayes had what people referred to as the Coleman blue eyes and nose. "Just let me know how we can help."

Hayes sighed and rubbed his gloved hands on his legs against the morning chill still lingering in the air. The storm Marcus had predicted had arrived, bringing several inches of snow and temperatures that hovered near zero. It had warmed up to the high twenties the past two days, and the sun appeared to be ready to make an appearance as golden spears of light shot across the sky.

"Honestly, I don't know what Bon and I would have done if you and Britta hadn't been here to lend a hand. We're both so thankful for your help."

Bryce shook his head. "We're the ones indebted to you two for letting us stay in Ava's house. If we'd had to spend one more day in the manor, I'm not sure we would have survived."

Hayes chuckled. "I would have run screaming into the woods weeks before you gave up trying to live there. Stay in Ava's house as long as you like.

It's nice having someone live there again, instead of the place sitting empty. Pops would be glad to know you're making the place into a home, even if it's only temporary."

"I've been looking at a piece of land that adjoins the ranch to the south. You know anything about the Bennett family?"

The rest of the way to the barn, they discussed the adjoining ranch, what Hayes knew about the current owners, and the top bid he'd be willing to pay for the place if he were the one doing the buying.

Bryce liked the idea of purchasing the property that adjoined Elk Creek Ranch. It would add to the Coleman holdings and essentially extend the ranch. He had no intention of running his own ranch simply because he wouldn't have time once he took over Lennox Enterprises, but he did like the idea of having his own place to live, out in the country, where he could rest and relax and be at peace. He could keep a few horses there, and Britta could have chickens and a milk cow, and whatever else she wanted. Josh was going to need a dog. Every boy needed a trusty canine companion.

He was sure Britta preferred a simple country life to the society life his mother and sisters led. She'd been happier baking cookies with Mamie than she'd been at any of the events the women in his life had dragged her to.

He tried to envision Britta at one of the boring high society dinners he'd attended with Grandfather Lennox. The people were stuffy and stodgy and full of self-importance. Britta would feel out of place and nervous that she might do or say something wrong, but he pictured her looking like a queen with her golden hair piled on her head and wearing one of the fancy evening gowns Susie had added to her wardrobe.

One of the things he loved about Britta was the fact that she had no idea of her beauty, or how she garnered second looks whenever she walked into church or a business in town. She was incredibly lovely no matter what she had on, but now that she wore her hair in a popular style and dressed in the latest fashions, she looked like any other American girl.

He'd hoped no one would take a look at her and Josh and stereotype them as German because of their blond hair and blue eyes. The only one who'd made that comment had been Kate. He didn't know what Carrie had said to her, but that was the first and last mention anyone made of Britta being a German spy. It must have bothered his wife, though, because Britta had taken to wearing a small V for Victory pin on her coat anytime she went into town.

"If I did buy that place, do you think you might want to use the ground for pasture?" Bryce asked his cousin.

Hayes gave Bryce a look that let him know he was asking a question he already knew the answer to as they loaded the wagon with hay for the evening feeding.

"Do cows moo?" Hayes grinned. "Of course, I'd use the ground for pasture. I might even put in a field or two of hay where they had corn planted last year. What would you charge for rent?"

"How about you agree to keep an eye on the place and whatever critters we have when I have to be out of town on business? If you do that, we'll call it even."

Hayes stuck out his hand. "Now that's a deal I'll gladly shake on. Do you really think you'll purchase it? If you do, we could put in a road between the two places so we didn't have to drive the long way around. Mamie seems to have taken quite a shine to your wife, and I think the feeling is mutual. Bonnie said she doesn't know how we managed before Britta arrived. And I could be wrong, but Britta seems to thrive out here. She's like a different person than the one we met when you two lived in town."

"I agree. Being part of the Lennox empire isn't an easy thing for anyone, but especially not a girl who prefers fresh country air to attending the opera."

"Well, you two can stay in Ava's house as long as you like."

Bryce thumped his cousin on the shoulder. "Thank you, Hayes. If I can strike a deal with Bob Bennett, we might just have our own place soon, but don't say anything to Britta. I want it to be a surprise."

"I hope it works out. Bonnie and I sure wouldn't complain about having you and Britta as neighbors. And the kids think the world of Josh. The girls would pack him around like a doll if he weren't nearly as big as they are. Gosh, that little guy is as smart as a whip, isn't he? Yesterday,

Chance was helping me fix a leaky pipe in the bathroom. Josh wandered in and just by watching what we were doing, he picked up a wrench and handed it to me when I needed it."

Fatherly pride filled Bryce, and he smiled. "He is incredibly smart, and he's strong and big for his age, but he's a sweet boy. I've only ever seen him throw temper tantrums a handful of times, and that was when he was overly tired, not just because he didn't get his way."

"He sure looks like his mama. What did his father look like?"

Bryce shrugged. "I don't know. Britta's never shown me a picture of Henri. She may not even have one. Things were remote where she lived. No electricity. No telephones. It was almost like stepping back in time."

Hayes's eyes widened. "You mean all of this," he swept a hand out to encompass not just the ranch but American life, "is all new to her? Phones, radios, electricity, cars?"

"Oh, she'd seen cars and trucks from the Germans driving by, but I don't think anyone in the area had a vehicle. She had to walk a few miles to reach the nearest village. She used to have a team of horses and a horse for riding, but they were confiscated by the Germans. The only reason she still had her milk cow and chickens was because she hid them in the woods behind her place anytime she heard a vehicle approaching."

"Gee, she must have had it rough with a baby and no husband or family. If for no other reason than giving her and Josh a better life, I'm glad you married her." Hayes offered him a teasing grin. "But any knucklehead can see you're crazy about her."

Bryce nodded sheepishly. "I guess I am, but you can't blame me. Britta is beautiful, smart, and kind, and she can cook as good as Mamie. Not only that, but she isn't afraid to work hard, and she even knows how to ride."

Hayes snickered. "I saw you two riding the other day. She does know how to handle a horse—and you."

Bryce scowled.

Hayes guffawed as he slapped Bryce on the shoulder. "Come on, Cousin, let's head to the house and see what your wife and Mamie have hot out of the oven. I heard Mamie mention something about cake earlier. I'm sure glad the women decided to hoard their sugar rations for Christmas treats. For the record, I'm glad you married Britta and not Kate. I never liked that girl. Bonnie said she makes her think of a snake, just waiting to strike her next victim."

Bryce wondered how Kate would react to being compared to a serpent, not that anyone would dare say it to her face. It made him smile as he pictured her coiled and ready to strike. Kate certainly would never have spent time in the kitchen with his grandmother, sharing recipes and traditions as Britta had done the last week.

Mamie had been making all his favorite treats, like *lebkuchen* and the crescent-shaped *vanillekipferln.* Britta had introduced them to French sweets like *madeleines* and *palmiers*. Bryce didn't think there was a thing wrong in blending their varying traditions, especially when it came to satisfying his sweet tooth.

"Can you smell that?" Hayes asked as they reached the back porch.

"Is that cinnamon? Do you think Mamie made a coffee cake? Or maybe Britta made the cookies she dips in cinnamon and sugar."

Hayes rushed to stamp the snow from his boots. "Count yourself blessed your wife can do more than boil water and burn toast."

Bryce chuckled. "I am blessed for many reasons, but your Bonnie is the perfect wife for you and this ranch."

"That she is," Hayes agreed, then frowned. "I worry about her and this baby. I pray every day they'll both be healthy."

"We all are praying for that, Hayes." Bryce waited as his cousin opened the door and stepped inside. The warmth of the kitchen engulfed them, surrounding them with the aroma of spices and coffee.

"I can't believe it!" Mamie said, turning to her grandsons. "Guess what Britta and I discovered this morning?"

Bryce kissed his grandmother's wrinkled cheek as Britta pulled a pan of little cakes from the oven. Jam dotted the tops of them, and they were the reason the house was redolent with mouth-watering spices. "We'll never guess, so you'll have to tell us."

Mamie excitedly looked at Britta. "Her father told her about my family's bakery. He grew up in a nearby town and went there as a boy. Can you believe it?"

Britta smiled at his grandmother with such pure affection, it made Bryce's heart feel as soft as warm butter.

"The world is sometimes a wonderfully small place, or at least God makes it seem so," Britta said as she drizzled sauce over the cakes that appeared to already have cooled. "Papa spoke of the *puddingbrezel* they made there as though it was the finest thing to eat in all the world."

"My mother gave me that recipe. I haven't made it in years. Oh, we must make some today," Mamie declared, hurrying across the kitchen to the wooden box filled with her treasure trove of hand-written family recipes. Although his grandmother had been raised in America, her mother had grown up in Germany in a bakery that had been in their family for generations. According to his grandmother, the bakery was famous for the sweets it created. She'd lost track of the family she had left there during the Great War and no one had heard from them since. Bryce had hoped after the war to visit the bakery and meet his grandmother's extended relatives, but that was not to be. Maybe someday in the future when the war was a distant memory, he could take his family there. He felt it was important for Josh and Britta to retain their French and German roots.

Bryce sidled up behind Britta as she continued pouring sauce on the cakes. "Mmm. Something sure smells good," he said as he slid his chilly fingers down the neck of her shirt, making her gasp in surprise. She spun away from him, trying not to drizzle the sticky sauce over the floor.

"You better behave or no *nonnettes* for you," Britta warned, grinning at him over her shoulder. With flour smeared across her cheek, mirth twinkling in her eyes, and her feminine fragrance blending with the delicious scents of holiday treats, Bryce had a hard time taking a step back from her instead of pulling her into his arms.

"What are *nonnettes*?" he asked, needing a distraction from his gorgeous wife.

"Gingerbread cakes filled with jam and topped with a lemon sauce. The translation is 'little nuns' and the cakes have been served for centuries. My mother always made them to share at our Christmas Eve service at church."

"That's great," Bryce said, leaning around her and snatching one of the still-warm cakes. He broke it in half and gave part of it to Hayes.

Mamie swatted both of them with a dish towel, making them all laugh as Josh, Pearl, and Ruby raced into the kitchen.

"Cookie!" Josh asked as he ran over to Bryce and leaned against his legs.

"Cake," Bryce said, bending down as he broke off a small bite. "Cake," he repeated.

"Cake!" Josh said, opening his mouth like a baby bird as Bryce gave him the bite. "Mo cake, Daddy. Mo cake, pease?"

Bryce's legs felt like they might give out on him. It was the first time Josh had referred to him as his parent. Hearing the little boy call him daddy nearly left him undone. Britta didn't say anything as she studied him, appearing to wait for his reaction.

Carefully, Bryce knelt in front of the child he considered his son, fed him another bite of cake, then pulled him into a hug.

Josh sighed and rested his head on Bryce's shoulder. "Mine daddy."

"All yours," Bryce said, his throat thick with emotion. "Josh's daddy."

Josh leaned back, then patted Bryce's cheeks. "Wuv Daddy."

"I love you, too, son." Bryce kissed his cheek, hugged him again, then set him on the floor. Josh and the twins scampered off to the front room to play, unaware of the storm of emotion he'd unleashed in Bryce.

Heart full to overflowing, Bryce took a deep breath before he stood and faced Britta. She dabbed at tears with the back of her hand while his grandmother used the hem of her apron to mop at her tears. Even Hayes looked a little misty-eyed over the exchange.

Bryce pushed aside Britta's hands, wiped her tears with the pads of his thumbs, then pulled her to his chest and kissed the top of her head. "He called me daddy."

Britta nodded.

Bryce tipped her chin up until he could look into her face. "Does that upset you? If you'd rather he didn't …"

"No," Britta said, reaching up with her hand and cupping his cheek. "It's perfect he thinks of you as his daddy, because you've been the only father he's known. I'm pleased, Bryce, and I'm grateful to you for being so good with my son."

"Our son," he corrected, then smiled at her. "And loving that little rascal gives me great pleasure. Now, since I had to share my cake, how about another one with a cup of coffee?"

"Coming right up," Britta said, imitating a southern-born waitress who worked at the diner in town, making them all laugh.

They'd barely sat down to enjoy the morning snack when the back door slammed open and Zach rushed inside.

Caught off guard, Bryce and Hayes both hopped up. Jace, who'd joined them for cake and coffee, slowly rose from his chair.

"What are you doing charging in here like that, son?" Jace asked, pointing to the still-open door. "We taught you better manners than that, and even if we didn't, I know you learned them from Lorna."

Zach looked like he might roll his eyes and offer a smart retort, but instead, he motioned to Bryce. "We don't have a minute to waste. They just received a telegram at the depot that the scrappers are coming for Hope today."

"For Hope?" Britta asked, clearly confused. "Who is Hope? What is a scrapper?"

"Hope is our train engine and scrappers are the men who gather up old metal things to be melted down and used for the war."

Mamie gasped. "They can't destroy Hope. They just can't. It's the engine Jace was driving the day we met. All three of you boys used to ride on it. And Zach, you've spent years keeping her running. We just can't let them destroy her. Can't we give them something else?" She turned to Bryce. "Can't Lennox Enterprises buy them more metal?"

"We aren't going to let them destroy Hope, Mamie," Zach said. Bryce watched as his father gave his grandmother a comforting hug. "But if we want to save the engine, we have to go now. We're going to have to move it. We only have an hour before the next train is due to arrive."

Bryce and Hayes hurried to pull on warm coats and gloves, then tamped their feet into their boots. They were settling hats on their heads when Bryce saw his grandfather yanking on his coat. "Where are you heading, Gramps?" he asked.

"With you boys. That engine is as much mine as anybody's. I was the first one to drive it, and if Hope ends up as another casualty of the war, I intend to be the last one to drive it."

Bryce looked to his father who shrugged.

"Come on, then," Zach said, placing a hand on Jace's back. "Let's go. I figured we can hide the engine in the Yellowbird Mine."

It didn't take them long to drive into town and head straight for the engine house at the depot. The old steam locomotive hadn't been used for years, but Zach had kept it in fine running condition. Jamie Milton, one of Charles Milton's boys, waved to them as they walked inside the building.

Bryce hated to think of the devastation the Milton family had endured. During the Great War, four of the six Milton sons had died in France, leaving behind widows and several children with no fathers. Jamie was one who'd grown up without his father and had spent a great deal of time with the

Coleman family. Uncle Mike had a plumbing business he operated with his two sons. Uncle Tim, the youngest of the six brothers, took over the feed store and garage. His two oldest sons were currently fighting in the war: one in the Army in France, the other in the Marines somewhere in the Pacific. The youngest child, Rand, was only four, and as full of pluck and sass as his older brothers.

"I hear we're liberating ol' Hope today," Jamie said with a grin. "What can I do to help?"

Zach had already built a fire in the old steam engine before he came out to get Bryce and Hayes.

"I'll serve as the fireman and keep the fire going," Bryce volunteered, excited to once again be on an adventure in the old engine with his family. His grandpa and dad had taught him how to do every job there was to know when it came to trains. He could repair an engine, hook the cars, serve as a brakeman, and even drive one as the engineer. But he loved riding in the old steam engine with his grandpa.

"You sure you feel up to it?" Zach asked, glancing at him in concern.

"I'll be fine, Dad. Are you or Gramps driving this old gal out of here?"

Jace looked at Zach. "I think you better drive, son. I'll take a turn once we're out in the open."

"Sure thing," Zach said, smiling at his father. "Hayes, if you'd drive to the location I mentioned earlier, you can pick us up there and give us a ride back."

"It'll take me longer to get there, so I'll head out now," Hayes said, jogging out of the engine house.

"Are you sure this is going to work?" Jace asked as Zach fiddled with a few switches while Bryce shoveled in more coal. From trips with his dad and granddad, he knew how important it was to keep an even level of heat in the firebox.

As he worked, he thought of all the fun times he'd spent with the two men in his younger years. George Lennox might have owned Hope and the track she rolled on, but the engine belonged to the Coleman family. Grandfather Lennox had never understood the sentimental value of the old steam engine, eager to replace her when better, faster models came along. But it didn't stop Zach from keeping the train in prime condition or taking them out on fun jaunts in it.

Bryce's mouth watered as he thought of the steaks his grandfather used to cook on a clean shovel placed in the firebox. Too bad they hadn't thought to bring some with them today. By the time they stowed the train in an abandoned mine shaft a dozen miles from town, it would be nearly noon and they could have enjoyed a feast.

"Hey, Dad, remember when you used to …" Bryce laughed when his dad held up a box containing four thick steaks.

"I grabbed some steaks on my way out the door. Maude won't tattle on me," Zach said with a grin. "We have to enjoy one final meal in Hope."

"That we do, but we'll have to remember to save one for Hayes. He'll be as mad as a hornet if we eat them all before he gets there and don't share." Bryce went back to shoveling coal.

Jamie pulled open the door in the storage section of the big engine house, and Zach eased Hope ahead on the track that ran through the building.

Bryce felt the pull of his muscles as he continued shoveling coal into the firebox and a strain on his side where the scars from his burns were still tender, but the physical exertion felt good.

His father guided the train out onto the main tracks, and they headed north in the direction of the mines and lumber mills.

Years ago, the discovery of gold had led to the boom that had founded the town of Holiday. One by one, the mines had played out and closed. One of the most lucrative had been the Yellowbird Mine. Not long after his grandfather Lennox had moved to Holiday, he'd purchased a share in the mine. When it had closed, he'd bought out the other partners, and now the land belonged to Lennox Enterprises.

The fact that Bryce essentially owned the mine was the reason his father had chosen it as an ideal place to hide the engine. Bryce had no doubt the men coming to collect Hope would search for it, and they might even look in the mine, but he knew of one tunnel where the engine would be undetectable.

"Are you taking it to the hidden tunnel?" Bryce asked as he leaned on the shovel and caught his breath as the train rolled down a grade in the mountains. It was beautiful out there, with the sun glistening on the snow and trees frosted in white.

Thoughts of trees reminded him they still needed to cut down their Christmas tree. Britta had asked a few days ago if he would mind retrieving a small green trunk that had come from her home in France from where it had been stored at Lennox Manor. Bryce had gladly hauled it out to the ranch, and she'd pulled out an assortment of antique decorations that had to have been in her family for generations. She tucked a dozen ornaments back into the trunk, but she set the other things out around the house they currently called home.

Bryce wanted, so desperately, to have a home and a future with her. The past few days, Britta had seemed more receptive to his attention. His heart melted all over again when he thought of Josh calling him daddy. It touched him in ways he'd never expected or anticipated to know the child loved him.

No matter what the future held for him and Britta, Bryce knew he'd do anything for Josh. Anything to keep him safe and happy and well. But he'd do the same for Britta; if she'd let him.

"You drive, Dad," Zach said, stepping back and letting Jace take over the controls. Bryce shoveled more coal into the firebox as they went up a grade, and then Zach took a clean shovel from where he'd stored it, dropped on a big glob of butter, and stuck it into the firebox.

"We better start cooking the beef, or we'll be eating cold, raw meat for lunch," Zach said over the noise of the engine.

Bryce glanced over at his grandfather as he shared an elated grin with him. He hadn't seen his grandfather look this happy and pert for ages. If they got caught, all three of them could end up in jail, or at least paying hefty fines. Bryce wasn't worried about the cost of the fines, but was concerned about the black spot it would leave on their reputations.

Then again, no one who mattered would fault them for doing their best to save the old steam engine that had run on the tracks between Baker City and the mines above Holiday for more than forty years.

When they could see the mine up ahead, Jace stepped back and let Zach take over the controls. He slowed the train and eased it along the tracks. They waved at Hayes as he arrived and hurried to move a downed tree branch out of the way. Zach drove ahead then backed the train into a tunnel where gold ore had been hauled out for nearly thirty years. The tunnel was wide enough and tall enough for the engine to fit inside, even as it curved back into the mountain. Zach stopped when they could no longer see any daylight from the opening of the tunnel. Hayes ran in with a flashlight in each hand to give them light to work by in the mine's dark recesses.

While Jace watched the steaks and Zach readied the engine for a long winter's rest, Hayes and Bryce shoveled rocks and dirt over the tracks, so it wasn't readily apparent they'd been recently used.

By the time they finished, the steaks were cooked, but Zach had forgotten to bring along utensils. They ended up using their pocket knives to cut the meat and eating it straight off the shovel as they sat outside on stumps. Bryce didn't know when anything had tasted any better as the meal eaten in the fresh winter air with the town of Holiday and the valley below them.

After they made sure the train was secure and settled, they piled into Zach's car and headed home. Jace was worn out and declared he needed a nap. Hayes went to check on Bonnie, and the rest of the ranch house was quiet.

Bryce made his way to Ava's house. He opened the back door and was greeted by the sound of the radio he'd bought and set up in the living room playing a popular new tune called "Mairzy Doats." He grinned as he slipped off his boots and shrugged out of his coat, leaving it hanging on a hook by the door.

On silent feet, he made his way to the doorway of the living room and watched Britta as she ironed one of his shirts. She'd changed from the dress she'd worn earlier into a pair of jeans with the cuffs rolled up just enough to show off her white socks and brown oxford shoes. She wore a white blouse with dark red polka dots, and her hair was fashioned in the twin braids she'd worn in France until the day he'd agreed to marry her.

She snapped a piece of gum and wiggled her backside to the music as she worked, pressing out the wrinkles from the shirt sleeve.

Amused by the sight of her looking so young and carefree, he leaned his shoulder against the doorframe and watched.

When the song ended and Bing Crosby began to sing "Happy Holiday," Bryce couldn't help himself. He crossed the space between them, took Britta in his arms, and danced around the room. At first, she looked at him as though he'd lost his mind, but then she laughed and followed his lead.

He was sure she had no idea about American dance moves, but she owned a natural rhythm that made it easy to dance with her.

The joy on her face and the twinkle in her eyes as they moved to the upbeat tune made him glad he'd arrived home when he did. When the song ended, he pulled her closer and swayed to the slower tune of "Somewhere Over the Rainbow."

"You're a wonderful dancer," Britta said in a whisper as she looked up at him. If he wasn't mistaken, she appeared to have her heart in her eyes.

"You're not so bad yourself, wife." His thumb traced the curve of her cheek and trailed down to her lips. He wanted to taste them, savor them. Before he could talk himself out of it, he inched closer to Britta and slowly lowered his head to hers. When their lips connected, he found hers to be sweet and willing. In no rush, he tantalized her mouth, exploring, learning, and accepting what she offered in return.

As the kiss deepened, he tightened his arms around her, nearly lifting her off her feet as he lost himself in the kiss, in the enticing fragrance of her, in the feel of her soft curves against his hard angles.

A moan of pleasure from Britta made him even more intent on finally claiming his wife as his own. He started to nudge her backward, toward the bedroom, when she seemed to suddenly snap out of the trance they'd been in. She took a step back, staring at him as though he'd turned into an enemy instead of her husband and friend.

Uncertain what else to do, he pointed toward the ranch house. "Where is everyone?"

"Chance and the girls went with Guzzy to give the horses some carrots," Britta said, referring to the older ranch hand who also served as the bunkhouse cook. He sometimes took the kids out to feed the horses and see the pigs or let them stay in the bunkhouse as he prepared a meal.

At his nod, Britta continued, "Mamie decided to take a nap, and Bonnie was asleep too. I decided to bring Joshua back here for his nap and get a little work done. You know he can sleep through anything."

Bryce had noticed Josh could sleep through a bomb explosion, due to the fact he'd spent the first two years of his life in a war zone where artillery fire was a common occurrence.

"So, Josh is asleep and everyone else is busy or resting. Hmm. I guess that means I've got you all to myself for a while." Bryce waggled his eyebrows suggestively, making Britta laugh, as he knew she would.

"You're such a tease, Bryce Coleman."

He stepped forward, settling his hands on her waist. "Maybe I'm not teasing, Mrs. Coleman. Maybe I would like some time alone with you. Maybe I'm tired of you sleeping way over on the other side of that big bed. Maybe, just maybe, I'm ready for the woman I married to truly become my wife."

Britta backed away from him until she stood with the ironing board between them. "Bryce, you shouldn't say such things. Not when …" She looked like she was about to cry, and that was the last thing he wanted. "You just shouldn't."

"I only say things I mean, Britta. I'm not joking around. What do you expect from me? I'm only human, and you are a beautiful, desirable woman, not to mention my wife." All the anger, frustration, and pent-up longing he'd tried to ignore abruptly spilled over. He moved around the ironing board, but she skirted to the other side of it.

"If you think I'm going to spend the next fifty years living like a monk while you love and cherish a ghost, you better think again!" Temper reaching the boiling point, he scowled at her and raised his voice, angrier than he'd ever been. "You need to decide if you are going to spend your life in the past with a man who's dead or live in the present with the one who loves you now. The one who is very much alive. The one who wants you more than anything."

Before he said something else he shouldn't, he stormed into the kitchen, yanked on his boots, and slammed the door behind him. Anger fueled his steps as he strode toward the barn, intent on taking a ride on his horse. Maybe that would help him calm down and clear his head.

That woman—that infuriating woman—had him so tangled up inside, he could hardly think straight. Was it so wrong for a husband to yearn for his wife? To want to hold her and love her?

A strong, primitive urge swept over Bryce with such force, he turned around and started back toward the house. He'd taken three steps when he stopped and expelled an irritated breath. He couldn't storm into the house and carry her off somewhere. He wanted to force her to listen to him until she saw reason or willingly surrendered to his need to love her, but now wasn't the time. Especially not when Josh would soon be up from his nap.

Exasperated, he turned around again and smacked into Hayes.

"What?" he barked at his cousin.

Hayes held up his hands in an innocent gesture, but then he smirked. "You have the look of a man who's just been set on his ear by the woman he loves." His cousin gave him a shove toward the barn. "Saddle Wren and you can help me check the fence line this afternoon."

Bryce nodded. Anything was better than being near Britta when she was working so hard to keep him at a distance.

Chapter Nine

Britta winced when Bryce slammed the door. She wanted to run into the bedroom, curl up on the bed, and cry.

Instead, she hurried into the kitchen and watched him storm off, stop, start to come back, then go off with Hayes. She wondered what he would have done or said if he'd returned inside.

Part of her wished he had come back and finished what he'd started. The kiss they'd just shared had left her lips tingling, her heart racing, and her wits scattered. She'd never been kissed with such consuming passion, such unfiltered longing.

She and Henri had been in love, but they'd also been so young when they wed. Henri was the first and only man she'd ever kissed until Bryce. And disloyal as it might be to Henri's memory, she couldn't help but compare the two men.

Everything about Henri had been quiet and reserved. Purposeful. He wasn't one who made grand gestures or flowery speeches. He didn't spout poetic phrases, flirt, or waste energy on things that were frivolous. He simply loved her and that had been enough.

Then Bryce had shown up on her doorstep and changed her life. Changed it in so many ways, she wasn't sure she could even count them all. It was amazing to think one choice, one single choice of opening the door to the two Americans who came to her house one summer afternoon would have such a profound and lasting effect on her life.

Bryce was so different than Henri. So full of life and fun, laughter and teasing. She knew even from the few times she'd listened to his telephone conversations with business associates that he had a keen mind and sharp intellect. He was passionate and confident, daring and strong. Even when he'd been bedridden with his injuries and stuck in her cellar, she knew if she'd needed his help, he would have climbed the stairs and stood beside her.

But Bryce came from a world so different than her own. The weeks spent living at Lennox Manor had made that irrefutable fact abundantly clear. Oh, Britta knew she had an education on par with that of Bryce and his sisters. Her father had seen to that, even if he had taught her at home. But she'd been raised in a simple country home. She didn't know which of the six forks at the table setting to use first or the proper way to accept a calling card, as Bryce's snooty sister Ardith had so enthusiastically pointed out.

When she was around Bryce's mother and sisters, she felt like a country bumpkin. Lorna had done her best to make Britta feel welcome and at home, as had Bryce's sister Carrie. But that atrocious woman who'd kissed Bryce on the first day they were in Holiday had done her best to make life miserable for Britta. She'd called her a German spy, made fun of the way she spoke with a slight accent, and even mentioned to the pastor at church her concerns about the "depraved woman" Bryce had married. Of course, she'd spoken to the pastor within Britta's hearing and had given her a nasty glare as she'd flounced away.

Britta had wondered what Bryce had seen in such a harsh, selfish girl, but she was beautiful. There were even moments she'd wondered if Bryce had been seeing Kate in secret; since Kate hinted as much, but Carrie had assured her Bryce had wanted nothing further to do with the woman after he'd arrived home with her and Josh. Even without Carrie's reassurance, Britta knew Bryce would never break the vows he'd made on their wedding day.

Bryce had played the role of doting husband and father to perfection. When they'd been at Lennox Manor with his family nearly smothering him with attention and keeping her so involved in various activities that she could hardly catch a breath, he'd still made sure they'd spent time together tucking Josh into bed at night.

Britta had worried about sharing a bed with Bryce, but he'd told her the first night they were at the manor he wasn't going to give anyone any reason to gossip about them being in separate rooms. As a couple that had recently wed, he expected her to sleep in the same bed. And that's all they did. Sleep. At first, it was a relief to Britta. But then, as she began to see Bryce not just as the hero who'd so nobly forfeited his future to give Josh a chance for one, but as a virile, handsome man who was gentle and caring, she felt powerless to keep from falling for him.

Yes, she still loved Henri. Still missed him. Still wished circumstances had been different and he was alive and well. Yet there was part of her that couldn't help but feel gratitude for the unexpected turns in her life, albeit some of them unbelievably painful, that led her to Bryce.

In the months since they'd wed, she'd seen so many sides of him. She'd seen him as a comrade well liked by those with whom he served. She'd seen him as a wounded man in need of care as well as an impatient patient. She'd seen him take on the persona of president of an important company and that of loving son and grandson. But the Bryce she liked the best, loved the most, was the one he'd been since they'd arrived at the ranch to stay.

He had been so relaxed, so happy, so full of laughter and joy. Sometimes watching him was like observing an overgrown boy, intent on having fun and sharing it with others. The first time she'd seen him wear a cowboy hat and boots, she felt dizzy with desire, especially when she pressed her nose to the window and watched him ride across the pasture with Hayes, thick thigh muscles encased in snug blue jeans.

There was no denying Bryce was an attractive man, and she was fiercely attracted to him, but before she took that next step of becoming his wife in every sense of the word, she wanted to make sure he was for keeps. She didn't want him to decide a year from now he'd grown weary of her and Joshua and turn them out to make their own way in a strange land full of strangers.

Then, that very morning, when Joshua had called Bryce daddy, she'd seen the big man humbled to the point he was nearly in tears. In that moment, as Bryce had held her son—their son—she'd known no matter what the future might bring, she could count on Bryce to stand beside her.

When he'd come in earlier and danced her around the room, Britta had felt so light in her heart, she thought she might have floated to the ceiling if Bryce hadn't held her close. Then she'd spoiled everything when she'd stepped away from him. It was just too much, too fast, or so she told herself.

Britta sighed and returned to her ironing. If she cared to admit the truth, which she didn't, she was scared of Bryce, of how he'd react to her. He was a man with a commanding, larger-than-life presence, and it intimidated her. How would she ever fit into his world of big business and corporate events? She would walk away from him and never look back before she'd willingly embarrass him in front of his peers. Carrie and Ardith had mentioned some of the grand events they'd attended that were hosted by Lennox Enterprises. Britta could no more picture herself making small talk with some corporation owner's wife than she could sitting at a table and skillfully maneuvering through sixteen pieces of silverware for one meal.

If Bryce had been a poor man or even a man of average means, she wouldn't have had any reservations about joining her life to his. However, nothing about Bryce was average. Not his looks, not his wealth, not his personality, not his intelligence, not even his heart.

She knew how big it was every time she looked at her son laughing with his cousins. Because of Bryce, they'd gone from being completely alone in the world in a house where they survived, to having a family that cared about them in a place they loved to live.

Britta wished they could just stay in the little house where they currently lived and pretend that was where they belonged. Not in the big marble-floored house in town that made Britta feel like a trespasser in someone's fancy castle.

She finished the ironing and hung up the clothes before Josh awakened from his nap. After giving him a snack of bread with jam and a glass of milk, she bundled him into his coat and returned to the ranch house where she'd left *bœuf bourguignon* simmering on the stove for dinner. Mamie had made the danishes filled with cream she'd mentioned that morning for dessert. They'd decided to serve the rich beef stew with Mamie's biscuits, and Britta's stewed apples.

Josh giggled and laughed all the way to the house, romping in the snow and playing with one of the ranch dogs when it ran over and licked his face.

Britta had given up on keeping the tongues of the ranch dogs away from her son's face. She'd seen the canines licking Chance and the twins and decided the germs wouldn't kill Josh if they hadn't hurt them.

The stew filled the house with a delicious,

beefy scent as they stepped inside the kitchen. Josh started to dart off in search of his cousins, but Britta grabbed him before he tracked snow across the clean kitchen floor.

"Not so fast, cowpoke," she said, then rolled her eyes, realizing Bryce's nickname for her son had finally stuck. "Let's take off your coat and boots, baby. Then you can play."

"Off, Mama! Go pway! Go now!" Josh wiggled and squirmed as she yanked off his stocking cap and his coat, and sent him on his way. "Peawl? Wuby?" he called as he ran down the hall toward the girls' room. Britta heard all three of them laughing as she removed her coat and hung it up. She pulled on an apron and set about peeling and coring the apples, then slicing them into a large pot with a spoonful of butter. She added maple syrup and cinnamon, placed a lid over it, then made a pot of tea she sweetened with honey. She set cups and the teapot on a tray, added napkins and a plate of cookies, then carried it to Bonnie's room.

The poor woman was propped up in the middle of her bed, a pile of catalogs and magazines around her, while Mamie sat in a rocking chair in the corner, repairing a pair of Chance's worn-out boots. Britta had been amazed to learn Mamie had learned the cobbler trade from her father. Since they'd been at the ranch, Bryce had been asking her to teach him about it and they sometimes spent an hour after dinner by the fireplace as he worked on practice projects and his grandmother tutored him.

"Would you ladies care for tea and cookies?" Britta asked, feigning a British accent.

Mamie smiled and took the cup Britta held out to her. "Anne Milton was British. Did you know she and I rode out here on the same train?"

"You did?" Britta asked, trying to recall if she'd heard the story.

Mamie nodded. "We were both mail-order brides. She came to marry R.C. Milton, the brawny blacksmith, and I was to wed Jace's brother. Only it was Jace's father who actually sent for me on Jude's behalf, but that's a story for another day." Mamie sipped her tea. "Anne made the best tea I've ever tasted. I watched her make it many times, but mine never turned out like hers. The only one of her girls who came close to making it the same was Ellery. I sure miss Anne, and we hardly ever see Ellery anymore, now that she and Tom have moved to Boise to be close to their son and grandchildren."

Britta set the tray on what was left of Bonnie's lap, lifted a cup of tea and a cookie for herself, then took a seat on the end of the bed. Bonnie got so bored stuck in the room alone, Britta and Mamie had made it a point to come visit her a few times a day.

It was through the visits with Bonnie and looking through the magazines everyone seemed to bring her that Britta had studied American fashions and hairstyles, and read about music and movies and books. She wondered if Bryce would take her and Josh to the movies sometime. Bonnie had mentioned there was a movie theater in Holiday. Perhaps after Christmas she'd ask him about it. He'd already been so good about introducing her to things she'd never had, like candy and spearmint gum.

She'd been as excited as a child when he'd arrived one afternoon with the radio that he'd set up in the living room at their little house. Britta loved listening to music and found it made the time pass quickly when she sang or hummed along as she worked. Of all the singers she'd listened to, her favorite by far was the crooner named Bing Crosby. Yesterday, when she'd listened to him sing about a white Christmas, it brought tears to her eyes as she thought of all the soldiers still fighting the war. She prayed by next Christmas, they'd all be home.

As it was, Bonnie was happy to answer any questions Britta had about American mannerisms and gave her useful tips for practical things.

"You should look at this," Bonnie said, stretching out her hand and grabbing a thick book on the bed. "It was supposed to have arrived back in October, but I just got it in today's mail."

"What is it?" Britta took the book, reading *Sears, Roebuck & Co Christmas Book* on the cover.

"A wish book for Christmas. Sears puts it out every year. It's too late to order this year for Christmas gifts, but it's fun to look through," Bonnie said, then bit into one of the spice-laden cookies left from those Britta had helped Mamie bake the previous afternoon.

Britta sipped her tea and thumbed through the catalog. There were pages filled with home goods, toys, candy and fruitcake, and many clothing selections. Her eyes landed on a page of nightwear and she envisioned wearing one of the lace and satin gowns for Bryce. Heat filled her cheeks, but she couldn't force herself to turn the page.

Bonnie strained to see what she was studying and grinned. "They have a dress shop in Baker City that carries those types of things. You ought to go."

Britta closed the catalog and set it on the bed, shaking her head. "I couldn't. I don't need anything. Bryce was quite generous in providing a new wardrobe for me when we were in Charleston."

Bonnie looked at Mamie with a raised brow, then back at Britta. "He did provide a wonderful wardrobe for you, but there are some things a wife just needs to have, like what you were looking at, Brit."

"I agree with Bonnie. You think she'd be stuck in bed awaiting the arrival of their fourth child if all she wore was high-necked flannel?" Mamie asked, making both girls laugh.

Bonnie rubbed her mounded stomach and sighed. "Maybe you shouldn't listen to me. Just look at the kind of trouble it might get you into."

Britta saw the covers jump as the baby kicked and placed her hand on Bonnie's belly. She smiled as she felt the baby kick again. As active as it was, she couldn't help but wonder if the baby was a boy. She was sure Hayes was hoping for another son.

She smiled at Bonnie and pulled back her hand. "I would be thrilled to trade places with you. I love babies and would happily carry a dozen."

"Then you definitely need to run into Baker City to the dress shop," Mamie said with a grin. "The first Christmas Anne and I were here in Holiday, we went shopping with Jace's Aunt Mae. Oh, but she was wonderful. We went to Maggie's dress shop and tried on the most exquisite creations. Of course, we had no money to buy gowns. Imagine our surprise when Jace and R.C. presented us with the dresses we liked as Christmas gifts. I still have that dress tucked away in a trunk. It was a beautiful red dress with lace, and the nicest thing I'd owned until Zach married Lorna and suddenly money was no longer a concern."

Bonnie nodded. "Bryce has been so generous."

At Britta's confused look, Bonnie smiled. "Bryce has paid for many of the improvements here on the ranch. He calls them investments, but Hayes is determined to pay him back."

"I'm sure Bryce wouldn't have spent the money if he didn't think it was a wise investment," Britta said, patting her friend's hand. "He is generous."

"And kind," Mamie said.

"And incredibly handsome," Bonnie said, making an exaggerated lovesick face that drew out Britta's laughter.

"Seriously, Brit. You should go to Baker City tomorrow. You can leave Josh here or with Lorna or Carrie. You deserve a day to enjoy yourself," Bonnie said, giving her an encouraging look.

"I don't know. I don't want to impose on anyone, and I'm not certain I should go off alone."

Mamie gave her a sly glance. "You could always take Ardith with you. She loves to shop."

"Mamie! Don't even suggest she spend a day with that dreadful woman," Bonne chided. "She might be related to you and Hayes, but I don't have to like her."

"I love her because she's my granddaughter, but she has too much of George Lennox in her for my liking," Mamie said, then looked to Britta again. "Don't forget tomorrow night is the annual Christmas party at Lennox Manor. You could have your hair done while you're in Baker City and come back just in time for the party. There will be so many people buzzing around the big house, it shouldn't be any trouble for someone to keep an eye on Josh. In fact, why don't you ask Zach to watch him? He'd love to spend time with his newest grandson."

"Really? You don't think he'd mind?"

Bonnie made a snorting sound. "Zach loves kids of any shape or size. He'll be happy to have Josh to watch and will use watching him as an excuse to not get sucked into all the craziness of getting ready for the party. Last year, he came and hid out here the whole day until it was time to go back to town to get ready."

"I think you talked me into it," Britta said, smiling from Mamie to Bonnie. "Is there a place I can get my money exchanged? Everything I have is from France."

"Go to the bank in Baker City and ask for Samuel Harter. He's one of my cousins. If you tell him Bonnie sent you, he'll take good care of you."

Britta squeezed Bonnie's hand, then rose to her feet. "Thank you. Should I call Zach tonight or wait until the morning?"

"I'd wait until the morning, but call early, before breakfast. Lorna and the girls will already be rushing around like mad to get things ready. Who knows, if you're at the depot in Baker City, you might even run into our friend Nick," Mamie said.

Britta had asked her about the man who reminded her so much of Santa Claus. Mamie had shared a similar story of encountering a man whose description was just like the person Britta had spoken with, one who'd made Mamie feel all warm and happy inside, then he'd just vanished. She knew there was no possibility it could be the same man, but it was fun to think about someone magical keeping an eye on them.

Mamie pushed herself up from her chair and finished the last sip of tea from her cup. "I'll whip up some biscuits to go with that stew. By the time they are ready, the men should be in to eat."

Because Bonnie seemed so tired of being alone in her room, Britta suggested they take their plates to Bonnie's room and dine there. Jace and Mamie sat in chairs, but the rest of them had an impromptu indoor picnic on the floor. The children thought it was a grand adventure and asked if they could do it again soon.

Bryce kept looking at her as they ate, but she pretended not to notice. She could tell he was no longer upset with her, but she wasn't quite ready to speak to him from her heart. She liked the idea of a day alone to get her thoughts in order. She hadn't had more than an hour or two to call her own since Joshua was born. It would be nice to have an entire day.

She remained silent as Hayes and Bryce recounted what they'd heard from Zach about the scrappers arriving to find the old steam engine missing.

"Dad said they were ready to blow a fuse when they couldn't find Hope," Bryce said, grinning at his grandfather. "He said they interrogated everyone at the engine house, including him, harangued the sheriff to arrest someone, then went up to the mines and snooped around. When they couldn't find Hope, they came back to town, threatening to arrest everyone who had anything to do with the engine's disappearance."

"Well, good luck to them in proving anything," Jace said, lifting a glass of milk in a toast to his grandsons.

The men laughed, but Britta shared a concerned look with Bonnie, hoping that would be the end of the matter.

The following morning, she rose while Bryce was still sleeping, pulled on a pair of jeans, a blouse, and a warm sweater, then tied a scarf over the hair she'd tied up in rags after Bryce had gone to bed while she'd pretended to read by the fire. After checking to make sure Joshua still slept, she pulled on her boots and coat and made her way along the path their frequent trips to the ranch house had packed down in the snow.

Inside the house, she removed her boots and coat, turned on the stove to heat, and started breakfast preparations. Mamie, who was always an early riser, joined her twenty minutes later. She made coffee while Britta kneaded loaves of bread that would be studded with fruit and nuts before they were baked. For breakfast, she stirred up batter for crepes and retrieved what was left of a baked ham from the refrigerator. After cutting the meat into small pieces, she stirred it into a mixture of eggs and cheese, then poured it over leftover boiled potatoes she'd thinly sliced and layered in a large baking pan coated with butter. She slid the dish into the oven and grinned at Mamie.

"Is it too early to phone Zach?" she asked in a whisper.

The older woman shook her head. "I doubt it. Zach is probably sitting in the kitchen sipping Maude's coffee, wondering how he can escape."

Britta grinned and walked over to where the phone hung on the kitchen wall. She dialed the Lennox Manor number and waited as it rang three times before someone picked up.

"Lennox Manor," a voice answered, sounding tired and perturbed.

"Dodi? This is Britta, Bryce's wife."

"Oh, darling! How are you? Are you enjoying the ranch? Isn't it splendid out there?"

Britta laughed as Dodi's voice changed from annoyed to cheerful. "It is splendid here. I love it. We are all well and looking forward to the party this evening. I'm sure if you need another set of hands, Bryce would be happy to help."

Mamie smiled and nodded her head at Britta.

She grinned at the older woman, then returned her attention to the conversation. "I was wondering if Zach is available, by chance. I needed to speak with him for a moment."

"Of course, darling. He was here just a second ago. Let me find him before he makes an escape for the day."

Britta listened to the sound of footsteps clacking across the kitchen tiles and pictured Dodi marching down the hall to find Zach. It wasn't long until she heard steps returning, then a deep voice on the line.

"How is my favorite daughter-in-law today?" Zach asked.

"I'm very well, sir. Thank you."

"What did I tell you about this sir business?" he asked in a teasing tone that sounded so like Bryce, it warmed Britta's heart.

"I'm sorry … Dad, but I was hoping you might be able to keep an eye on Joshua for me today. I have an errand I need to see to in Baker City, and I'd rather Bryce not know about it, with Christmas and all."

"I understand. How about this? I'll insist Lorna give him something to do here in town to keep him occupied and I'll come out there. I wouldn't mind spending time at the ranch where people aren't rushing around like they've lost their ever-loving minds. If you set out the clothes you want Joshie to wear tonight, I'll make sure he's clean, dressed, and ready for the party when you get back. I assume you'll be coming straight to the manor instead of going back to the ranch."

"That was my plan, and thank you, Dad. I appreciate this so much."

"You're welcome, Britta. I'm more than happy to spend time with my cute little grandson. Did he master saying the letter R yet?"

"He's working on it. It won't be long until Ruby is no longer Wuby."

Zach laughed. “Thank you for calling, Britta. I’m glad to have a reason to come out there today. Do you want someone to tag along with you? One of the Milton girls would no doubt be happy to go.”

“I think I need a day just to myself, but thank you. I’ll see you in a little while. Oh, and what time does the train leave?”

“You’ll want to take the train at eight. It will put you there right when the shops open. The hotel is a great place to go for lunch, or ask at the dress shop for a recommendation.”

“How did you know I planned to visit the dress shop?” she asked, curious.

A chuckle sounded across the line. “Just call it a family tradition. Have fun, Britta.”

“I will, Dad. Thank you.”

Britta hung up the phone and was surprised when Mamie gave her a warm hug.

The older woman pulled back and smiled at her. “I’m glad you’re going today. You need a little time for yourself. We all do. Do you have enough money? If not, I have some set aside.”

“Oh, I think I have plenty, Mamie, but thank you for being so sweet and offering.”

“If you need more, just tell them at the bank you are Bryce’s wife. They’ll trip all over themselves catering to you if you do.”

Britta would have laughed, but she could easily envision that very thing happening, which was why she intended to be nobody but Britta today. Not a wife or a mother or a daughter-in-law or cousin or friend. Just Britta.

Excited, she finished breakfast preparations

with Mamie's help and by the time everyone wandered in for breakfast, she could hardly contain her anxiousness. They'd just finished the meal when the telephone rang. Hayes answered it, then handed it to Bryce.

Britta had to work to subdue her urge to giggle when he rolled his eyes and kept saying, "Yes, Mama. I know, Mama. I'll be there, Mama," interspersed with beleaguered sighs. He hung up the phone with an annoyed growl.

"I've been summoned by the queen to the castle," he said, making everyone laugh.

"Have fun, Bryce. It should be quite a day." Hayes thumped him on the back as he carried dirty dishes to the sink.

Bryce scowled at him, ruffled Josh's hair, then kissed Britta's cheek. "It seems I'm to get there right away. If you need me, call the manor. Otherwise, I'll see you this afternoon. I can come back and get you and Josh."

"That won't be necessary. We'll catch a ride with someone. Take your suit with you, then you won't have to make a trip back out."

Bryce gave her an odd look but nodded, then hurried out the back door.

Britta almost asked if she could ride into town with him, but then she'd have to make up an excuse or story about why she wanted to be dropped off at the depot. Instead, she hoped Hayes wouldn't mind giving her a ride. She waited until she saw Bryce drive down the lane to bring up the subject as she washed the dishes.

"Will someone give me a ride into town?"

"I may be old, but I can still get you to Holiday," Jace said with a wink. "You go get ready, honey, and I'll warm up the car."

"Thank you, Gramps." She kissed his weathered cheek and raced out the door. She hurriedly changed into a dark blue suit with a soft yellow blouse, styled her hair, slipped on her watch, and pulled on a pair of dressy snow boots Susie had insisted she'd need. At the time, it had seemed frivolous to purchase them, but now she was glad she had them. She pinned on a hat, slipped on her coat, then took all the money she had and stuffed it deep into her handbag. Bryce gave her money from time to time, but she rarely spent it, so she'd use it for her train ticket today.

At the station, Jace dropped her off at the step so she wouldn't have to walk in the snow, told her to have fun, then gave her several bills of money and asked her to pick up something he'd ordered for Mamie at the dress shop.

"I will happily do that, Gramps. See you tonight," she said, kissing his cheek then bounding out of the car and into the depot office to purchase a ticket that cost a fraction of what she'd expected to pay.

The train was packed, but Britta didn't mind. It was fun to see people excited about heading somewhere for the holidays, many of them laden with colorfully-wrapped gifts tied with string.

When she reached Baker City, she followed the directions Bonnie had given her to the bank, asked for Bonnie's cousin, and soon left with her purse full of American money. It was far more than she'd anticipated when she'd tried to guess the conversion rates. Giddy to have plenty of money to spend, she went straight to the dress shop and was greeted by two beautiful women she assumed had to be sisters from their similar appearances.

"Good morning," the taller of the two said, greeting her. "Welcome to Maggie's. How may we assist you today?"

"My husband's grandfather asked me to pick up something he ordered for his wife. His name is Jace Coleman."

"Mr. Coleman? You must be married to Bryce," the shorter sister said.

"Yes, that's right." Britta followed the two of them over to a counter set against the wall nearest the door. "Do you know the family well?"

The two sisters looked at each other and smiled. "Lorna Coleman and her daughters have been shopping here for years, and so has your husband's grandmother, Cora Lee, along with those lovely Milton ladies. Our grandmother started the shop. For years after she retired, our mother ran it, and now we've taken over management. Maggie was our grandmother's name. I'm Ansley," the shorter one said, then pointed to her sister, "and this is Ella."

"It's lovely to meet you both. Bonnie Coleman said you had such lovely things here. If it would be all right, I'd like to look around."

"Please do," Ella said, motioning to the racks of dresses. "While you browse, we'll wrap Mr. Coleman's gift."

"Thank you." It didn't take long for Britta to

find a dress she absolutely loved. It was the perfect shade of deep Christmas red with short fluttering sleeves, a round neckline, and a waist with inverted pleats. The fabric glided through her fingers.

"You would make that dress look amazing," Ansley said as she stepped beside her.

"Oh, I really don't need another dress." Britta released the fabric and stepped back.

Ansley looked at her sister, and the two of them laughed. "There's no such thing as not needing another dress. That's like saying you don't need another pair of shoes."

Britta grinned. "Well, I suppose it wouldn't hurt to try it on."

"Of course not. I'll hang it in a dressing room for you." Ansley took the dress while Britta continued browsing. At the far corner of the store behind a tall screen that blocked the view of anyone coming in the door, she found what she'd traveled to Baker City to buy. She had never even known attire like the exquisite nightgowns existed until she'd seen them in Bonnie's catalog. Now, she struggled to decide which one would be best for charming her husband.

There wasn't a single thing in the world she could purchase for Bryce that he didn't already own or couldn't buy for himself. But there was something she could give him she was sure he wanted, something she hoped he'd love—her. Her future. Her trust. Her heart. Her love.

"It's hard to choose, isn't it?" Ella asked from behind her, making Britta jump. The woman smiled and placed a hand on Britta's shoulder. "I didn't mean to startle you. Have you purchased a peignoir set before?"

"No. I have no idea what to buy, but I wanted to surprise Bryce."

Ella's smile broadened. "With your coloring and that gorgeous hair, the peach one would look best. It's too bad we don't have one in bright blue because the color would be stunning on you."

Britta picked up a peach gown of satin accented with white lace. It truly was lovely.

"Why don't you try it and then decide?" Ella suggested.

By the time she left the shop an hour later, she'd purchased the red dress, the peach peignoir set, and gifts for Mamie, Lorna, Bonnie, and Carrie. Bryce had assured her he'd taken care of gifts for everyone, but she wanted to give the people who were special to her something special. The things she purchased weren't elaborate, just meaningful.

Ansley had kindly called the beauty shop and scheduled an appointment for Britta at three. It would give her just enough time to get her hair done, return to the shop and change into the red dress, then make it to the train and back to Holiday in time for the party that began at five.

She thanked Ansley and Ella and left their shop, making her way to the general store Mamie had recommended. Britta selected books as gifts for Jace, Zach, Carrie's husband, and Hayes. For Chance, who loved to listen to the country-western hour on the radio, she purchased an authentic Gene Autry flat-top guitar. Ruby enjoyed drawing, so she chose a blackboard easel with butterflies painted across the top and three boxes of colored chalk. Pearl loved to sit with her books by the fire in the evening, so Britta chose the complete works of Mother Goose for her.

It was hard not to want to buy everything in the store for Joshua, but she settled on a fold-out farm book. Each page was connected and folded out so when the whole book was extended, it was almost six feet long. Each page was cut into the shape of the animal featured on it, like a sheep or a pig. Her son would love it. She also added a toy duck connected to a string to her gifts for Joshua. When the string was pulled the duck waddled along and quacked. She could almost hear his squeals of delight at finding it beneath the tree.

It was then Britta realized they still hadn't put up a tree. Bryce had mentioned it several times, but in all the excitement of hiding the old steam engine and her planning this trip, she'd completely forgotten they were supposed to cut down a tree today. Perhaps they could do it in the morning and still have most of the day to enjoy it.

She was just about ready to check out when a toy train set caught her eye. It looked so much like the steam engine Bryce and his family had been so adamant about saving, she thought her husband might get a kick out of it. The train came with several pieces of track and cars, and there were even little trees and bridges he could set out. She pictured him on the floor with Joshua, his dark head bent over her son's golden curls as they set it up together.

In a festive mood, Britta added a few boxes of

candy, a canister of tea for Mamie, and a spool of red ribbon to her purchases. "Do you, by chance, make deliveries to the depot?" Britta asked as the clerk rang up her purchases.

"Sure do. I can get this there for you. Which train should they be on?"

"The Holiday Express, please."

The clerk nodded. "Name for the crate?"

"Coleman. Mrs. Bryce Coleman."

Slowly, the clerk raised his head and eyed her, then smiled. "Sure thing, Mrs. Coleman. Would you like the gifts wrapped?"

"Oh, yes, please. That would be most helpful." Britta grabbed a package of gift tags to add to the pile on the counter. She hastily wrote names on them and placed them with the appropriate gift.

"Anything else?" the clerk asked, clearly pleased at the large sale.

Britta added a box of spearmint gum to the purchases. "I believe that's all I need today, but thank you." She paid him then strode out the door and headed to the hotel for lunch. The dining room was opulent with a spectacular skylight. Christmas decorations gave the place a cheerful atmosphere. Britta enjoyed every bite of the succulent roasted chicken and wild rice she ordered, along with a slice of coconut pie.

She still had almost two hours before her hair appointment, so she went to the theater and watched her first movie while eating popcorn and drinking a cold bottle of Coca-Cola. The newsreel at the beginning of the show made her sad for the soldiers still fighting for what was right, yet grateful she no longer had to fear for Joshua growing up in a Nazi-controlled country.

The romantic comedy starring Cary Grant and Priscilla Lane made her laugh and took her mind off thoughts of the war, the party that evening, Christmas plans, and how she could best go about seducing her husband. Instead, she allowed herself to relax and enjoy the show.

After it ended, she raced to the beauty shop, then hurried back to the dress shop to change. Ella had boxed up her other purchases and already sent them ahead to the depot. The two girls wished her well; then she rushed to the depot, stopping just long enough to buy a pair of heels that matched her new handbag. At the depot, she hoped to run into the mystical Nick, but he didn't make an appearance.

Forty-five minutes later, she stepped off the train in Holiday, feeling renewed. It had done her a world of good to get away and the excursion gave her time to think. Time to decide what she wanted. What she wanted most was to spend a long and happy life with Bryce. She didn't want him to ever think he was second to Henri, because he wasn't. Henri would always be her first love and Joshua's father but Bryce was her son's daddy and the reason she had a new light shining in her heart.

Because of Bryce she now had a family, even if some of them drove her batty. And she had a home, not just for the holidays, but forever. Her home wasn't Lennox Manor or the little house out at the ranch; it was with Bryce. Wherever he was, that was her home.

Nervous about seeing Bryce, but looking forward to surprising him with her new outfit and newfound confidence, she smoothed a hand down the skirt of her new red dress, then went into the depot office. She asked for the crate and the packages from the dress shop to be delivered to the house at the ranch, then tipped the man five dollars if he ensured the delivery was made right away.

She'd just stepped out of the office when she heard someone call her name and turned to see Zach and Joshua waving to her. Her son had on a cute little pair of blue checked pants with suspenders and a white shirt. His coat dangled off one arm since he was going through a phase of not wanting to wear it. Zach was dressed in a suit and tie. Distinguished and handsome as he appeared, she couldn't help but think he'd be much happier in jeans and a flannel shirt.

"You look like you had a wonderful day, honey. Did you have fun?" Zach asked, kissing her cheek as she rushed up to them.

"I had an incredible day, Dad. Thank you for watching Josh. I hope he wasn't any trouble."

"Not at all. We had a grand day at the ranch. Mamie even let us help taste the treats she baked." Zach grinned and handed Joshua to Britta.

"Mama!" Joshua gave her a tight hug, then started babbling so fast, she had to work to pick out words she recognized. She heard Wuby and Peawl, and something about the woof-woofs. No doubt the kids had played with the dogs.

"Are you ready for this?" Zach asked, holding out his arm to her.

"No, but I suppose it's too late to claim we don't feel well."

Her father-in-law laughed as they made their way to the car. Since Britta had slipped on the heels she'd purchased and sent her snow boots out to the ranch, she carefully made her way through the snow. Joshua climbed into the car as soon as Zach opened the door, eager for a ride.

"Bryce has been so busy running errands for Lorna today, he only had time to call the house three times and ask to talk to you. Each time, Mamie made an excuse. I had no idea my mother was so good at subterfuge."

Britta giggled. "I bet she enjoyed every minute of it. I do so appreciate your help—everyone's help. I found just what I wanted for Bryce, and hope he'll like the surprise."

"I'm sure he'll be thrilled with whatever it is because it came from you and was given in love."

Britta realized Zach's words rang true. Everything she'd purchased today had been bought with love and affectionate thoughts of the recipients. Especially Bryce.

When they reached the house, cars were already parked all along the driveway and along the street. Lights glowed from what seemed like every window. Fat, fluffy snowflakes fell from the sky, infusing the evening with an even greater holiday feeling.

"Wow!" Britta whispered, impressed by the appearance of the manor and the greenery draped across the front, accented with fluffy red bows. Huge wreaths hung on the doors and from the balconies. Lights strung along the hedges and wound around the trees glowed and twinkled against the dusky evening sky.

"Wow!" Joshua repeated, rising to his feet and leaning against her.

"The first party at Lennox Manor was held the year I asked Lorna to marry me. That year, she invited everyone in town to come for lunch and purchased gifts for every child in town. After that, we switched to a dinner celebration, but we still try to make certain every little one in attendance receives a present."

"It's a beautiful gesture, Dad, and such a lovely tradition. I'm so pleased to get to be part of it."

Zach grinned at her. "You say that now. Wait until you've shaken hands with a hundred people and smiled until your cheeks hurt."

Britta laughed as Zach drove around back and onto the walk that had been shoveled to the kitchen door.

"This will be easier for you to navigate than trying to reach the walks at the other doors," he said. "I'll be in as soon as I park the car."

Britta leaned over and kissed his cheek. "Thank you, Dad. For everything."

"You betcha, honey." Zach winked at her as she helped Joshua out of the car and took his little hand in hers.

Together they hurried up the walk and in the back door to the kitchen.

"Hi! Hi!" Joshua said, smiling as Dodi and Maude greeted him with warm smiles.

"Oh, he's just cute enough to eat," Dodi said,

picking up Joshua and removing his coat then giving him a hug.

Joshua patted her cheeks, then pointed to Britta as she took off her coat and left it with her handbag on a hook by the door. "Mama, pwetty! See mine Mama! Pwetty!"

"Yes, little man, your mother is pretty and beautiful both inside and out." Dodi smiled at her as Joshua squirmed to get down. He took off running from the kitchen and Britta gave the staff a helpless look as she chased after him.

Britta caught up with Joshua near the front entry. Lorna had already picked him up and showed him off to a guest Britta didn't recognize. There were many people milling about that she'd never seen before and wondered if they lived out of town.

A warm, familiar, masculine scent that she found entirely enticing, reached her nose a second before Bryce settled his hands on her waist and his breath stirred a curl by her ear. "You look ravishing, wife of mine. Is that a dress I haven't seen before? And your hair looks different. Lovely, but different. Let me get a good gander at you."

Britta turned and smiled at him, pleased he'd noticed her appearance. She waited as his gaze traveled over her from the top of her head to the toes of her heels and back to her face. "Absolutely gorgeous. By far, you're the prettiest girl here tonight."

"You do go on, don't you, Mr. Coleman?" Britta offered him a coy look, attempting to flirt with her husband. She'd never flirted with Henri. He hadn't been the type to enjoy it. But Britta had been reading Bonnie's magazines and it seemed American men enjoyed a little flirting from time to time. "Flattery like that might get one of us into trouble."

He raised his eyebrows and gave her a puzzled look, as though he couldn't figure out what had happened to the Britta he'd grown accustomed to. He finally shifted so he stood beside her and slid his arm possessively around her waist before tipping his head down so his mouth was near her ear. "What did you do today? Each time I called to talk to you, Mamie assured me you were busy and couldn't come to the phone."

"Oh, this and that," she said in a vague reply. "You know how it goes."

Bryce gave her another odd look but nodded and smiled as Lorna motioned for them to move forward and greet guests. Britta was introduced to so many people, she had no hope of ever keeping their names straight.

The party was fun and joyful, though, and her favorite part was watching all the children receive a gift from a man dressed in a Santa Claus suit. She was fairly certain Santa was played by Mike Milton, and he did a grand job of portraying the jolly old elf.

For a moment, Britta thought she caught sight of the man named Nick she'd met at the depot in Baker City back in October. The old fellow grinned and waved at her, but she blinked, and then he was gone.

Once the party ended and the guests all left, Lorna begged them to stay. Bryce, Britta, Joshua,

Mamie, and Jace spent the night there, after phoning Hayes to let him know they wouldn't be coming back that night.

It was barely past five the next morning when Britta was awakened by something cold on her face bringing her instantly awake. When she opened her eyes, it was to find Bryce standing over her fully dressed and holding a snowball in his hand.

"Ready to get going?" he asked, poised to drop the snowball in the bed with her. "We have a lot to do today."

"Are you sure you wouldn't rather stay in bed?" she asked in a hushed voice, offering him a heated look as she stretched lazily with her arms over her head.

Bryce's grin melted off his face and he held the snowball against his neck. "If you play with fire, little girl, you are apt to get your fingers burned."

Before she could reply, he turned and rushed out of the room.

Pleased with his reaction, Britta smiled as she got out of bed and dressed in one of the outfits she'd left in their room at the manor. Once she was ready, she checked on Joshua. He was still sleeping peacefully. She saw no need to awaken him this early in the day, so she went down to the kitchen where Bryce and Zach cooked eggs and bacon while Lorna hid a sleepy yawn behind her hand.

"I see they forced you out of bed too," Lorna said, motioning for Britta to join her at the table. She had on a pair of woolen trousers and a cashmere sweater. It was the first time Britta had seen her wear anything other than a dress. When

Britta sat beside her mother-in-law, the woman reached over and gave her shoulders a hug. “You looked spectacular last night, Britta. Everyone was talking about Bryce’s beautiful, sweet bride.”

“Because she is beautiful and sweet,” Bryce said, winking at her as he turned slices of bacon in the frying pan.

“Did you have a good time?” Zach asked over his shoulder as he continued scrambling eggs.

“It was fun, and the food was delicious, but I think my favorite part was singing carols together after everyone went home.” Britta had been tired, but when Lorna had suggested they sit by the fire and sing carols while enjoying cups of spicy cider and cookies, they all joined in. As they sang the carols, Britta thought about Mary and Joseph. Like Bryce, Joseph had loved a child that wasn’t his, and that love had blessed him and his family.

She hoped Bryce’s love for Joshua would bring blessings to him; because it had certainly blessed her and their son.

How a man, any man, could so willingly, so readily accept a child that wasn’t his baffled Britta, but Joseph had accepted Mary’s child, and Bryce had accepted hers. If the Lord blessed them with more children in the future, Britta would love them all, but she didn’t think the relationship between any children she and Bryce might have could be as meaningful and precious to her as the bond he’d created with Joshua.

Without hesitation, Bryce had taken Joshua as his own, and she could picture them in the future, as Bryce guided their son to grow up to be a good, strong, and kind man. A man like his daddy.

Britta had been nearly overwrought with emotion by the time they'd finished singing carols the previous evening. She'd hardly said anything to Bryce as they tucked in Joshua and then settled on their own sides of the bed in their room.

Starting tonight, though, Britta intended for them to never again sleep with so much distance between them. Not when Bryce had so fully claimed her heart.

Chapter Ten

"I didn't think he'd ever go to sleep," Bryce whispered as he carried a box into the living room and set it by thc tree.

Britta leaned back against the couch as she sat on the floor, wrapping gifts for the cowboys at the ranch. Bryce had bought new gloves for all of them, then stuffed a twenty-dollar bill inside each glove. Britta had offered to wrap them while Bryce read Josh a few stories.

He'd saved *The Night Before Christmas* for last, and Josh had asked "mo?" the first two times Bryce had finished reading the story. Finally, the little one had fallen asleep as Bryce had read the last page of the book for the third time.

Britta's gaze shifted from him to the tree they'd chopped that morning in the woods at the back of the ranch and later decorated. They'd left Josh with Lorna while Zach accompanied them out to cut down trees; then Lorna had driven out for lunch and brought Josh with her.

Together, they'd decorated the tree in the ranch house and the one in Ava's house. Lights twinkled on the fragrant pine tree and added to the festive atmosphere of their little home.

If someone had told Bryce back in August that he'd be home for Christmas, married, with a two-year-old son, he would have called them plumb daffy. But here he was, eager to set out Josh's gifts, and so excited about the gift he'd arranged for Britta that he could hardly wait until morning to give it to her.

Tonight couldn't be a more perfect Christmas Eve. Carols played softly on the radio. A fire crackled in the fireplace. And one of Mamie's bayberry candles blended with the smell of the Christmas tree in a heady, familiar fragrance that took him back to some of his favorite childhood memories.

He glanced at Britta, admiring the way the firelight highlighted her golden curls and creamy skin. He'd been hard-pressed to keep his hands to himself all day. Yesterday, when he'd looked up and seen her walking down the hallway at the manor, he almost hadn't recognized the mesmerizing beauty as his wife. It wasn't the new hairstyle or even the new dress and shoes that had caught his attention. It was the confidence in the way she walked toward him that had changed everything.

People he hadn't seen in years came up to him and congratulated him on marrying such a mesmerizing woman. What none of them knew was that Britta was pretty from the inside out, beautiful in all the ways that really mattered. Although he wouldn't complain at all about her spectacular appearance.

In fact, as she'd stood on a stool earlier, hanging ornaments on the tree and stretching to reach a high branch, it was all he could do not to run his hand over her backside. He figured it would have earned him a slap in the face, but it might have been worth it.

She'd started out the morning shamelessly flirting with him, and he had no idea what to make of it. Maybe she'd been picking up a few tips from Bonnie, Carrie, and their friends. Up until yesterday, he wouldn't have thought Britta even capable of flirtatious behavior, but she'd flirted with him throughout the evening last night.

The coy smiles and saucy looks had left him so discombobulated, Bryce had hardly slept a wink. At four, he'd awakened and just watched Britta sleep. Like Josh, she always had one hand out of the covers, lifted above her head.

He thought about how easy it would have been to slide over and kiss her awake this morning, but he didn't want to scare her off or ruin their Christmas Eve by pressing his amorous attentions on her if she wasn't yet receptive to them.

From the signals she'd been sending out all day, though, he thought perhaps she was open to the idea of moving their relationship to the next level. Perhaps they could start slow with some kisses by the fire and see where things led from there.

As it was, Bryce felt like every nerve in his body was strung so tight, they might explode. Earlier that evening, Bonnie had begged and pleaded to attend the Christmas Eve service at church, so Hayes had packed her out to his car; then the rest of them had piled in, although Bryce would have happily driven his vehicle so they weren't so crowded. As it was, Hayes, Bonnie, and their kids occupied the front seat while Gramps, Mamie, Bryce, Britta, and Josh sat in the back. Gramps held Josh while Britta settled onto Bryce's lap and smiled at him in a way that made him think she'd intentionally arranged for their crowded trip to town.

Throughout the children's program, he'd only half-listened to the performers, even though Chance was one of the sheep in the play. Then the pastor had started talking about Jesus not being Joseph's child, but how much he was loved by a man who wasn't his father. Bryce could relate so well to the man who had loved a child that wasn't his.

He'd loved Josh since the moment the little boy had appeared by his bed in Britta's cellar. And each passing day Bryce loved him more. Just like he loved Britta more and more each day. Although he had no idea what their future might hold, Bryce prayed they'd hold onto each other.

Following the service at the church, they'd all gone to the park where the gazebo lights were turned on and the community joined together for carols, cocoa, and cookies. His mother had started the tradition thirty years ago, and he couldn't imagine a Christmas Eve without the special time together.

After that, they'd returned home, given Josh a bath, and tucked him into bed.

"What's in the box, handsome?" Britta asked,

then snapped the piece of spearmint gum she was chewing. He grinned and took out the cowboy hat, boots, chaps, and saddle he'd purchased for Josh.

"Please tell me there isn't a pony outside for him." Britta couldn't hide her smile as she admired the little western clothes.

"No pony, for now. I'm saving that for his birthday." Bryce smirked at her and set a few more gifts beneath the tree; then he took three stockings from the box and hung them from the fireplace mantel. "I know you said you never had stockings hung by the fire, but I thought you might enjoy the tradition."

Britta rose and hurried over to admire the stockings, then gave him a concerned look. "What will we put in them? I didn't buy anything special for stockings."

"Not to worry wife. I've got it all taken care of," Bryce said. He stuffed a wooden top and a set of nesting blocks with nursery rhymes printed on them into a blue sock with Josh's name embroidered on the front. Bryce added an orange, a peppermint stick, a small glass train filled with colorful candy, and a few pieces of chocolate wrapped in red and green foil.

"Joshua will love it all," Britta said, leaning against his arm. Either he'd been standing by the fire too long, or she was the cause of his temperature suddenly spiking.

"Are you finished with the gloves?" he asked, needing a distraction from her before he lost the tenuous hold he had on his self-control.

"One more pair and I will be," Britta resumed

her seat on the floor and returned to wrapping the gloves.

"I appreciate you doing that for me," he said, as he quickly filled her stocking. He had one very special gift he hoped she'd like that he'd tucked inside the toe. He added an orange and candy to his, not expecting there to be any gifts because Britta hadn't known what he'd planned.

It had been a pure delight to see Christmas through her eyes and Josh's. The things Bryce had always taken for granted had been such wonders to them both and made him grateful again for all he'd been blessed with, especially them.

"I think I'll get ready for bed," Britta said, as she rose and put away the scissors and string she'd used to wrap the gifts, blew out the candle, then left the room.

He thought he could hear the bathwater running and wondered if she planned on a long soak or just a quick bath. Visions of her in the tub covered with bubbles made him step out into the cold and gather another armload of wood. Once the wood box was full, he set all the gifts for the hired hands in a box, then piled the gifts that would go up to the ranch house in another. He'd been amazed when Britta had shown him the gifts she'd purchased for Chance, Ruby, and Pearl. He knew the kids would love them, just like Bonnie would love the soft robe Britta had purchased for her. How she'd managed to sneak off and go shopping without him knowing about it amazed him. His dad had mentioned something about Britta needing a day to find herself.

If her new confidence was the result of it, he'd encourage her to take more days just to enjoy herself.

He couldn't imagine any woman fitting into his family as well as Britta. His parents adored her, his grandparents thought she was wonderful, Hayes and Bonnie said she was the best thing that ever happened to him, and he had to agree. Even Ardith had been mostly civil to Britta at the party last night, and that was saying something.

While he waited for Britta to finish her bath, Bryce went into the kitchen and washed his hands, got a drink of water, then paced back to the living room. He'd just bent over to unplug the tree lights when he looked up and saw Britta leaning against the doorway wearing something that looked like it came right out of one of his dreams.

A satin robe the color of peaches was trimmed in lace and cinched in at her waist. She'd pulled the pins from her hair and brushed it out so it hung in thick curls around her shoulders and down her back. The scent of her luscious fragrance reached him just as her gaze entangled his.

She studied him a moment as he continued to gape at her, still half bent over the light plug. He unplugged the strand, then straightened, facing her as she strolled into the room, hips swaying invitingly. When she stopped a foot away from him, Bryce's mouth went dry.

"What are you doing?" he croaked, wondering how much control she thought he possessed because he'd reached his limit. He was just a man, after all, and one with a lot of hot red blood pumping through his veins.

"I know your family exchanges gifts on Christmas Day, but I wanted to give you a gift tonight. A special gift."

"That's fine, Britta." His voice sounded strained, even to him. "What is it?"

"The gift," she said, moving closer, her eyes never leaving his. In their bright blue depths, he could see love mingling with hope, a hint of mirth, and yearning. Yearning for him. "The gift," she repeated, "is me."

"You?" he rasped, trying to force his muddled brain to understand what she was saying.

"Me." She offered him a seductive smile, then put the ends of the cloth belt tied around her waist into his hands. "Want to unwrap your present?"

"Do I?" Bryce no longer felt uncertain about her intentions. "You can't begin to know how long I've wanted to do that very thing, Britta. I love you so much. I've loved you since I looked up the day I collapsed on your kitchen floor and thought I'd been saved by an angel."

"I'm no angel, Bryce, and I can't promise I'll always be the wife you want, but I'll do my best to be the one you need. I love you, too. And before anything else is said, I want you to know that I will always love Henri, but that doesn't mean I don't love you as much, because I do. In some ways, I love you far more. You are a miracle and a blessing, and I pray I never take you or your love for granted. You mean the world to me."

"You, my darling wife, have become everything to me. Everything," he said, leaning down and capturing her lips in a gentle kiss that rapidly gained heat until Bryce thought he might combust. He pulled back and smirked at her then stepped over to the fireplace and fished his fingers into the stocking he'd hung for her. He pulled out a small box, dropped to one knee in front of her, and opened the lid.

"Britta, when we wed in France, it wasn't a grand ceremony, and you married someone you barely knew, but I do love you. I love you with all my heart, and I hope together we'll have a wonderful future full of love and joy. Would you do me the great honor of becoming my wife, my real wife, and allowing me the privilege of courting you for the rest of our lives?"

She nodded, tears in her eyes, as he slipped a diamond ring on her finger next to the plain gold band she wore. The ring had belonged to his grandmother Lennox and his mother had given it to him to give to his bride years ago. It wasn't any surprise to him that it fit Britta's finger perfectly.

"The ring was my grandmother's, Mama's mom. I want you to have it."

"And I'll cherish it always, Bryce. Just like I'll cherish you," she said, holding out her hand and admiring the way the firelight played off the oval diamond.

Bryce rose to his feet. Slowly, he untied the belt of her robe and pushed it off her shoulders, letting it fall to the floor. He took his time gazing at the peach-colored satin and lace confection she wore that accentuated her curves and left him without a shred of restraint.

He swept Britta into his arms and kissed her all the way to their room, knowing this Christmas was the happiest he'd ever known.

The next morning, after they'd eaten breakfast at the ranch house and exchanged gifts with everyone there, Mamie and Gramps volunteered to keep an eye on Josh while Bryce insisted on taking Britta for a drive.

"We don't have time for a drive, Bryce. We need to finish getting things ready to take into town to the manor for Christmas dinner. Mamie will need help with the dinner rolls, and I promised I'd make more gingerbread cakes."

Bryce shook his head as he climbed in the car then gently tugged on Britta's hand to slide closer to him. Since last night, since they admitted their love for one another, he couldn't get enough of touching her, holding her, kissing her, loving her.

"I promise this won't take long," he said, heading down the lane to the road. "Besides, if you don't make the gingerbread cakes, the world won't end. There are enough sweets at Mama's house and the ranch house to rot the teeth out of every child in Holiday."

"Not quite that many," Britta said, glancing down at her hand where the ring he'd given her last night glittered in the morning sun. "The ring is gorgeous, and it means so much knowing it belonged to your grandmother. Thank you. Thank you for everything and for all the fun things you bought for Joshua. If you aren't careful, you'll spoil him."

"Me? I'm not the one who bought him that

blasted duck that hasn't stopped quacking since he opened it this morning." Bryce grinned at her and she laughed.

"Maybe we'll tell him it's a toy he can leave at Lennox Manor."

"That's a grand idea." Bryce chuckled, then raised Britta's hand to his mouth, kissing her fingers. "Thank you for the train set. It's perfect and looks so much like Hope. I love it. Next year, when Josh is big enough not to trample all the pieces, it will be fun to set it out around the Christmas tree."

"I'm glad you like it. I thought it would be something the two of you could enjoy together."

He turned and drove down a lane, then parked in front of the house he now owned. A house he'd purchased from Bob Bennett two days ago. The family had moved out last month, so the place was empty. Bryce had hired a crew to clean it from top to bottom; then he'd purchased a few things and brought them out yesterday when Britta was busy helping Mamie cook their Christmas Eve feast.

"Who lives here?" Britta asked, looking around, noticing the barn at Elk Creek Ranch was barely visible in the distance. "Is that the ranch?"

"It is. This property connects to it on the southern border. In fact, Hayes and I have discussed putting in a new road so it will only take five minutes to get from this house to his instead of driving all the way around on the county road."

She frowned. "Why would you do that? Is one of your relatives moving in here? Or a Milton? I heard one of Uncle Tim's girls talking about hoping her beau would propose. Is she getting married?"

Bryce shook his head, hurried out of the car, and ran around to open Britta's door. He took her hand in his, laced their fingers together, then led her down the walk and up the steps.

One of the ranch's hired hands had hustled over an hour ago and boosted the heat setting on the furnace, lit one of Mamie's bayberry candles, plugged in the string of lights on the tree Bryce had set up and turned on the brand-new RCA Victor console radio Bryce had hauled in the previous afternoon.

As they lingered on the porch, he gave Britta a long look, then pushed open the door, swept his wife into his arms, and carried her inside. She laughed and looped her hands around his neck, and for a moment, he forgot about the house and anything else as he lost himself in a passionate kiss.

He toed the door shut behind him and eventually set Britta on her feet. Although the house was devoid of furniture, the radio sat in a corner of the living room, playing Christmas songs, while the tree filled the space in front of a big picture window. The fragrance of the pine mingled with the scent of the candle, creating a wonderful holiday aroma.

"What is all this?" Britta asked, stepping further into the house that was drenched with light from the many windows. She seemed to enjoy sunny spaces as much as Bryce.

"This, Britta, my love, is our home. I know you hate living in town, and I do too. This way, we'll be close to everyone at the ranch, but still have our own place. Hayes is going to run cattle on the pasture and plant hay in the fields, but you can have whatever animals you want here. In fact, I have one more present for Josh, if you approve."

He picked up an open-topped box by the tree and held it out to her. Britta gazed down at the sleeping puppy and gave him a look so full of love, Bryce thought his heart might burst.

"Every boy needs a good dog," he said, brushing a finger over the puppy's head before he set the box on the floor.

"Oh, he's perfect and Joshua will love it." She threw her arms around his neck and kissed him, then pulled back and took his hand. "Show me the house. Tell me everything."

Bryce laughed and led her through the house that had four bedrooms, a space for him to have a home office, a large sunny kitchen, and a spacious living room.

Above the fireplace, Bryce had hung a photo he'd received in the mail from Colonel Lee Thompson. Britta noticed it and raced over to study the image of the two of them on their wedding day. The photographer had captured them smiling at each other while Josh ate a piece of cake. Together, they looked like a happy family.

And that's exactly what they were.

"Colonel Thompson sent the photograph and some others, although that one is my favorite. I've got the rest of them back at Ava's house, but I wanted to show you this one first," Bryce said, wrapping his arms around Britta from behind and resting his chin on her shoulder. "I'm so glad you married me."

"I'm so grateful you married me, Bryce. You saved me and Joshua and gave us a hope for the future, and a forever home in your heart. Thank you for loving me, for loving our son. I can't believe you bought me a house for Christmas."

"Not a house, wife of mine, but our home for all the holidays to come."

She turned in his arms and they shared a tender kiss. Bryce lifted his head when Bing Crosby began to sing, "Let's Start the New Year Right."

Britta lifted an eyebrow in invitation, and soon the two of them were dancing across the floor.

"Let's do what the song says, Britta. Let's start the new year right. We've got a new home, a new future, and a new love. What could be better?" Bryce asked as he swung her around, then pulled her close against his chest.

"Nothing. Nothing in the world can be any better than this unless you want to give me another baby to love."

"Now that would really start the new year right." He kissed her soundly, looking forward to the years ahead of them, knowing no matter where life took them, they would always have a home together, in each other's arms.

Gingerbread Madeleines

Years ago, not long after Captain Cavedweller and I married, we were visiting his grandparents. Grandma Nell handed me two baking pans with little shell-shaped molds, and simply said, "He likes these." I had no idea, at the time what "these" were, but I soon learned they were madeleine pans, and CC had a fondness for the traditional French cakes. This version offers a little holiday flair with gingerbread and spices. Happy baking!

1/3 cup granulated sugar
2 eggs
1 teaspoon vanilla extract
2 tablespoons molasses
1/4 teaspoon ground ginger
1 teaspoon pumpkin pie spice
1/4 cup melted butter, additional for the pan
1/2 cup all-purpose flour, additional for the pan
powdered sugar, for dusting

Preheat the oven to 375°F. Brush softened butter onto a madeleine pan, then sprinkle flour into the molds. Tap out the excess flour.

Beat the sugar and eggs together until pale yellow, about 1 to 2 minutes. Add the vanilla, molasses, and spices. Mix to combine. Scrape the bottom of the mixing bowl, then mix again to combine.

Alternating, add part of the butter, then the flour on low speed. Continue adding and mixing until well blended.

Use a tablespoon to scoop out 1 tablespoon of batter into each madeleine mold. Bake the madeleines for 8 to 10 minutes, until they spring back when gently touched on their tops.

Use a knife to gently wedge the madeleines out of the pan and onto a wire cooling rack. Cool completely then dust with powdered sugar.

Author's Note

Thank you for coming along on another Holiday Express adventure. I hope you enjoyed sharing the journey with Bryce and Britta to their happily ever after!

I don't know about you, but Josh, that sweet lil' cowpoke, sure captured my heart.

When I was working on ideas for this series, I knew I wanted one of the books to take place during World War II. It always grabs onto my heart with both fists when I dive into the research of this era. I continue to be amazed and awed by all that was sacrificed by the people who served and those who kept things running at home.

Before I begin a book, I always select a song (sometimes several, but usually just one) that I listen to on a loop while I'm writing. For this book, I knew the song I wanted to listen to the moment I decided Britta should be a widow with a toddler. "It Wasn't His Child" by Trisha Yearwood is such a sweet, beautiful song that made me think so much of the love of a wonderful man for a child that wasn't of his blood, but instead of his heart. If you've never heard it, give it a listen.

As I sank deeper into my WWII research for this story, I was trying to figure out a way to tie Bryce to railroads. (He's a Coleman–there had to be trains!). It was then I stumbled upon information about the 727th Railway Operating Battalion. The mission of a railway operating battalion was to manage and maintain a specific section of railway in a theater of operations and to be prepared to destroy the line if necessary.

In March 1942, the 727th Railway Operating Battalion, sponsored by the Southern Railway Company, became the first battalion to be activated after the war began. Although most of the officers and many of the enlisted men were experienced railroaders, the new battalion included men drawn from Army training centers who needed to be trained. The men had to learn to work together efficiently as units, and on-the-job training came from contracts by the War Department with commercial railroads. An untrained Army train crew would accompany a train manned by civilians to learn rules for operating as well as preferred techniques. The 727th went to Camp Shelby, Mississippi, to train on the Southern Railroad between Meridian, Mississippi, and New Orleans, Louisiana.

As the war effort increased, the War Department activated additional railway battalions. In November 1942, the Transportation Corps assumed responsibility for the Military Railway Service (MRS) operated by the Corps of Engineers. During World War II, the MRS operated in every theater of operations where there were American forces. At its peak, it included eleven divisions, thirty-three railway operating battalions, and eleven railway shop battalions. A variety of engineer, signal, and military police units provided support to the railroaders. Also, in December 1942, two railway operating battalions deployed to theaters overseas: The 711th went to Iran while the 727th headed for North Africa.

So, that's why and how Bryce ended up in North Africa. From there, the 727th served in Sicily, then Italy, and then in France where they were stationed at Lyons.

Have you ever thought about what it would be like to try to wrap a pile of Christmas gifts without Scotch tape? It almost makes me want to cry, because I love to wrap gifts and Scotch's satin tape is my sticky substance of choice when it comes to holding the wrapping paper in place.

In the 1920s, Richard Drew, a young research assistant at 3M's Minnesota headquarters, was working to develop an adhesive tape that would allow a precise two-tone paint job without mixing or bleeding colors. His prototype didn't have enough stickiness to it, and he was told he was being "Scotch," or stingy, with the adhesive. By 1929, DuPont had developed transparent cellophane, and it was being used in all sorts of packaging. Producers wanted a tape that could match the vitreous appearance. After more trial and error, Drew and his team developed Scotch Brand Cellulose tape. I'm so glad they did!

But during the war, Scotch tape was as hard to find as silk stockings. I happened upon an advertisement from 1944 of an exasperated woman trying to wrap a Christmas gift using a spool of string. A cat plays with the spool and the paper won't stay in place. Above the ad, it reads *Home Front Headaches: No "Scotch" Tape*. Below the illustration of the woman is a soldier telling her to be patient because Scotch tape is on the war front, doing things like sealing Army containers.

Another advertisement shows a running soldier carrying a box of dried blood plasma that's been taped shut using Scotch tape. Who knew something we take for granted every day (and never have enough of when wrapping that last gift on Christmas Eve) was so useful and vital to the war effort? I certainly had no idea.

In this story, you might have noticed I mentioned an assortment of food. I could happily live at Elk Creek Ranch for a variety of reasons, but I would thoroughly enjoy Mamie and Britta's cooking.

I almost included the recipe for crepes in this book instead of madeleines. The reason for that is because:

1. I love them
2. So does Captain Cavedweller
3. They are so delicious

Even though I didn't include the recipe, you can find Christmas Crepes on my website. I don't always make them for Christmas. And sometimes I make them for no other reason than CC has the day off and we can enjoy a leisurely breakfast.

I was in the seventh grade the first time I had crepes. Our teacher decided to give us all some culture and let each of us select a country to study up on and do a presentation complete with props. One of the girls chose France. Her mother brought in a hot plate and helped her make crepes for the class. They were delightfully wonderful and so different from anything I'd eaten. When she passed out copies of the recipe, I immediately went home and begged my mom to let me make them. She did, and I've been making them since. They are light and delicious – just right for a morning brunch before a big holiday meal! We like to fill our crepes with berries, or bananas (or both!), and freshly whipped cream.

As I mentioned in the author's note for *Holiday Heart*, the inspiration for Lennox Manor comes from the Pittock Mansion in Portland. If you ever have an opportunity to visit it – go! It's such a spectacular example of not just architecture, but an entire way of life from a specific slice of history.

When I was digging out my research book for this series, I found a book I'd forgotten I'd ordered last year after Christmas. It's the 1942 edition of the *Sears, Roebuck & Co Christmas Book.* Oh, my gracious! Talk about tripping down memory lane! (To clarify, this came out decades before I was born!) But there are so many things in the book that I remember seeing at my grandma's house and it filled me with what my cousin Julie would refer to as "happy-sad" nostalgia. How I wish I could be ten years old again, just for an afternoon, and stroll through my grandmother's house, admiring all those treasures once again. Also, it was such fun to see both everyday and special gift items available back then, like Britta's peignoir set, and the glass train full of candy

Bryce tucked into Josh's stocking.

If you'd like to read more about the Milton family, be sure to read my modern-day Holiday Bride romances. Samuel Harter (Bonnie's cousin at the bank in Baker City) is a descendant of Seth Harter who you can read about in *Dumplings and Dynamite*!

Thank you to Katrina, Allison, Alice, Linda, and all of my Hopeless Romantics Street Team for their help with this book. I appreciate you so much!

I hope, dear reader, you'll do as Bryce and Britta did at the end of the story and "start the New Year right" with a heart full of joy and a home full of love.

Happiest of Holidays to you!

Shanna

Thank You

Thank you for reading *Holiday Home*! I hope following Bryce and Britta's journey to a happily ever after brought you joy and warmed your heart. If you did enjoy it, I'd be so appreciative if you'd consider leaving a review so other readers might discover the book, too.

Holiday Express

Four generations discover the wonder of the season and the magic of one very special train in these sweet holiday romances.
Find them on all Amazon

Also, if you haven't yet signed up for my newsletter, won't you consider subscribing? I send it out when I have new releases, sales, or news of freebies to share. Each month, you can enter a contest, get a new recipe to try, and discover details about upcoming events. When you sign up, you'll receive a free digital book. Don't wait. Sign up today!

Holiday Love Excerpt

Will delving into the past kindle a forever love?

Kali Hoyt loves old things. Old books. Old dishes. Old cars. Old love stories. Hired as the director of the newly-formed preservation society for the town of Holiday, she can't wait to begin digging into the history of a place she enjoyed visiting during her childhood summers. When her cousin introduces her to his best friend, Kali has no idea the grease-covered redneck will have such a monumental influence on her future.

Trace Coleman has spent his life being groomed to take over his family's vast Lennox Enterprises empire. Astute at running the company, he much prefers to spend his days tinkering with the old steam engine that his great-great-grandfather worked on as a mechanic in the Holiday engine house. When he encounters the newly hired director for the preservation society he founded, he knows her presence in Holiday is going to change his life in ways he can't begin to imagine.

Will two reluctant hearts succumb to the magic of the holidays? Find out in this sweet holiday romance filled with humor, heart, and love.

A fresh summer breeze carrying the hint of pine trees and cinnamon drifted in the open windows of Kalista Hoyt's vintage Jeep Wagoneer, stirring thoughts of the holidays, even though a few days remained of August. She breathed deeply and smiled. It was good to be back in Holiday.

The small Eastern Oregon town where her aunt, uncle, and cousins resided wasn't on the way to anywhere except higher into the mountains, but starting today it was her home.

She inhaled another breath, filling her lungs with the clean Christmas-scented air, feeling more relaxed than she'd been in years. With her elbow propped out the window, Kali leaned back in the seat and hummed along to one of her dad's favorite tunes from the 1980s, about ruling the world.

Fingers tapping on the steering wheel, she slowed to a crawl and studied the businesses on Main Street, surprised to see several new places open since the last time she'd been in town six summers ago.

A bakery sign for Sunni Buns caught her eye. She grinned at the logo of a sun rising over a big cinnamon bun. Leave it to her cousin to come up with such a unique, amusing business name.

The sound of a horn blaring behind her made her jerk the wheel to the right. A lunatic in a beat-up pickup that had more rust than paint on it swerved around her and zoomed down the street. That was the sort of thing she would have expected in Los Angeles where she'd spent the past two years working at an award-winning museum, not in a friendly little town like Holiday.

"What a jerk!" she said, annoyed by the maniac driver. Granted, she had been driving slower than a snail, but in all fairness, it was early and hardly anyone was out. Kali had been so excited to reach Holiday, she'd left the hotel where she'd stayed in Boise last night a little before five that morning. It had taken her almost three hours to make the drive to Holiday, but now that she was here, she could hardly contain her excitement.

On Monday, she'd begin her position as director of the Lennox Heritage Preservation Society. Funded by Lennox Enterprises, a world-wide corporation with deep pockets, the preservation group had been recently founded and concluded they needed someone to oversee it.

At first, Kali had thought she was interviewing for the role of director for the Holiday Depot Museum that was slated to open in November. What she'd realized during her first virtual interview with two of the board members was that they wanted her to be in charge of all the old buildings in town being renovated through the LHPS. She'd been so excited and giddy, she'd nearly grown lightheaded. It would take years and years to get all the facilities restored and open, and she loved the idea of the stability that would come with the position.

Two additional virtual interviews later, she'd danced around her apartment as the newly hired director. It had taken her three weeks to wrap up things at her position in LA, pack her belongings, and pay a quick visit to her mother in San Diego before she made her way to Holiday.

Now that she was here, she couldn't wait to get started. Kali pulled over and parked, then walked across the street to the bakery. The aroma of cinnamon and yeast made her stomach growl with hunger. She pulled open the door and stepped inside, then jumped as she was yanked into a tight, nearly suffocating hug.

"Here she is! Our favorite California girl," her cousin Matteo said, giving her one more squeeze before he let her go. "Welcome to Holiday!"

"Thanks, Matt. It's so good to be here," Kali said, happy to see her only male cousin. She turned and faced his four sisters: Julie, Vicki, Sunni, and Tori. The entire Lopez family was attractive, but Kali was always taken aback by how stunning the girls looked in person. Their mixed heritage of Italian, Cuban, Mexican, and Irish had blended in the most beautiful way.

"What are you all doing here?" Kali asked as she was hugged and kissed and hugged some more.

"We always have breakfast together on Saturday. No kids. No spouses. Just us," said Sunni, the owner of the bakery with a personality that matched her cheerful name. She pushed Kali into a chair and set a cup of iced Mexican coffee in front of her along with a warm cinnamon bun.

"That's awesome. I had no idea you all did that." Kali accepted the fork Julie handed to her and took a bite. She closed her eyes in calorie-laden bliss, and smiled. "Mmm. So good! They taste just like the ones Nana used to make."

Sunni beamed and went to help a customer who walked in.

Kali looked around the bakery, taking in the shiny glass display cases full of tempting treats, and the assortment of tables and chairs that looked inviting. One corner of the shop had overstuffed chairs with a coffee table in front of the grouping. It would make a wonderful place to linger on a cold winter day.

When Sunni rejoined them, Kali reached over and patted her hand. "You've done an amazing thing opening this shop, Sunni. Nana and Papi would be so proud."

"Thank you," Sunni said with a sniff, then hopped up to help another customer.

Their beloved grandparents had died two years ago when they'd been driving through Colorado on their way to Florida. Their car had slid on a patch of ice and crashed, killing them both instantly. At least they'd been together. Kali couldn't picture one of them without the other. They'd always been so close, so loving. Even though their grandfather had been a third-generation Italian-American raised in New Jersey, and their grandmother had been a baby when her parents migrated from Cuba to Miami, they'd had a long, loving marriage.

That was what Kali was holding out for and wanted. She wouldn't settle for anything less than a marriage based on love, fueled by passion, and sustained with friendship. Since she'd not met anyone who would come even remotely close to her ideals of the perfect man for her, she rarely dated. She'd been too busy earning her Master's degree, and then building her resume and experience in the world of museums and preservation to have time for meaningless connections with men she'd likely only see once or twice before she tired of them.

"Did you just get into town?" Matt asked as he sipped a cup of plain black coffee.

"I did. I spent the night in Boise and left there around five."

He grinned at her. "Always the early bird, aren't you?"

"You know it." When she had visited her cousins in the summers of her youth, she was always the first one up. She would torment Matt by doing things like turning the dogs into his room or using a feather to tickle his nose to get him out of bed. The people sitting around her had not only been her cousins but also her friends through the years, and another reason she was so thankful to now be in Holiday close to them.

"Do Mom and Dad know you're here?" Tori asked as she refilled cups of coffee from a pot behind the counter.

"Not yet," Kali said, eager to see her aunt and uncle. "I didn't want to show up on their doorstep too early. Besides, I thought I'd explore the town a little. So much has changed since the last time I was here."

Matt nodded. "Three brothers—Carson, Colton, and Kaden Ford—moved to town. Since then, it seems like things have been changing for the better."

Vicki bumped his arm and shook her head. "I'm sure their arrival has nothing to do with the new businesses going in, or the expansions. Carson took over his aunt's ranch, the Flying B. Colton married Piper Peterson. Do you remember her? Her grandpa is Rand Milton. Anyway, she and Colt bought the feed store and Millcreek Acres, the old Milton place, from Rand. The store and the house have been updated since the last time you were here. Colt and Piper manage both together. Piper seems to be collecting rescue animals while Colt has started a horse breeding and training business. Kaden married Katherine Kelly in May. She is a manager at the bank and he has a software company that creates apps for agriculture applications."

"Well, aren't you in the know," Julie said sarcastically as she stirred cream into her coffee.

Vicki shrugged. "You just have to know who to talk to."

Tori leaned forward and stage whispered, "She means the busybodies at Golden Skies Retirement Village. Vicki gets all the gossip since she works there as a nurse."

Matt smirked. "Better known as the Hokey Pokey Hotel, or so I've heard."

Kali laughed. This was what she'd missed most. Being with her family, listening to them talk and banter. "Hokey Pokey Hotel?"

Vicki nodded. "Katherine told me it's what the Ford brothers call Golden Skies. Their aunt Ruth married Rand Milton. Katherine's aunt Lou is there too, along with Matilda Dale."

"Oh, Matilda. I'd nearly forgotten about her," Kali said.

Matt snorted. "How could you forget the most colorful resident of Holiday?"

Kali recalled the last time she'd visited. She'd gone to the grocery store with Julie and Vicki and couldn't help staring at a woman dressed in a neon pink tunic splashed with bright yellow and orange flowers over purple leggings. The apple-green shoes she wore, along with an assortment of colorful, chunky bracelets gave her quite an eccentric appearance. "Mrs. Dale is hard to overlook."

The girls talked about people who'd moved away, and people who'd moved to town. About marriages, and births, and a few people she knew who had passed.

"Tell her about the buildings. That's what she most cares about," Matt said, helping himself to one of the fruit and cheese filled pastries Sunni had placed in the center of the table.

"She'll find out all about them on Monday," Tori said, sipping her coffee.

Matt shook his head. "Not all of them. Just the buildings the Lennox group is restoring. She should know about the florist shop, and the hotel, and the others."

"Others?" Kali asked, eager to hear more. "What others?"

"Well, you may have noticed the florist shop has moved into what was once the old general store. It's really cute inside," Sunni said, motioning out the window to a building across the street. "And a young couple from Seattle bought the hotel. It's been boarded up so long, no one really paid any attention to what was going on there until they installed new windows, but they've almost finished the restoration. They plan to have it open in time for the holidays."

"Really?" Kali felt excitement bubbling in her. The greater number of old buildings that were open and operational, the better it would be for the whole town. Instead of trying to get people to come to Holiday to see one museum or shop in a store, like the drug store or Milton's feed store, that had been open for more than a hundred years, they could promote the entire town. "That's incredible news. Wouldn't it be something to have even more old places reopen, like you've done with the bakery, Sunni. Even if it used to be an assayer's office, the building has such character. People are going to love coming here for your wonderful sweets, but also just to see the unique architectural design."

"I agree," Julie said, brushing crumbs into her hand then dumping them onto Matt's lap.

Kali bit back a grin as he scowled at his oldest sister, then turned to her. "Sarah took the kids to see her sister this weekend, so if you want someone to hang with, I'm available."

"That's great, Matt. If you have time, and don't mind, I'd love to walk around town and have you point out things of interest. The more I know about Holiday, both past and present, the better I'll be able to serve as director of the preservation group."

"I'm happy to do that. We can go whenever you're ready. I'll call Mom and let her know to expect us for lunch."

"Great. Thanks." Kali smiled as Matt got up and went outside to place the call. She finished her cinnamon bun and coffee while visiting with her cousins about their families. When Matt returned inside, she was ready to join him for a tour of Holiday.

"Thanks for breakfast," she said, giving Sunni a hug. "I'm so proud of you and the bakery."

"Aw, thank you, Kali. It's something I always wanted to do. Now that the kids are old enough to go to school, I can pursue my dreams. Have fun with Matt. Don't let him walk your legs off."

Kali laughed. "I won't." She hurried out the door Matt held open and fell into step beside him as they strolled down the street. Since it was still early, few of the shops were open, but she looked forward to exploring them all.

Matt's phone buzzed and he took it out, typed a reply, then grinned at her. "Want to go look at some trains? My buddy is at the old engine house with a crew, working on Hope."

"Are you serious?" Kali hastened her step and Matt laughed.

"You don't have to run there. It's not like the trains are going anywhere."

She slowed her pace, slightly. "I know, but I can't wait to see it. It's amazing that old steam engine survived all these years, especially after the Coleman family hid it in the Yellowbird Mine to keep it from being destroyed during World War II. They had no way of knowing the mine would collapse a few months later and leave the train buried for decades. Do you think it will ever run down the tracks again?"

"That's the plan, but you know that from the info the preservation society sent to you." Matt looked at her. "For the record, I'm happier than you can know to have you here. If there's anything you need, you ask. Okay?"

"Thanks, Matt." Kali gave him a warm smile as they turned and headed down Park Street toward the depot. As an only child, she'd loved all her cousins, but Matt had filled the role of brother to her, and had always been her favorite.

Movement caught her gaze and she came to a stop in the middle of the sidewalk, staring at the park where a half-completed gazebo stood.

"No way," she said, unable to mask her surprise or delight.

"Yes way," Matt laughed and took her arm, propelling her forward. "They just started on the gazebo last week. It was a shame they finally had to tear down the old one, but it was a rotting eyesore. This one is going to look exactly like the original, complete with pillars, flowerboxes, curved dormers—the whole works."

"Oh, I can't wait to see it lit up for Christmas." She pulled her gaze from the two men working on the gazebo and looked at Matt. "They will put lights on it, won't they?"

"I think that decision is up to the director of the preservation society," he winked at her, "but you could check with the mayor, since it is in the town park. I have a feeling the two of you will spend a lot of time together."

"I'll do that," she said, taking out her phone and making a note to introduce herself to the mayor next week.

When they reached the old train depot, Kali stood and stared at it, feeling like she was perched on the edge of diving into a childhood dream. When she used to come to Holiday to visit, she wondered what was in the old buildings, and why they'd been locked and left to deteriorate.

From what she could see, all the buildings at the depot complex had been meticulously restored. They looked even better than she'd imagined.

"Come on." Matt led the way over to the massive engine house that had served the engines of Holiday since the 1880s.

The most famous of all the engines was one named Hope. It had been used on the Holiday Express line for almost forty years, or so she'd read in the history she'd dug up on the town. Jace Coleman had been the first engineer, and, if legends were true, he'd been on it with his son Zach and grandson Bryce when the three men hid it in the mine all those years ago.

She turned to smile at her cousin and noticed the rust-bucket pickup that had honked at her earlier parked near the engine house. She hoped the driver wouldn't be as rude in person as he was on the road.

Anxious to see the old steam engine and the other trains in the building, she followed Matt inside. Odors wafted around her, stirred by the breeze blowing in the open windows, bringing to mind creosote, sweat, and campfires.

A filthy cat meandered over and brushed against her, smearing grease across her bare legs. Kali reached down and rubbed it on the head, pleased when it started to purr. She pulled her hand back and looked at the dirt coating her palm and fingers.

"That's Mutt," Matt said, giving the cat a scratch behind its ears before he straightened.

"Mutt? Who names a cat Mutt?" she asked, indignant on behalf of the feline. "And why doesn't someone give the poor thing a bath?"

"Because Mutt lives here in the engine house. She catches mice and keeps watch over things. And she does get a bath from time to time, but as you can see, she likes to rub on everything."

Kali watched as the cat rubbed against a greasy piston and sauntered off with a fresh streak of black on her side.

Since this was her first time in an engine house where trains were serviced, repaired, and housed, she looked around with interest. Giant wrenches and a variety of equipment looked old and authentic to the era when the engine house was originally constructed.

"Wow! This is so cool," she said as Matt led her through a maze of equipment to where several men worked. The majority of them were older, and all of them wore striped bib overalls with what she thought of as an engineer cap. Apparently, playing with trains was something some men never outgrew, and she was glad of it, since their efforts had resulted in the old engines running once again.

"I'm going to see if I can locate Three. Wait right here," Matt said, then strode through an open doorway.

Kali couldn't help moving closer to a big locomotive where several men labored. A younger man, probably closer to her age, stood inside the smokestack working on something she couldn't quite see.

Focused on getting a better look instead of watching where she was walking, she moved closer. She took another step toward the engine, but when her foot should have connected with the cement floor beneath her, it kept going. She glanced down and realized she'd walked right over one of the pits beneath the tracks that extended from one end of the building to the other. The openings in the floor provided access to the undercarriage of the trains.

She threw out her arms to regain her balance, but the forward momentum was too much to overcome. Closing her eyes, she wondered how many bones would break when she hit the concrete in the bottom of the pit and the tools she could see on a narrow table.

As suddenly as she started to fall, she was yanked backward. An arm with muscles that felt like a steel band encircled her waist, nearly knocking the wits and air right out of her.

"You better pay more attention to what you're doing, Toots, instead of ogling the help," a deep, teasing voice said near her ear. In fact, the man stood so close to her, she could smell the minty flavor of his gum mingling with a spicy, woodsy fragrance and a musky, manly scent that rendered her slightly woozy.

She spun around and glared at a person so handsome he might have been a cover model if his face hadn't been a tad too long to be considered absolutely perfect.

But he was about as close to perfection as most humans would get with thick, wavy black hair, stunning blue eyes, a slender nose, square jaw, and a defined chin covered in black stubble. His lips—oh, mercy—those lips kept her gaze lingering on them, wondering what it would be like to kiss them.

Aware of her perusal, the man offered her a cocky smirk.

"Like what you see?" he asked, stepping back from her and narrowing his gaze as he studied her.

"I'm not … I didn't … I wasn't …" Aware she

sounded like a stammering ninny, she took a deep breath and tried to gather her discordant thoughts together. "Thank you. I wasn't ogling the help. It's the engine that held my interest."

"Right," he said, sounding dubious. "This building isn't open to the public, Toots. I'm sorry, but you'll have to go."

"But, I …" Distracted when she realized the tall, hunky guy was wearing just the bibbed overalls with no shirt beneath, she could see mounds of muscle covered by golden skin. Her mouth went dry, and she tried to remember what it was she intended to say.

"Three! There you are. I've been looking all over for you, man." Matt hurried over to them, smiling. "Hey, you met my cuz. Kal, this is my longtime friend and cohort in crime, Three."

"Three?" she asked, gaping at her cousin in disbelief. From the time Matt was thirteen, she'd listened to him rave about his friend, Three. She'd always thought it a ridiculous name and had asked many times if the name was real, or a nickname. Matt always assured her it was his friend's name.

"Three. That's me," the man said, grinning at her as he pulled a rag from his back pocket and wiped off his greasy hands. It was then Kali glanced down to see big greasy smears across her white blouse.

He followed her gaze and shrugged, as if to say it wasn't his fault she hadn't been paying attention.

Normally, she was a reasonable person not given to snap judgements. However, in that moment, she felt a strong and undeniable urge to slap the ridiculing smirk right off his fine-looking face.

Instead, she clenched her hands at her side and latched onto her sense. "You don't, by chance, drive the exceptionally rusty pickup parked outside, do you?"

"As a matter of fact, I do. It was my grandpa's

pickup."

"Figures," she muttered to herself, then looked to Matt. "I believe I've seen enough of the engine house today."

"But, Kali, we …" Matt snapped his mouth shut at her glacial glare, and nodded once. He turned to his friend. "Hey, man, I'll swing back around later."

"Sounds good, Matt. See you then." The man tossed her a glance, one devoid of expression, then hopped down into the pit beneath the train.

In spite of her fury at him, she couldn't help but watch all those muscles bunch as he moved.

"What's up with you?" Matt asked when they were outside.

"I, uh … I think the long drive caught up to me. Do you mind if we head over to your mom and dad's house?"

"No, that's fine. If you don't feel like walking back to your Jeep, I'll go get my pickup."

"I can walk, Matt, but thank you."

Hours later, she slid between the cool, fresh sheets in the apartment over her aunt and uncle's garage. The apartment had been Matt's when he first wanted to move out on his own. Now, Aunt Bee and Uncle Ike used it as a place for guests. Fully furnished, with a small kitchen and bathroom, Kali planned to stay there while she looked for a house to buy, one she loved, since she planned to remain in Holiday.

She expelled a long breath, excited to be there, but unable to relax as she thought about the incredibly strong, unbelievably annoying guy from the engine house. How could a conceited man named Three be her cousin's best friend? And how, in all the times she'd visited Holiday, had she never met him? If he was always as obnoxious as he'd been that morning, she was glad she hadn't encountered him.

Perhaps she wouldn't have to see him with any frequency. After all, she was about to step into a new position with the newly formed preservation society, and she knew the board of directors had an aggressive agenda heading into the holiday season.

She closed her eyes, willing herself to rest, yet irritated to find a scruff-covered jaw and a pair of incredible blue eyes taunting her while a deep, intriguing voice called her Toots.

Available on Amazon

About the Author

PHOTO BY SHANA BAILEY PHOTOGRAPHY

USA Today bestselling author Shanna Hatfield is a farm girl who loves to write. Her sweet historical and contemporary romances are filled with sarcasm, humor, hope, and hunky heroes.

When Shanna isn't dreaming up unforgettable characters, twisting plots, or covertly seeking dark, decadent chocolate, she hangs out with her beloved husband, Captain Cavedweller, at their home in the Pacific Northwest.

Shanna loves to hear from readers. Connect with her online:

Blog: shannahatfield.com
Facebook: Shanna Hatfield's Page
Shanna Hatfield's Hopeless Romantics Group
Pinterest: Shanna Hatfield
Email: shanna@shannahatfield.com